THEATER VOICES

Conversations on the Stage

STEVE CAPRA

THE SCARECROW PRESS, INC.
Lanham, Maryland • Toronto • Oxford
2004

SCARECROW PRESS, INC.

Published in the United States of America
by Scarecrow Press, Inc.
A wholly owned subsidiary of
The Rowman & Littlefield Publishing Group, Inc.
4501 Forbes Boulevard, Suite 200, Lanham, Maryland 20706
www.scarecrowpress.com

PO Box 317
Oxford
OX2 9RU, UK

British Library Cataloguing in Publication Information Available

Library of Congress Cataloging-in-Publication Data

Theater voices : conversations on the stage / [interviews by] Steve Capra.
    p. cm.
  Includes bibliographical references and index.
  ISBN 0-8108-5047-8 (alk. paper)
  1. Theater—History—20th century. 2. Theater—Interviews. I. Capra, Steve, 1951–
PN2189.T497 2004
792'.092'2—dc22

                                                            2004006283

∞™ The paper used in this publication meets the minimum requirements of American National Standard for Information Sciences—Permanence of Paper for Printed Library Materials, ANSI/NISO Z39.48-1992.
Manufactured in the United States of America.

An actor should look at the theater like "This might be my last day on earth. I might never survive this. I might never survive this."

JULIE HARRIS

CONTENTS

Foreword

THERE'S A FINE LINE BETWEEN an interview and a conversation. Let's hope that I've had the sense to leave the talking to the extraordinary individuals I've met.

I've discovered in the process of collecting these interviews an intriguing triangle. The first and most evident side is the *work itself*—the staging, the writing, or whatever it may be—that makes us *attend*. I expect that the reader is familiar with the work of the various professionals presented here. If not, drop this book and go to the theater.

The second side is the *ideas* expressed herein. They are as diverse as stage designs, and they create between these covers a dissonance that reflects the protean nature of the theater.

Then there are the *personalities*, the third side of the equilateral. It's the relationship that each personality has to his or her work and to his or her statements that I've found most interesting. We are, after all, dealing with some of the most creative minds of three generations, and the active reader will find the character behind the words.

It's been suggested that I limit the scope of the book to a single discipline—to exclusively interview directors, for example, or critics. I can only respond that the fact of our working in the theater is more important than the particular function we serve. Indeed, we find that theater professionals take multiple roles. To cite only two examples: Robert Brustein is a director, playwright, critic, and teacher; Michael Shurtleff is a teacher, casting director, and playwright.

And what of the reader? If he or she has a role in the theater, I warrant it is more than one. A student's curiosity, or a maven's, will be catholic.

It's been suggested that I explain what I've learned about the theater from writing this book. The reader can learn for himself or herself, from those more articulate than I.

It's been suggested that I cut the text to the bone, as if statements existed outside of a context. But it would be misrepresenting my late friend Quentin Crisp to limit his conversation to a point. And if Zerka Moreno should drop a bit of gossip about Peter Lorre or Eleanora Duse—well, no sentient writer could deny the reader this.

Nor could I "correct" the grammar of the interviews, as if the words had been written, not spoken.

It's been suggested that some of the reviews are no longer young. But neither is Aristotle's *Poetics*. An idea is not more true because it's more recent. Fortunately, my Scarecrow editors have had better sense.

Each individual I've interviewed is an undisputed authority on the theater. But an authority's word is not the last word. It's only the first word. We want to know what you think of these discussions—what surprised you, what you disagree with, what you can confirm. Please join our discussion by visiting the book's website: www.theatervoices.net.

I'd like to thank the twenty-seven people who consented to talk with me. They were, individually and collectively, utterly gracious.

Notes on Awards

The ASCAP Awards are given by the American Society of Composers, Authors, and Publishers.

The Critics Circle Award is given by the Critics Circle, an association of U.K. theater critics.

The Drama Desk Awards and the Vernon Rice Awards are given by the Drama Desk, an association of New York critics.

The Edwin Booth Award is given by the City University of New York.

The Elliot Norton Awards are given by the Boston Theatre Critics Association.

The George Jean Nathan Award for Dramatic Criticism is given by Cornell University.

The London Evening Standard Awards are given by the *London Evening Standard* newspaper.

MacArthur Fellowships are given by the MacArthur Foundation.

The National Medal of the Arts is given by the National Endowment for the Arts.

The New York Drama Critics Award is given by a consortium of New York arts journalists.

The Obie Awards are given by the *Village Voice* newspaper, New York.

The Olivier Awards are given by the Society of London Theatre.

The Peter Brook/Empty Space Awards are given by London Theatre Reviews and the Theatre Museum.

The Pulitzer Prize is given by the Pulitzer Prize Committee and Columbia University.

The Roger Machell Prize is given by the English Authors' Union.

The Stubby Awards are given by *Hampton Shorts* magazine.

The Tony Awards are given by the American Theater Wing and the League of American Theatres and Producers.

Sheridan Morley
London, March 15, 1995

I think you experiment in rehearsal, or you experiment in workshop. But to experiment in front of people who've paid twenty dollars seems to me chutzpa of a kind I'm not entirely sure I would encourage.

SHERIDAN MORLEY IS THE London drama critic for the *International Herald Tribune* and the *Spectator*. In addition, he writes for the *London Times*, the *Sunday Telegraph*, and the *London Evening Standard*. He's also been arts editor and drama critic for *Punch*, and he was named BP Arts Journalist of the Year in 1989. His several books include biographies of Sir Noel Coward, Dirk Bogarde, Audrey Hepburn, Elizabeth Taylor, Gertrude Lawrence, and Sir John Gielgud.

SC: What has become of the English theater in the past ten or twenty years? What do you expect will become of it? And what can you tell me about the West End?

SM: I am slightly more centered on the West End than a good many of my colleagues. I think, if you look around the English press, you will find very largely that, unlike America, we have about twelve national critics, if you count the daily press, the Sundays, and then places like the *Spectator*, the weekly press, and the *International Herald Tribune*. We form a kind of jury—it's a matter of twelve people—men, women, all ages, colors, sexes, whatever.

Now, what's interesting about that jury is that it splits—like any jury—into component parts. You will find on that jury some very academic critics, writers who work from the word out, who start with, if you like, a professorial brief. Then there are some who work very much on a political/sexist brief, going for those plays which alter the agenda, which are particularly good to ethnic or female writers.

Then there are a few writers—like me—who have an old-fashioned, kind of commercial theater background. I grew up in a family of actors. My father was Robert Morley, and my mother's mother was Gladys Cooper. So I was brought up in a very commercial environment, where the theater was business, not an art form, where it was a matter of getting people into shows, where the actors were very dominant. In my father's day, it was he who, very often, chose the play, the producer, the cast, the theater.

Now, that is almost entirely gone. There are very few examples left of an actor's theater. We moved from that in the 1940s—in my childhood—'50s. We moved towards a writer's theater with John Osborne, with Harold Pinter. We have now moved to a director's theater, where all the big subsidized companies—be it the National Theatre,[1] be it the Barbican[2]—are run by directors. We now live in a world where directors are dominant.

Now, the West End has fallen, really, out of critical favor, in much the way that Broadway has. We are going in that direction—we are not going as fast as Broadway. We haven't got as many theaters that are dark. But the truth is that we are now, more and more, seeing the West End as a transfer house. Most of the straight plays in the West End have come either from the subsidized areas, the National Theatre, the Royal Shakespeare Company, or—and now a much more fruitful area—they have come from the fringe, what you would call the off-Broadway, off-off-Broadway, or the regions.

So, very seldom does a straight play actually start in the middle of London. Of course, there are exceptions. If you have Edward Albee's *Three Tall Women*,[3] and you have Maggie Smith, then you can certainly afford to go straight to the West End, and you will indeed sell out night after night. But it's interesting that even that would have been a much more risky prospect if it had been one without the other. If it had been Maggie Smith in, say, a new play by an unknown playwright, or if it had been Albee with an unknown cast, that show would not have been as cast-iron a hit as it is. You now have to have both. But if you're a musical—yes, you can do without the stars if you've got chandeliers crashing in *Phantom*,[4] or you've got helicopters crashing in *Miss Saigon*.[5]

The only way round that is, as I say, to come in from the fringe, come in from the pubs, from the clubs, from the regions, where you have an already known quantity, because then you've got original reviews. You've got the word of mouth that says this is a great show.

The danger with all this is that the West End then becomes kind of inert. It becomes a resting place for things that have already happened elsewhere. Or it becomes a home for great musicals.

Now, I, unlike a lot of my colleagues who will tell you this is really all terrible, I actually have a lot of time for Cameron Mackintosh, for Lloyd Webber. I believe that a truly great musical—I would say *Miss Saigon*—I would say *Les Miserables*[6]—can actually, at its best, be as good as anything by Chekhov or Shakespeare, or Ibsen, or Albee, or Tennessee Williams. Now, that is not widely believed. The theory is that even a great musical is somehow inferior to a middle-of-the-road play. I think you can have great musicals, but the danger is you can have too many of them. And if you have a West End that is now almost entirely composed of musicals that have been there five, and in some cases ten years—we're talking about ten years of *Cats*,[7] of *Starlight*,[8] of *Phantom*—there starts to be a real problem, which is that the place begins to look a bit dusty, and it looks a bit ancient. And then you start to add the revivals—*Crazy for You*,[9] which is a disguised revival in that it's really *Girl Crazy*[10] done over as a new show, or *Carousel*.[11] There is a problem of museum theater—that you're going to get a West End that is really only a resting place for things that are old transfers.

But having said that, the single great change of the last ten years has not been much to do with the RSC or the National Theatre. The single great change has been Cameron Mackintosh—has been the bringing of these enormous shows not just to London, but all over the world, the cloning of *Phantom*, of *Miss Saigon*, the marketing, the franchising whereby you go to fifteen airports from Reykjavik to Rio de Janeiro, and you get off the plane, and what do you see? You see the poster for *Cats*, the poster for *Phantom*—you see those logos.

Now that has been an extraordinary commercial change, and it's affected everything else, because if you're going to spend twenty-five or thirty pounds in English money, and you're then going to take somebody with you, and you're then going to go out for a meal, and park the car, and get a babysitter, you're in for about a hundred pounds of English money. It makes the musical more attractive, because you can see where your money is going. If you can see forty dancing cats, you kind of see where your money has gone, and in a recession that's always very valuable.

If you look at the 1930s, the whole Busby Berkeley world of Hollywood musicals was entirely an escape from the big Depression of 1929. In the same way, we are not in a very economically easy time, and we are getting a lot of safe shows—shows that take your mind off the present situation. In a good time, like the 1960s, when there was a lot of money around, theaters were indeed being built, then you could afford revolution, and the plays were indeed very anti-government; they were anti-authority, they were anti-conservative.

What we are now seeing is an extraordinary kind of paralysis, whereby very few writers are actually writing plays about the state of Britain in the '90s. It was as though Mrs. Thatcher paralyzed a whole generation of playwrights, who were so horrified by the conservative triumph that they couldn't bring themselves to write about it. It's really only David Hare who has been looking at the state of the Church of England, in *Racing Demon*.[12] He's been looking at the state of the judiciary in *Murmuring Judges*,[13] and he had a play about the Labor Party in disarray.

It seems to me that that is quite frightening, and I think it's to do with the fact that we just don't have the confidence, either economic or social, at the moment, to deal with revolution, or to deal with dissent, or to deal with disarray.

SC: Isn't that particularly surprising if many of those shows come from the fringe? I would expect them to be more bold.

SM: It's surprising . . . In a way, they are bold, but they're not politically bold. They are bold sexually. We've gone into a much more personal area, where plays now tend to be people agonizing over their sexuality, or their mothers, or their childhoods, or their whatever. But it's not about England. Somehow the nation has ceased to be on the agenda, and plays have gone. This is partly the result of economics. The pub theater shows tend to be very small—they tend to be two or three characters, and with two or three characters, there isn't a lot you can do about the state of the nation. So what you're getting are much more intimate, personal shows.

SC: In terms of employment, my English actor friends are always complaining—but actors always complain. Is it becoming difficult for an actor to earn a living?

SM: I think it's difficult outside London. There is still a lot of television going on here, a lot of radio drama, and a good deal of work in the subsidized companies. But the problem is that if you go to, say, the Royal Shakespeare Company, a hundred and fifty pounds a week is about the bottom of the scale. You are on a two-year contract; you're working in Warwickshire at Stratford. You can't then do the voice-overs, the commercials, the one-day jobs that pay the rent. It's always been a tough life, and, indeed, 90 percent are unemployed at any one time in Equity. This is true for actors—not true for stage managers. If you're in the backstage crews, you can usually get work, but if you're an actor . . .

SC: I'm sure you're familiar with New York theater. When I look at the fringe theater here, I find that it's healthy, in terms of audience, in terms of the number of shows, but I do not see here the bold, new forms that I see in the East Village.

SM: You mean things like performance art and all of that?

SC: Audience-activated theater, improvisational theater, theater off the text . . .

SM: I think we are still, in some ways, quite conservative. We still believe that, even if you go to a pub theater, and you only pay, maybe, fifteen dollars, you don't want total anarchy. You want somebody to have written a play, actors to have learned the lines, someone to have designed a set. We are not a nation, I think, that believes that the audience is going to have to take part.

There is still a certain distrust of shows that depend on the audience. We are not a very active audience. We believe that, if we go to a theater, we have bought the rights to be told something, or shown something, or made to laugh, or made to cry, but that we ourselves should not have paid money to join in. If we want to do that, we'll give a party, or we'll become actors, or we'll become directors.

And I'm not sure that's a bad thing. A lot of very sloppy, lazy theater gets by now in the terms of innovation, or experiment. I'm not entirely sure you ought to experiment with ticket-paying customers. I think you experiment in rehearsal, or you experiment in workshop. But to experiment in front of people who've paid twenty dollars seems to me chutzpa of a kind I'm not entirely sure I would encourage. It seems to me that there is such a thing as professionalism, and that does not come from encouraging an audience to mess around.

Notes

1. The Royal National Theatre, London.
2. The Barbican Theatre, London.
3. *Three Tall Women*, by Edward Albee, opened off-Broadway and in the West End in 1994.
4. *The Phantom of the Opera*, music by Andrew Lloyd Webber, lyrics by Charles Hart and Richard Stilgoe, book by Richard Stilgoe and Andrew Lloyd Webber, opened in the West End in 1986.
5. *Miss Saigon*, music by Claude-Michel Schönberg, lyrics by Alain Boublil and Richard Maltby Jr., book by Alain Boublil and Claude-Michel Schönberg, opened in the West End in 1989.
6. *Les Miserables*, music by Claude-Michel Schönberg, lyrics by Herber Kretzmer, book by Alain Boublil and Claude-Michel Schönberg, opened in the West End in 1985.
7. *Cats*, music by Andrew Lloyd Webber, lyrics by T. S. Eliot (based on his collection of poems *Old Possum's Book of Practical Cats*), opened in the West End in 1981.
8. *Starlight Express*, music by Andrew Lloyd Webber, lyrics by Richard Stilgoe, opened in the West End in 1984.
9. *Crazy for You*, music by George Gershwin, lyrics by Ira Gershwin, book by Ken Ludwig, opened on Broadway in 1992.
10. *Girl Crazy*, music by George Gershwin, lyrics by Ira Gershwin, book by Guy Bolton and Jack McGowan, opened on Broadway in 1930.
11. *Carousel*, music by Richard Rodgers, book and lyrics by Oscar Hammerstein II, opened on Broadway in 1945.
12. *Racing Demon*, by David Hare, opened at the Royal National Theatre in 1990.
13. *Murmuring Judges*, by David Hare, opened at the Royal National Theatre in 1993.

Vjachelslav Dolgachev
New York, August 12, 1998

OLEG KHEYFETZ, TRANSLATOR

2

It seems that the time of avant-garde theater is lost.

VJACHELSLAV DOLGACHEV, ONE of Russia's foremost directors, has directed regularly at the Moscow Art Theater for more than ten years. He's particularly well known for his productions of Dostoyevsky's *Bobok* and Tolstoy's *And Light Is Lighting Up the Dark.* His productions have toured internationally. He's taught at many studios, including the Moscow Art Theater School and the Actors Center, in New York, and he is the head of directing at the Russian Academy of Theater Arts in Moscow.

SC: We connect the Moscow Art Theater[1] so much with Stanislavski.[2] Do the acting techniques that you teach—have they changed very much from the techniques he wrote about in his books?

VD: Stanislavski was great because he discovered the laws which determine human beings' behavior on stage—as well as in life. The laws of human behavior are really endless. So you could work forever in this way to discover newer and newer laws. Stanislavski showed us this way, and all his successors, all other generations continue to work this way—the whole twentieth century continues to work this way.

Of course, we're talking about those who've focused on psychological theater. The main problem Stanislavski considered was to find the way to the subconscious of the actor—he worked to get from conscious to subconscious. In his last long book,[3] Stanislavski wrote that he had reached the conclusion that it makes sense to influence the subconscious of the actor directly, not to go through the conscious, like he thought at the beginning. He wrote about it in terms of his future work, but he was unable to develop in this direction, because he died. The twentieth century has continued this search. Stanislavski put the main results of his work on paper, and his last point concerned *radiation* and *absorption.* He only just mentioned this point—he didn't work with it. The discoveries of the twentieth century continue to work in this direction. That's why you could say that the method of Stanislavski doesn't stay still—it's going forward constantly.

SC: American acting has been so influenced by Stanislavski, and by the Moscow Art Theater's tour in the 1920s. Do you find that the acting you see in New York today—the best acting in New York—is very different from the acting I would see in Moscow?

VD: It's difficult for me to comment on it, because I haven't seen a lot—and what I saw probably wasn't the best.

SC: Does the Moscow Art Theater produce any *avant-garde* forms, any *new* forms, any experimental theater?

VD: It depends on what you mean when you talk about *avant-garde*—and what you mean when you talk about *experimental* theater. The Moscow Art Theater tries to be a contemporary theater that expresses contemporary processes of life. It seems that the time of *avant-garde* theater is lost. Its time was 1960, 1970. In different times, different things become important in the theater. And now, it seems that, at least in Russia, the most significant problem is not the search for new *avant-garde* forms, but the quality of real life in actors. Something that we call *director's theater* brought a lot of new forms, new ways of expressing content, but today's the time of the actor, not the time of the active director.

SC: I was very impressed by *Three Sisters*.[4] Can your actors use the same techniques to approach Beckett, or Ionesco?

VD: One of the biggest impressions I got of the theater recently was the production of Beckett's play *Happy Days*[5] that was directed by Peter Brook in Switzerland. This show was done as a perfect example of the technique of Moscow Art Theater.

SC: You mentioned Peter Brook. I know he was present at the Moscow Art Theater's international meeting last year, along with many other of the foremost people in the theater. What should we know about that incredible meeting of theater professionals?

VD: It was the hundredth anniversary of the first meeting of Stanislavski and Nemirovich—the meeting that took place in a restaurant. A lot of directors from around the world made speeches at the conference. They all shared the ways that the Moscow Art Theater and Stanislavski had influenced them.

SC: Did the Moscow Art Theater state a mission for the future?

VD: The hundredth anniversary of the theater comes next month. It's a great milestone—a good occasion to come to some conclusions about our mission. Every three or four years, Stanislavski thought about a new way to develop the theater. He didn't have it in mind that the theater would exist a hundred years! He actually wrote that every fifteen years the theater should be renewed—and everyone should be kicked out!

SC: I see!

VD: So nobody knows how long the Moscow Art Theater will exist. I was constantly surprised when I studied the theater's history. In spite of the repertory system it used, it didn't have the stable cast. At moments, when a really nice company got together, something really great happened. And then it disappeared—time after time. And then again a new company would appear, and again something great would happen. It's difficult to say what will happen in the future—who will stay, who will go . . . I don't know if I'll work with the Moscow Art Theater in the future. It depends on a lot of factors, including what company will be there—whether they'll be people I'm close to.

SC: In light of the fact that there are film and television in the world, can theater ever be as important for ordinary people as it was for Stanislavski's audience?

VD: Of course—because they're absolutely different genres, different styles, different kinds of art. They give audiences absolutely different impressions. Only in the theater does the audience have the opportunity to observe the real event—the *life* of the event. Only in theater does the audience have the opportunity to influence what happens on the stage. We can't have influence on the television or the screen. My tears, my laughter, my reactions as an audience can influence the people on the stage. That's why theater will always interest people.

SC: In England, ordinary people go to see the theater. In America, they don't. Most people—95 percent of the people in the country—never see theater. What's it like in Russia? Is theater still very important?

VD: My impressions are not deep, but as far as I can see, dramatic theater hasn't yet been born in the United States. That's why audiences don't go to the theater—because there is nothing to go to. It's not just because there are television and movies—they're everywhere. But in Russia, and in England, there is the theater as well.

SC: *Three Sisters* was certainly very well received here. Do American audiences experience it differently than Russian audiences? Do audiences around the world experience theater the same way?

VD: In different ways—and not. There's a lot of common ground. All people have similar emotions, but different nations have different cultural traditions. There are different cultural traditions in the United States than in Russia. In American theater, I've often gotten the impression that the audience would like to laugh as much as possible. They search for reasons—excuses—to laugh. In Russia, and in London, the audience doesn't go to just laugh. They believe in the artists, and they're ready to follow them wherever they go.

Notes

1. The Moscow Art Theater was founded in 1897 by Konstantin Stanislavski and Vladimir Nemirovich Danchenko.

2. Konstantin Stanislavski (1863–1938), Russian director and actor, a founder of the Moscow Art Theater.

3. Part One of *An Actor's Work on Himself*, by Konstantin Stanislavski, was completed in 1936. Part Two was never completed.

4. *Three Sisters*, by Anton Chekhov, was first produced in 1901, by the Moscow Art Theater. I'm speaking of the production that the Moscow Art Theater brought to New York in 1998.

5. *Happy Days*, by Samuel Beckett, was first produced in 1998.

Peter Hall
London, March 9, 1995

The theater's been dying for two thousand years, and I'm sure will continue to.

SIR PETER HALL FOUNDED the Royal Shakespeare Company in 1960 and remained its managing director until 1968. He was the director of the British National Theatre from 1973 to 1988, and has been the artistic director of the Glyndebourne Festival Opera since 1984. His many honors include two Tony Awards, for his direction of *The Homecoming* and *Amadeus*, and an Olivier Award for Lifetime Achievement. He's been decorated Commander, Order of the British Empire; he was knighted in 1977.

SC: In your latest book,[1] you say you want an ensemble company trained in the classics but expert in modern drama. Could you say more about what classical techniques we can apply to modern drama? After all, Martin Esslin wrote that we need a new acting for a new drama.[2]

PH: Well, I spent twenty years of my life creating the Royal Shakespeare Company, and at the same time doing Harold Pinter, Samuel Beckett, Edward Albee, and I don't believe myself that the classical disciplines are at all out of date, or at all outmoded, when it comes to working on texts of real style and particularity. Most actors nowadays are faced with rather sloppily written texts where what is unsaid is more important than what is said, and what is said covers up what is unsaid. This is why quite dreadful dialogue in films in the hands of Spencer Tracy can sound quite true—because his subtext is so absolutely accurate. But the fact remains that the reality of any great dramatic writing still resides in the style. And the voice of Ibsen—I have a little Norwegian, and I've translated Ibsen—the voice of Beckett, the voice of Pinter, the voice of Albee, the voice of Tennessee Williams are not at all naturalistic.

I've done a lot of Tennessee Williams plays, and about four or five years ago, I did a Tennessee Williams play in New York with an entirely American cast. And I was extremely saddened to find that the natural instinct of every American actor, given the Stanislavski naturalism tradition, was to split those long sentences of Tennessee's down into little gobbets, which ruined the rhythm and ruined the actual lyricism of it. And I had to actually teach them to speak their own language.

SC: In the same way that you say the line of meaning in Shakespeare is pentameter.

PH: Yes. And Shakespeare's whole being is in preserving the identity of the line. The irregularities from the line are what give the tempest and the passion and the emotion. So the classical disciplines are no different to the musician's disciplines—the discipline of rhythm, or the discipline of pitch. If Beckett writes an antithetical speech, then you need to know about antithesis. If Pinter asks for a pause, you have to know why, and you have to actually observe that. So the kind of discipline that Shakespeare gives an actor I find completely transferable to all the great writers. Because all great writers gave form, and if actors come in hobnail boots, trampling over the form of a writer, saying, "Never mind about his commas, never mind about his full-stops, never mind about his sentences, never mind about his antithesis—I want to be real," they are actually raping the form—which is to me quite comparable to a singer refusing to observe the actual phrasing of Mozart.

You can't sing Mozart by saying you'll breathe when you feel like it. And you can't actually play Shakespeare by saying, "I'll breathe when I feel like it." Shakespeare tells you when to breathe, and if you don't breathe then, you're in trouble.

SC: You define the play, then, very largely in terms of the language.

PH: Yes. Theater—our theater, the western tradition of theater—is defined by language. In that sense, in the beginning, certainly, was the word. *Word* defines space in the theater; *word* defines silence; *word* defines *no word* in the theater. Not, of course, true in movies, where words take a secondary place. And there are forms of theater, obviously, which are nonverbal, but not many of them survive, in historic terms. The main way theater has survived is by printed or preserved text. Of course, that's only half the story. A Shakespeare text is only half the reality—it has to live. But it's a great beginning.

SC: You've mentioned the western tradition. While we're putting theater into a tradition, you mention that the general level of creativity in London has increased, although going to the theater had become, or is becoming, little more than a tourist attraction, or an elitist art. What are we to make of the fact that, while work seems to be developing greater diversity, it seems to be less vital to the people as a whole?

PH: I'm not sure I agree with what your question's driving at. I think the theater is in a tremendous state of change at the moment. The West End theater, the commercial theater, is now more or less a tourist attraction. It has plastic musicals on for tourists in their eighth or tenth year, and you will notice they are the same musicals the world over, whether Helsinki or Tokyo, London or Chicago, Los Angeles—the same musicals. They're really part of a sort of a Disneyland culture. The theater-going public in London has increased and become actually more sophisticated, but it's fed by the National Theatre,[3] the Royal Shakespeare Company, and the Royal Court,[4] rather than by the West End. That's just something that's happened partly for economic reasons, and partly for social reasons.

But I don't despair about the future of the theater. The theater's been dying for two thousand years, and I'm sure will continue to. It goes through various convulsions. But theater remains the only place where people can have a live experience, and where they can actually debate and think about the issues of their lives in living, active terms, and I think the appetite for that will increase.

SC: Even though we have television and film.

PH: This is passing. It's passing. If you see Shakespeare on the screen, I don't think it works, because Shakespeare entirely depends on the imaginative game of make-believe played between the live actor and the live member of the audience—whereas film is about fantasy reality. Shakespeare doesn't work, to me, on the screen. It works at a certain point, like the reproduction of a picture may not be as satisfactory as the picture. If you see Shakespeare on the screen, it's more likely to make you go and see it in the theater.

SC: I'm happy to hear you're so optimistic!

PH: Yes, I mean, the main problem the theater faces is economic. Theater is a very expensive form of activity. It's kind of hand-built for you tonight. You can't have more than a thousand people in a building without ruining the experience. You can't amplify the actors. You can't make the actors play more than once a day, et cetera, et cetera. So it's becoming more and more and more expensive, as the standard of living rises. Therefore, the historical fact that the theater has usually been subsidized by somebody—by the court, the king, the state, the religion—has to be admitted. I believe the theater is an important social function in a democracy, and therefore merits subsidy, and I've always felt that.

SC: But acting as the manager and as the artistic director must have been so stressful. That's the impression we get from your books. Did that not affect your work?

PH: Well, it might have done. Who's to know? I don't know the work would have been worse or better if I hadn't been doing that. I did it for twenty-five years—ten years at the Royal Shakespeare and fifteen at the National, and I think I was very lucky to have that opportunity. All in all it was a rich experience, one that I wouldn't have missed. I think I became a better director because I was a manager, and I think I became a better manager because I was a director. That's what I think—others may not.

SC: In your diaries,[5] you mention several times the importance of ambiguity in a play, and yet you also quote a book called *How to Draw*, which accents the importance of clarity. How does the director deal with that tension between ambiguity and clarity?

PH: Well, by being clearly ambiguous. I think human beings are very contradictory. Human behavior's very contradictory. Human motivation is very contradictory. You ask four people to describe a conversation they all had in a room, they would all give you a slightly different description of it, yet they might all be truthful. If you preempt things by making a man, as it were, just plainly angry in a scene, that's a very boring and uninteresting— almost repulsive—simplistic emotion, which you very rarely see in life. I think, myself, that ambiguity in the theater is most clearly obtained, and should be clearly sought for, by the actor feeling completely truthfully his motives, but not necessarily sharing them. Often his mask—his words, his behavior—hides what he feels, and one of the curious puzzles about the theater is that audiences understand what an actor is feeling even if the actor doesn't tell them it. I mean, directing Pinter, who is the master of enigma, if you don't know the melodrama that is going on underneath the text of Pinter in very crude terms—who hates who, who loves who, who wants what—second by second, the play becomes pretentious and empty. Underneath all Pinter's text, there is a very strong sinewy melodrama, and I've often, when directing Pinter, worked with the actors on expressing that melodrama. And then, having found it, you then hide it, contain it, disguise it, with the text that he has written.

SC: You're expressing it through improvisation, then.

PH: Through improvisation, or even by using the actual text and playing it in vividly colored emotional terms. But then you must use the text to hide those emotions. Then the ambiguity is there, and the audience does understand it. It's not empty—it's quite full. It's quite full. The fascination of the theater to me is that it always oscillates between the said and the unsaid. Even in the most extremely clear and up-front writers, like Shakespeare— Shakespeare tells the audience what they are to think and feel on each line, but he sometimes uses underplaying also, and he sometimes uses words to disguise the feelings, too.

SC: So there is sometimes a subtext in Shakespeare.

PH: Oh, certainly. Quite often there's a subtext in Shakespeare—quite often.

SC: In one of my favorite passages in your book,[6] you say: "The openly public presentation of a true emotion is my aesthetic." Of all the possible focuses you could have for the theater, you choose the presentation of emotion. Could you say something about that?

PH: Theater has been and always will be about feeling. We go there for strong emotion. It's partly erotic, sexual. But that's why it's alive. That's why I think it will never die.

SC: You dislike musicals, in general, and yet you do so much work in opera.

PH: I dislike musicals because they trivialize, on the whole. There's no reason why they should. *Carmen*[7] is a great musical, but it doesn't trivialize. Most musicals have somewhere built into their mechanism a patronizing attitude towards the audience, which says that we will trivialize, and popularize, and simplify true emotion. Most musicals are not about ambiguity at all. They're not about richness or contradiction. They're very, very simplistic, very sentimental. There are some great musicals, but there aren't many. *Guys and Dolls*[8] is a great musical, because it deals within a fantasy. It's a complete masterpiece—wherever you hit it, it rings true. But I would be hard put to say any other complete masterpieces. A much loved and vaunted musical, *Carousel*,[9] I think one of the most sickening pieces of sentimentality and manipulation. It just happens to have some very good tunes. But, I mean, if you actually put *Carousel* on the stage as a play, people would throw things.

SC: So it's not innate to the form, then.

PH: I think it's partly a social thing. I mean "the musical" has really come almost at the same time, historically, as the popular press and the popular novel. There is a certain popularization of people, as it were, coming to the opera experience, but diluted. It's not as demanding. Whither the musical? I don't know. I find the current state of the musical really horrible. It seems to me bland, plastic, without any humanity—and yet it is popular the world over. But then so is McDonald's—so is fast food.

SC: One of the points you come back to a number of times in your diaries is that popular theater must to some extent be worthwhile theater, and you say you grew doubtful of that.

PH: Yes, I do grow doubtful of that. I think that what matters is standards. And I think "standards" really means that you have to understand that art is not a democratic activity. Art is something that you're given by the artist, who is particular, an individual, and sometimes quite alarming in his demands, in what he says, in what he tells us. The fact that a play is understood and loved by two hundred people or two hundred million people is actually insignificant in the beginning. What matters is the quality of the thing itself, and whether it will grow, and whether it will continue to find its public. So I think you cannot believe in art, which I do, and finally not be elitist, because part of the process of art is elit-ist. When Picasso began, he was elitist. He's not elitist now. I think what is very dangerous is to change the vision of the artist, or influence the vision of the artist, in the interest of popularity, or in the interests of immediate commercial popularity, because it always per-verts. It always perverts the vision.

SC: You talk about a voyage of discovery in the rehearsal process. Can you say some-thing about the process that you use to pull together disparate personalities?

PH: I have a terribly clear idea about which way the journey's going to take us; I'm not quite sure where we're going to end up. I don't tell them where I want to go. I hope that it will be obvious where we need to go. I hope that the actors will discover where to go them-selves. Because if they discover themselves, it will be much more creative. They will not feel as if they're in a revival, or in a figment of my imagination. They will feel that they're a part of a creative process.

I think the most important thing about directing is: you obviously have to make a group. There has to be some reason for the group to join together. It may be: "We want to do this Shakespeare play, and we are united in trying to find out what the man meant, what he wants, and we're united in trying to find out how to do it, technically." That will make a group. Any piece of fine writing will make a group that's the objective.

But there are other things. I did, a couple of years ago, a very wild production of *Ly-sistrata*, the Aristophanes play, and we were united there in using half-masks in order to re-lease anarchy, and it released some alarming things at times, alarming things in the people—grotesque, and funny, and wild. So there's always an outside objective. I don't think I can make a group by saying, "Hello. I am your leader. I am Peter Hall. I am your director. You are to be my group." There has to be an ideal—the play, the style, the mean-ing, the occasion—something. And then I think it's a question of measuring up to the ma-terial. The better the play, the better the rehearsal—no question about that.

SC: And, as I understand it, you're committed to keeping the play intact.

PH: Yes. I wouldn't be committed to keeping the play intact if the writer was alive, and was sitting by me, if I thought something needed changing or cutting. But I really am deeply tired of the abuse that we put to Shakespeare. We cut great lumps of him. We rearrange great lumps of him. I've done it myself. I've been guilty of it. And you do it partly because you think "Times have changed," or "This will go better"—or sometimes pure ignorance because you don't know how to make it work. But it is disgraceful, actually. There's a curi-ous duality at the moment. If we fell upon Wagner, and chopped great lumps out of him, and rearranged him, and buggered him about, as we do Shakespeare, there would be riots outside the opera house. But there's very little rioting outside Shakespearean houses, and of-ten critics don't seem to notice that the text has been rearranged or cut to shreds. He did know what he was doing. He is rather better than any of us, I think.

SC: Is there no problem, then, in jumping three hundred years of an audience?

PH: Yes, yes—of course there is. Of course there is. But that's the historical problem that you have with any work of art. There will come a moment when Shakespeare no longer speaks to the English—I would guess in about a hundred years. It really won't be comprehensible—it'll be like Chaucer.

SC: Because of the language itself.

PH: Yes, because of the language difference. We pronounce it completely differently now to how he was pronounced. So the sound experience is completely different. The world of Shakespeare is not our world. But what he said about his world is a metaphor which still says something very strongly to our world, and that would be my definition of a classic—that its metaphor speaks to the next age. It's fantastic that you can do Aeschylus, and you can do Aristophanes, and it still speaks. The world of Aeschylus is even further away from us than the world of Shakespeare. So it seems to me you have to find out what you think the man wanted—what he was trying to say—and then try to communicate it to your audience with as little abuse of the original as possible. It's used often as a free-for-all—to be silly, I think. It's much easier to do *Romeo and Juliet* on motorbikes than it is to do *Romeo and Juliet*—much easier. Concept theater is actually terribly easy, and very simple—it's not ambiguous.

SC: Yes, I understand. At some point in your diaries, you mention—I think it was during the year of the strike—that it would be nice to have theater without all this tech. You also mention Peter Brook's phrase "six actors and an empty space." Have you developed those ideas, or was that a reaction to the strike?

PH: Well, I would love to develop them, but one has to find a place and a space in which to do it which also makes economic sense. I work now with my own company in the West End, in conventional theaters. I work at the National. I work at the RSC; next year I'm going to do the *Oedipus* plays of Sophocles at Epidaurus, in Greece, and then bringing them to the Olivier[10] from there. And this autumn, I'm doing a production of *Julius Caesar* at Stratford,[11] and I'm going to bring it up in September for a day's work on the new Globe Theatre[12] stage. I'm really looking forward to that.

SC: It will be open, then?

PH: It will be workable. We're going to have some workshops there. I think theater as high tech—that's obviously a fashion of the late part of the century.

SC: That's good to hear!

PH: Oh, I'm sure of it. I'm sure of it. Theater finally comes back, always, to an actor, an audience, and the words—always. However much you try and slice it into something else, it always comes back to that. There was an absolutely brilliant high-tech production at the National a few months ago. The stage did everything. It was a brilliant production, but finally you thought: "It's not a very good text."

SC: Yet even Aristotle tells us that spectacle is an element of drama.

PH: Oh, I think it is! One of the dangers of the English tradition is that we are so text-bound, and we're so Puritanical, that we don't understand the visual strength of the metaphor. That's why Inigo Jones was initially unpopular, why Ben Johnson was thought to have sold out by writing masks. I've done a lot of work in Baroque opera. I love the idea of the theater as a metaphor, with the devils underneath, a man on the stage, and the gods above. That's very potent—and that still works, if you do it honestly, and you really respect it. So I think it comes back to that hoary old phrase "That's nice, but is it necessary?" If high tech—emblematic theater, visual theater—is not necessary to the moment, then you don't need it. You shouldn't *decorate* in the theater. If you can do it without it, you should do without it. I think that applies to practically everything.

Notes

1. Peter Hall, *Making an Exhibition of Myself* (London: Sinclair-Stevenson, 1993).

2. Martin Esslin, *The Theatre of the Absurd* (Garden City, N.Y.: Doubleday, 1961).

3. The Royal National Theatre, London.

4. The Royal Court Theatre, London.

5. Peter Hall, *Peter Hall's Diaries: The Story of a Dramatic Battle* (New York: Harper and Row, 1984).

6. Peter Hall, *Making an Exhibition of Myself* (London: Sinclair-Stevenson, 1993).

7. *Carmen*, by Georges Bizet, was first produced in 1875.

8. *Guys and Dolls*, music and lyrics by Frank Loesser, book by Jo Swerling and Abe Burrows, opened on Broadway in 1950.

9. *Carousel*, music by Richard Rodgers, book and lyrics by Oscar Hammerstein II, opened on Broadway in 1945.

10. Olivier Theatre, Royal National Theatre, London.

11. Royal Shakespeare Company, Stratford-upon-Avon.

12. Shakespeare's Globe Theatre, London.

Nicholas Barter
London, October 15, 1993

4

My generation had its shot—we had our opportunity to find our new audience, to say the things we wanted to say, to express the kind of issues that we wanted to express. I think now that each new generation has got to do that for itself.

NICHOLAS BARTER HAS BEEN principal of the Royal Academy of Dramatic Art since 1993 and has taught theater extensively. A board member of the National Council for Drama Training, he's also served on the Executive Committee of the Conference of Drama Schools, as well as on the Drama Panel, the New Writing in Theatre Committee, and other committees of the Arts Council of Great Britain. He's a fellow of the Royal Society of Arts. He's also a stage director and the author of *Playing with Plays.*

SC: In *My Life in Art*, Stanislavski says most acting teachers are charlatans.[1] It's been my observation that that's true today, in the States. What's the situation like here?

NB: I don't think the situation is quite the same here as it is in the United States. The acting teachers in this country tend also to be, on the whole, people who either are or have very recently been working directors. And the majority of the teachers who work at RADA—on the acting course, not on the stage management and technical course, where we do have a permanent staff—but all the teachers on the acting course are, in fact, free-lance teachers. They are, therefore, working out in the profession as well, so they're constantly reevaluating their work in the light of what is going on in the real world. Therefore, we, in a sense, tend to protect ourselves against the sort of hothouse atmosphere that sometimes grows up around the teaching of drama.

SC: Certainly, RADA would be above suspicion, in every way. Can we be as confident about individuals who are not associated with studios—or are there not so many of them here?

NB: I don't think you'll find that there are so many of them here. I don't think the situation is at all the same. There are people, for instance, teaching acting at the Actor's Centre, but they again tend to be working professionals. So there isn't the same structure of actors being able to book in for classes in a studio which has its own methodology, as there is in New York. When we audition students in New York for places here, I find that the majority of students are going to one or another studio for constant classes with acting teachers. We don't hold acting teachers in quite the same reverence.

On the other hand, it is true that our senior acting teacher here, Doreen Cannon, who was trained by Uta Hagen, certainly uses the methods that she has learned—and which, I think, are still used in the HB Studio[2]—Herbert Berghof's and Uta Hagen's approach to Stanislavski—that very much underpins the acting work here. And Doreen, of course, taught for twenty years at Drama Centre.[3] She's trained a whole generation of English actors, and indeed, has trained a number of people who are now teaching in other drama schools. So that method of teaching acting is very much, now, a common thing in England.

SC: That's very interesting. My next question would have been "There's so much talk about the difference between the British and American approaches. How true is that?"

NB: I think there is still a difference, because I think there's a sort of healthy skepticism in this country around any methodology. I think there's a healthy skepticism around anybody who says "This is the only way to do it." Because English acting traditionally has been so eclectic—it has drawn from many different traditions. I don't think you would ever find people taking the whole thing on board without asking some very challenging questions. And, of course, Doreen is not just working here—she's also running her own classes; she's also directing plays here and there, and she also directs plays for us with our third-year students. So, in sense, she is putting herself to the test constantly as director, as well as being a teacher of acting. And the two teachers who work with her—Davilia David was trained by her; Jennie Buckman, on the other hand, uses the same foundation methods, but Jennie comes from a different tradition—she's worked in different companies. So there is, if you like, a sharing of ideals, but the methodology is constantly being reevaluated and thought about.

SC: When I see fringe shows, it seems clear to me that the actors are better trained than New York fringe actors, physically and vocally, and not approaching it the same way.

NB: I don't know whether you can say they're *better* trained. The majority of good actors in this country have had some form of training, and it tends to be within one of the major drama schools. And because most of the drama schools are exposing them to outside directors, outside influences, as well as the ethos of the school, they very soon have to learn how to apply their acting technique in a number of different situations.

The acting technique is seen here, at RADA, as a fundamental; it's a safety net. If your imagination fails, if inspiration fails you, if your intuition fails you, here is a method which will always bring the scene alive, make it come up fresh—a procedure with which to approach your work, and a procedure which you can share with other actors. But you can't necessarily assume that all the actors you work with when you leave RADA, or Drama Centre, or LAMDA[4]—or any other drama school—will have been trained in this way. So what we're saying to the actors is that we're giving you a method by which to work, which will stand you in very good stead, but you can't just wait, like an empty jug, to be filled by a director who also knows this method, or, indeed, by other actors who also know this method. You will probably have to do a lot of this work on your own, and you may well have to work with actors who aren't familiar with the terminology, or with directors who are not interested in the terminology—so you've got to find a way of making this your own work.

I hope that we're sending out people who are properly trained but who are also capable of working in many different fields.

SC: There are a lot of new forms on smaller stages. Martin Esslin wrote that the new theater needs a new type of acting.[5] Is that true? Can we approach the new forms with the traditional structure of an actor, or does there have to be a new acting that goes with the staging of the past twenty or thirty years?

NB: There may need to be a different extension of the actor's technique, but that doesn't mean he isn't coming from the same place. The interesting thing about acting, it seems to me—and, indeed, I talk of myself, directing over the past thirty years—is that every time you start a production, you have to go back to square one. Every time you start a piece of work, you have to begin from the point of "Don't know—I don't know if I'm going to be able to do this. I don't know what's going to be required of me in order to achieve what I feel needs to be achieved." A fundamental technique that underlies all our work here is the Alexander Technique. The whole point of Alexander Technique is the ability to leave yourself alone and to start from where you are now—not to constantly what Alexander called "endgame," not constantly look to the end result.

Now, I think that every actor needs to start from where he or she is now, and then extend out. That means that the starting point is always the same, the fundamental techniques are always the same, because we're all starting from what we mean by truth—and that obviously begs a huge question of "Whose truth?" and "What is truth?" But that's the simple situation of starting with yourself and extending out into character—out, then, to work with your fellow actors. It's like a series of concentric circles, really: you begin with your self-knowledge; you extend out into the character to find how much of yourself the character needs, then how much that character has to interact with the other characters in the play, and, finally, the extent to which that interaction embraces an audience.

Now, that may mean that if the play has a very particular slant, or has a very particular way of expressing the meaning which includes extreme physicality, then you may have to extend a very long way out, into something very physical, or you may have to stretch the language, as somebody like Stephen Berkoff would do. He would stretch your vocal capability because of the very complicated linguistics of the play; the language of the play is a very important part of how the character expresses him- or herself. Now, I don't think that means that you start from a different point. It probably means that you end up at a different point.

SC: Can we generalize about the trends in staging in the theater today?

NB: No, I think it would be almost more difficult to do it now than at any other time, actually. I think there is more diversity of approach, and also at the same time more different kinds of theater. The theater is probably reevaluating itself. It seems to me that the theater is asking questions about itself at the moment; there has been a great deal of uncertainty. Writers have not been quite sure what it is that they're trying to express. If you look at the new writing which developed, say, in the 1960s and 1970s, there was a great clarity about what writers were trying to say, how they were trying to look at society, and the changes that were taking place in society. I think, since the 1980s, we've been in a time when the changes themselves almost overwhelmed the art. The writers haven't found a way, the directors haven't found a way, the actors haven't found a way of expressing what is going to meet a new audience's needs. I think we've been in a great state of *chassis*, as Jack Boyle says in *Juno and the Paycock*.[6]

SC: Is that an indication that theater is in a decline? Is it still vital, for most people?

NB: From where I'm sitting, it's extremely vital, because now at last there's a new sense of young actors coming along who have a very, very strong sense of what they want to do. And what, I hope, we're doing here is to empower each new generation of actors to remake the theater for their audience. My generation had its shot—we had our opportunity to find our new audience, to say the things we wanted to say, to express the kind of issues that we wanted to express. I think now that each new generation has got to do that for itself.

Now, the means by which it does that are severely reduced. The regional theaters in Britain are not what they were. There aren't the permanent companies; there aren't the long seasons; there aren't the diversity of plays for them to go into, so what we have to do is to empower our actors to be able to go out and work at the highest level in a constantly shifting landscape—to do television and make it stick. One play, in the regions—make it stick. A fringe play—make it stick. A commercial, a radio, a film—they're tending to do one-off jobs. Now that, obviously, makes it very, very difficult for them. And that's why we've extended our course from seven terms to nine terms, so it's a full three-year course now, in order to give them more continuity of experience of different kinds of parts in RADA before they leave, because they won't get that kind of experience in the regional repertory theaters, as they used to do.

SC: In the States, stage is an esoteric art. Essentially, no one goes to the theater. People are going to films and television.

NB: That's not quite true in this country. More people go to the theater in this country than go to football matches. That's a statistic which has been researched by the Arts Council.

SC: I see! Nonetheless, television and film are becoming increasingly important in the way people perceive themselves, in the way they perceive society. I'm wondering what you think of that. Can film and video reflect life with the subtlety that stage can? Can it do as good a job?

NB: I think it can, but it does it in a different way, doesn't it? The medium—you have a different experience when you go and sit and watch a film—it's a much more private experience than the theater. The theater is a much more collective experience, and that is one of its extraordinary powers—is that it brings an audience together, in a way. You are aware of sitting in an audience with the rest of the audience, in the theater, which you're not aware of in the same way in the cinema and certainly not sitting at home, watching a very small box in the corner of your room.

SC: Certainly, right. It is very solitary.

NB: It's a very solitary activity.

SC: In the States, every actor worth his salt has read Michael Shurtleff's book, *Audition*,[7] as well as either *Respect for Acting*[8] or *A Challenge for the Actor*.[9]

NB: *Respect for Acting* and *A Challenge for the Actor* are books that we'd recommend for our students here, partly because they help to reinforce the work that they will be getting in class.

SC: What else would you recommend to people?

NB: Well, I suppose you could recommend to the students *Building a Character*.[10] Of all of Stanislavski's books, as collated in English, it's probably the easiest for them to read. I think *An Actor Prepares*[11] is a very hard book for people to read, and it's a very hard book to apply. It's better to do the exercises—do the work, on the ground.

We don't require any sort of academic work in RADA at all—it's an entirely practical, vocational training. And I'm more concerned that the actors are learning through doing, rather than reading about it. We do have a class in contemporary text here, in which we introduce them to all the new playwriting over the last ten to fifteen years, and they often meet new writers and find themselves working on scenes, sometimes, from plays that haven't yet been performed or published. And that is, if you like, an evaluation for them of the way in which the theater is moving, the kind of issues that writers are dealing with, in the United States and Ireland and in mainland Britain. But that, I suppose, is the nearest thing to a contextualizing class that they get. Everything else is absolutely practical: movement work, acting, voice, speech, dialect, verse work, text work, stage fighting, physical skills—an all-round classical training.

SC: Yes, it includes just about everything except for stage direction.

NB: We don't have a directors' course—that's absolutely right.

SC: Why is that?

NB: It's been tried by a number of drama schools in this country, and it's never really worked, to be perfectly honest with you. One of the problems is: "Who do the directors train on?" Because it's quite dangerous, I think, for young directors who are learning their trade to learn on students, who are also learning to act. It's much more useful for the students who are learning to act to work with experienced directors—or actors who direct, who really know the business very well indeed. For a director's training, bringing in professional actors for them to learn on is prohibitively expensive. Most drama schools are very strapped for cash these days, because, as you realize, the majority of drama schools in this country are not state funded. We're private institutions. So I don't know what it is—we've just not found a way of training directors to our satisfaction. Directors in Britain have tended to come through the universities.

SC: Theater in this city seems to be very text oriented, as opposed to theater in the States. I've seen very little that was improvisational, that involved the audience, that deconstructed the text a great deal.

NB: Yes, I think that is fair, actually. Yes, I can't think of any company in this country that's working the way the Wooster Group[12] is working, or even the way that Schechner[13] was working twenty years ago.

SC: What direction would you like to see the theater in this country go in, artistically?

NB: I don't think that's for me to say. I think it's for the actors who I'm training to say that. As I say, I think my generation has had its shot. What I'm trying to do is put the tools into their hands to do what they feel is appropriate for the next generation.

Notes

1. Konstantin Stanislavski, *My Life in Art* (Boston: Little, Brown, 1924), 1. Stanislavski (1863–1938), the Russian director and actor, was a founder of the Moscow Art Theater.

2. HB Studio, New York; Uta Hagen's school.

3. The Drama Centre, London.

4. London Academy of Music and Dramatic Art.

5. Martin Esslin, *The Theatre of the Absurd* (Garden City, N.Y.: Doubleday, 1961).

6. *Juno and the Paycock*, by Sean O'Casey, was first produced in 1924.

7. Michael Shurtleff, *Audition* (New York: Bantam Books, 1978).

8. Uta Hagen with Haskel Frankel, *Respect for Acting* (New York: Macmillan, 1973).

9. Uta Hagen, *A Challenge for the Actor* (New York: Scribner's, 1991).

10. Konstantin Stanislavski, *Building a Character* (New York: Theatre Arts, 1949).

11. Konstantin Stanislavski, *An Actor Prepares* (New York: Theatre Arts, 1936).

12. The Wooster Group, New York.

13. Richard Schechner.

Julie Harris

5

Cape Cod, Massachusetts, February 23, 1996

An actor should look at the theater like "This might be my last day on earth. I might never survive this. I might never survive this."

JULIE HARRIS HAS RECEIVED six Tony Awards for her Broadway performances—for her work in *I Am a Camera*, *The Lark*, *Forty Carats*, *The Last of Mrs. Lincoln*, and *The Belle of Amherst*, as well as a Special Award for Lifetime Achievement. Her numerous other honors include two Emmy Awards, a Theatre World Award, and a National Medal of Arts. She's noted for continuing the tradition of touring with her productions; she's also been widely applauded for her work in film and on television.

SC: I'm so interested in what you have to say about the way the theater's developed in the past twenty years or so. Broadway has declined so much, in terms of the number of plays that have opened, and so much theater—so much more is being done in the regions. What do you think of that?

JH: Well, when I started in the theater, in 1945, the theater could give you a good living if you got a good start and were accepted. All the theaters seemed to me then to be full. Not everything lasted of course, but the season was full of plays, comedies, musical comedies. There was a lot of theater in New York. Now, it's diminished so that the great theaters—so many of them—are closed and becoming derelict. A friend of mine gave me a copy of Katherine Cornell's autobiography.[1] It came out in '48, or something like that, after her triumph with *The Barretts of Wimpole Street*,[2] and the long tour she took across the country. She and Ruth Gordon, and Helen Hayes, and the Lunts,[3] Maurice Evans, Judith Anderson, Fredric March—they all did a play every season and then took it on the road. And there isn't anything like that now. It's diminished, so that I have to think of other ways of working, myself, because I can't depend on being in a play on Broadway.

SC: Well, in your book,[4] you say that if you work hard enough, you have a good chance of making it. That was—twenty-five years ago that you wrote that? Do you think it's still true for a young actor?

JH: Oh, yes. To act, not to act in Broadway theater, but to act, to have a career as an actor. I think it is possible—I hope it is. I think some of my friends who are greatly gifted have had to give up because they couldn't find enough work to sustain them.

SC: Yes, yes—I see a lot of that.

JH: I mean, it does happen. The competition is so very strong. There are just so few parts, and so many of us. When I was in my thirties, forties, even fifties, I was always considered, but now I have a lot of competition. There's a great many of women who are my age who are out there—wonderful actresses—who are all competing for a few parts.

SC: But, nonetheless, you work regularly, don't you?

JH: Yeah! I work in little things. The movie I did last summer in Italy was really a thrill for me because it was a leading part. Mostly in movies now I get very small parts. I love to work in movies—like *Housesitter*.[5] That was a very small part. And the bigger parts like Jessica Tandy[6] would get, I don't seem to get.

SC: Really?

JH: So I have to think of things that I can do on my own, like these one-woman plays that I love doing, and love working on—that's something. That's an area where I can find my own work.

SC: In light of the fact that there are film and television, can the theater ever become as important as it was for Ibsen's audiences, or Shaw's audiences?

JH: Well, I think it has to be subsidized. I think it has to be government subsidized, and I don't know if that's ever gonna come around. The National Endowment for the Arts is almost going out of business. And I don't think Shaw and Ibsen and Shakespeare can sustain themselves without government help, without subsidizing. There were two Shakespeare movies this season—*Othello* and *Richard III*. I don't know how successful they are, how much they're big money-makers.

SC: They're certainly well reviewed.

JH: Yes, but I don't think you can compare them to *Mr. Holland's Opus*,[7] which was a huge success, and *Babe*.[8] I think *Babe* deserves to be a success. I think it's a particularly delightful and truthful and beautiful movie—but it's not Shakespeare. Always, when people have to sit and think and reflect and absorb, people don't want to do that very much. We have to train them. We have to train audiences always to think and sit and absorb things, new ideas, and be excited by it. I know that I am. I am, maybe, not your typical audience, but I love to be an audience. I've never gotten over that. You know, I'll go anywhere to see a play! I don't think people will do that as much. Tomorrow night, I'm going to Orleans to see *The King and I*[9] at the Academy[10] there, and I go all over the Cape[11] to see theater. I go to that wonderful theater in Wellfleet, the Wellfleet Harbor Actor's Theater, and my life wouldn't be as rewarding and exciting and richly endowed if I didn't go to see theater.

SC: Do you read many new scripts?

JH: Yes, yes . . .

SC: What do you think of them?

JH: Some are very exciting! The Beverly Hills Theater Guild has a playwriting contest.[12] I have to read the last five plays. There are a number of us that have to read the final plays. I find sometimes it's very hard to say "This one is the best." And I'm always reading plays that people send me. Some I like, and some I don't, but I find that people are writing plays—furiously writing plays—which is a good sign.

SC: That's good to hear, yes. I'm interested in what you have to say about the actors' unions, because so often the unions are criticized. Do you think that they support the art, or the industry?

JH: I don't know much about unions. I never have become involved. I know it's very important and that we fought very hard to have certain rights and benefits. But I've always felt like this profession is very delicately balanced, and the unions—when something is almost starving, the unions can't ask for things that you would from American Telephone Company. Our profession is not a prosperous profession.

SC: You've done so much work on Broadway, and you've done work in large regional theaters, and in small theaters on the Cape. Do the audiences differ?

JH: I don't think so. I think if a play is correctly constructed, then it has its own built-in responses from the audience. I find that especially in comedies. When you read or hear a reading just of *Romeo and Juliet*, the balcony scene, it still has the charm that it must have had originally and still gets the same laughs. You see, he really knew what he was doing. I mean, it's infallible, when the play is well constructed.

SC: When people come to see you in a show, they must come with so many expectations, and associations with other work that you've done. Does your celebrity in any way make it difficult to reach people, or does it . . .

JH: Oh, no. In my career, I've never played the same kind of parts. It's always been different. So I think audiences who know me are prepared for it not to be the same thing all the time. Sometimes, like *Ladies in Retirement*,[13] which was a very dark part, people say "Oh, we'd like to see you laugh more," but it doesn't keep them from enjoying the woman I'm playing at the moment. It's just that she's different. That's one of the thrills of the theater for me, that an actor can try to be almost anything.

SC: It's fun—no question! In your book, you use an interesting term. You talk about an "actor's intelligence." You write: "Actor's intelligence has to do with making choices. It's the tool of acting that serves as an umbrella for the rest."[14] I'm wondering what you mean by that, because so often it's just that problem of making the choices that we find so difficult.

JH: Well, you're led first of all by the playwright. For instance, if you are playing Amanda Wingfield[15]—everybody looks at something differently, you see. I see the mother in that play as stricken by her inability to help her two children, and that makes her sometimes mean and harsh and overbearing. Because she wants the best for them. She does it out of great love and devotion. She wants them to be perfect. She wants them to get ahead in the world. She wants them to be successful. She wants her daughter to be charming. And nothing is coming out right. So the choices for your intelligence are to follow that through, that theme of a character.

I saw once an amateur production of *The Member of the Wedding*,[16] a play that I had done for a long, long time. The girl who played John Henry's mother used a handkerchief, and I thought: "The author doesn't say she carries this handkerchief and waves it around a lot! Why was that a choice for her to do that?" The mother was a rather self-contained housewife who was careful and loving—and wasn't this flamboyant person who waved a handkerchief a lot. If I had been the director, I would have said to the actress, "Why are you doing that? Why do you think she would do that? She's rather a quiet little southern lady." And that, to me, was a wrong choice. So you should think about the choices you make, the kind of clothes you wear. That's what I mean by your intelligence coming into it. You're making a portrait, but you're always doing it with the playwright's guidance. You don't overrule what he's given you.

For instance, a friend of mine was doing a production of *Night of the Iguana*.[17] Shannon is all wrapped up, because he's having a sort of nervous breakdown. They've bound him, so he won't hurt himself. He's like the iguana—the iguana is lashed to a post there and can't get away. The lady who paints portraits comes out to sit with him and to bring him some tea and to try to soothe him. She wears an old Japanese kimono. And the director said to this actress, "I want you to come out in full Kabuki makeup." She looked at him and said, "I can't do that." He said, "Why? She's been to Japan." But it was so phony, so wrong, that she refused to do it.

SC: That type of thing is so tempting for a director.

JH: She held her ground and refused to put that white makeup on. And I thought: "I would have, too." I would have said, "Are you crazy? Where does that come from?"

SC: You were at the Actor's Studio. I read so much about the Actor's Studio, and I find that sometimes it's critical. A lot of teachers today consider it somehow emotionally excessive.

JH: *Acting* is emotionally excessive! It is! That's where you're going! You're going towards that being absolutely at one with the part, so that you can express every moment in the most alive way. On the stage we are vessels for these extraordinary emotions—and you have to be able to do them at the snap of a finger. It's life and death! We're the vessels for life and death. And slowly, slowly, you learn how to do that. An actor should look at the theater like "This might be my last day on earth. I might never survive this. I might never survive this."

SC: Ordinarily, a drama has a structure that holds the audience, and a set of events that holds the audience. How do you manage to hold so many audiences in plays like *The Belle of Amherst*,[18] when you don't have a dramatic structure, a strict plot?

JH: I find with those one-person plays that I am like an evangelist, and I want everyone to love Emily Dickinson, and to know her heart, as I do. It's thrilling to me to be a part of her thought and life. It's this absolute fierce conviction that I love the very words I'm speaking that makes people listen. I want them to get inside her heart. I want them to understand her. Not half-heartedly—I can't do those plays half-heartedly. There could be a fight between you and me if you didn't agree with me. She was this extraordinary human being!

SC: Those extraordinary letters . . .

JH: Yes! And she had a way of pointing things out to us. I used to feel at the end of that play like I was really floating on a magic carpet of her ideas, of her feelings—they were so extraordinary.

It's like any great spirit that's lived. I've always been drawn to Van Gogh and his paintings and his letters. He was a great letter writer. He was a great writer. You want people to understand what you feel you understand about this particular person. Charlotte Bronte— the life of the Brontes' has always excited me, and Mr. Luce,[19] who wrote *The Belle of Amherst*, also wrote *Bronte*[20] for me. First we called it *Currer Bell, Esquire*, which was the name she first published under. I think it's a more arresting title than *Bronte*. It's so interesting that women in Victorian times published under men's names. It was considered easier to get a publisher.

SC: Did you perform that as much as *The Belle of Amherst?*

JH: Maybe not quite as much, but then I did *Lucifer's Child*,[21] about Isak Dinesen, and Mr. Luce wrote that for me, too.

SC: I see. So a lot of collaborations.

JH: Yeah, yes. I also have done a play about Sonia Tolstoy, called *Countess*,[22] by Donald Freed. I never get to the end of fascinating ladies, to read about and think about and know that they would make plays.

Now, you haven't had anything to eat! That's Emily Dickinson's fruitcake, so you should have a little piece of that. That's her black cake. It's her recipe.

SC: How interesting! I lived in Amherst for a long time, so I was wondering . . .

JH: Did you know anybody who lived in that house then?

SC: Someone from Amherst College.

JH: They advertised for a caretaker to live in the house. I was tempted to write for the job. . .

SC: Miss Harris, do you teach very much?

JH: No, I don't teach.

SC: I'm surprised to hear that, because certainly every actor in the country would . . .

JH: Well, I love young actors, but I don't feel I'm together enough to teach. But I love to be with young actors! I think they're wonderful! A friend of mine who was a stage manager is now studying acting, and he's a wonderful character actor, but he has a nasal problem, which they are now concentrating on so that they can help him with that.

SC: That type of thing is so tough to deal with.

JH: I know! But you have to if you want to be an actor. Everybody has something they have to overcome. I didn't have much of a voice in the beginning, but I acted and I concentrated on it. I didn't train my voice—only by doing it did I train it. I always say to young actors you have to study everything. You have to study movement. You have to be a dancer. You have to be a singer. You have to play a musical instrument. You have to be a designer. You have to know about stagecraft, so that if you had to, you could say "This is the way it should look." You have to be complete, like Kenneth Branagh now, and Emma Thomson. You feel she could design her own sets if she needed to. And Laurence Olivier. Those people were actors—craft actors! They could do the whole thing. They knew what kind of material they wanted, what the movement should look like.

SC: Some teachers say that actors don't need directors. I was wondering what you think.

JH: Well, I think directors serve a great purpose in the theater. I mean, some directors have great vision, and not all actors have that capability. So we need directors, I think. Some actors have that capability and can do it all, like Orson Welles.

SC: Have you directed much?

JH: No, I've never directed a play.

SC: I'm surprised!

JH: More and more, I'm interested in all aspects of the theater. I have worked with a very gifted director, Charles Nelson Reilly. He did *The Belle of Amherst* with me, and *Bronte*. We've done a lot of plays together. We did a wonderful play by Moti Lerner,[23] an Israeli writer, about Else Lasker Schuler, who's a famous German poet and was persecuted by the Nazis.

You see! When I say "Nazi"—I was just watching a documentary about Winston Churchill. When he got up to speak, he pronounced that word, he said "Naaazis" with such contempt and fury: "Naaazis." We always say "Nazi" but he said "Naaazi."

SC: In that wonderful voice of his.

JH: Yes, that wonderful . . . There was an actress by the name of Fabia Drake, an English actress. I don't know if you saw *The Jewel in the Crown*.[24] She played the one who lived in the mountains, and the family came to visit her, and Peggy Ashcroft was her servant lady, her companion. And her husband had been in the army. There was the reception for the wedding of the young girl, and Peggy Ashcroft, I think, pointed to something, and Fabia Drake said "Chillianwalla."

I thought: "That name . . . what is that name?" It went right through me like a cold knife! This was known to be like, in our country, Gettysburg. An enormous number of Indians and English died in this battle, which was fought in 1849, in January, in terrible mountainous country, with freezing winter, and it was a slaughter on both sides. It was absolutely horrendous. Now, when she said that name, I didn't know what it was. And I thought: "Now that's the actor's job." When she said that word, my heart began to stop! If it hadn't meant that to her, it wouldn't have meant anything to anyone!

This is how things go through our lives and mean something to us, because we've seen them in the theater, or on the television, or on the big screen. And they become part of our life, if the actor's doing his job correctly. This is how the theater educates us. This is how it involves us in life. It's not so much what's going to happen in the future, or what's happening now, but we have to know what happened before. We have to have a sense of history, as people. We have to know what's gone into making us!

Notes

1. Katherine Cornell and Ruth Woodbury Sedgwick, *I Wanted to Be an Actress: The Autobiography of Katherine Cornell* (New York: Random House, 1939).

2. *The Barretts of Wimpole Street*, by Rudolf Besier, opened on Broadway in 1931.

3. Alfred Lunt (1892–1977) and Lynn Fontanne (1892–1983).

4. Julie Harris with Barry Tarshis, *Julie Harris Talks to Young Actors* (New York: Lothrop, Lee and Shepard, 1971).

5. *Housesitter*, a film directed by Frank Oz, 1992.

6. A year after this interview, Ms. Harris was nominated for a Tony Award for her performance in the role of Fonzia Dorcy in the Broadway production of *The Gin Game*, by D. L. Coburn, a role first made famous in 1977 by Jessica Tandy.

7. *Mr. Holland's Opus*, a film directed by Stephen Herek, 1995.

8. *Babe*, a film directed by Chris Noonan, 1995.

9. *The King and I*, music by Richard Rodgers, book and lyrics by Oscar Hammerstein II, opened on Broadway in 1951.

10. The Academy of Performing Arts, Orleans, Massachusetts.

11. Cape Cod, Massachusetts.

12. The Julie Harris Playwright Awards Competition.

13. *Ladies in Retirement*, by Edward Percy and Reginald Denham, opened on Broadway in 1941. Ms. Harris is referring to the Coconut Grove Playhouse Production that opened in 1995 with Ms. Harris, directed by Charles Nelson Reilly.

14. Harris with Tarshis, *Julie Harris Talks to Young Actors*.

15. Amanda Wingfield is a character in *The Glass Managerie*, by Tennessee Williams, which opened on Broadway in 1945.

16. *The Member of the Wedding*, by Carson McCullers, opened on Broadway in 1950 with Ms. Harris.

17. *The Night of the Iguana*, by Tennessee Williams, opened on Broadway in 1961.

18. *The Belle of Amherst*, by William Luce, opened on Broadway in 1976 with Ms. Harris.

19. William Luce.

20. *Bronte*, by William Luce, was first produced on radio in 1979 under the title *Currer Bell, Esquire* with Ms. Harris. It was produced on stage under that title in 1983, and produced under the title *Bronte* in 1986, both with Ms. Harris.

21. *Lucifer's Child*, by William Luce, opened on Broadway in 1991 with Ms. Harris.

22. *The Countess*, by Donald Freed, was first produced in 1986 with Ms. Harris.

23. *Exile in Jerusalem*, by Moti Lerner, was first produced in 1990 under the title *Else*. Ms. Harris is referring to the 1994 production directed by Charles Nelson Reilly at the Williamstown Theater Festival in Massachusetts.

24. *The Jewel in the Crown*, a television miniseries produced by Granada Television, 1984, based on the 1966 novel of that name by Paul Scott, Part I of *The Raj Quartet*.

Adrian Noble
London, October 12, 1995

6

If people say that the classics aren't about current life, it's because they've misread them—it's as simple as that.

ADRIAN NOBLE WAS an associate artistic director of the Royal Shakespeare Company from 1982 to 1990 and its artistic director from 1991 to 2003. He has worked as well with the Royal Exchange Theatre in Manchester, the Bristol Old Vic, and the Gate, Dublin, and Royal Court Theatres. A director of "straight" theater, musicals, opera, and television, he's received the Plays and Players London Drama Critics Award and two Drama Awards.

SC: You've called RSC[1] a classical company. I'd like to ask you about the problems that are involved in restaging classics, and how they're overcome. After all, we're taking a script from another culture. How do we deal with making that transfer?

AN: Are we taking a script from another culture? I mean, one will find, will one not, that there are echoes throughout western civilization, and if you say the fountainhead of western drama is Greek theater, you can also say the fountainhead of western civilization is Greek civilization. The next great dramatic flowering was the Renaissance, which had an impact that is still felt today. You can see links between our lives now and the drama of the Renaissance—or indeed the ancient Greeks. What one has to do is to recognize those connections.

I could talk for about an hour. Would you like me to talk about specifics of how one tackles a production, or talk more generally?

SC: Let me be more specific with the question. To start with: what about the language of Shakespeare, and the form of verse in plays, for an audience who wouldn't understand the original pronunciation of Shakespeare and are not used to hearing verse?

AN: Well, one discovers with Shakespeare, the more one works with him, is that he was a fantastically practical, pragmatic fellow, and that the key to Shakespeare's verse speaking is actually to recognize how practical and pragmatic his writing is. He was writing for a company of actors that rehearsed very, very swiftly—performed in large spaces with a huge capacity—and the composition of the audience was extremely catholic—i.e., from highly educated folk to completely illiterate people. Now, we *know* that. And you will find that what

28

maybe we regard in the modern age as the complexities of the verse are frequently there to offer the actor practical help with overcoming certain difficulties in holding an audience.

"O for a muse of fire"[2]—"O" gives the actor a moment—gives him the opportunity of controlling the house. It's a practical issue, as well as an expression of emotion, and all the other things it does, et cetera . . .

The verse line itself is more recognizable than one would first think. You will find that people tend to speak in pentameters, if you like—that's roughly how much language we have in one portion of a thought. And a verse line—the moment you recognize the primacy of the verse line over the sentence, you immediately recognize human behavior—that people don't speak in sentences. I'm not talking to you in sentences—I'm talking to you in thoughts, which means that I'll move to a sentence, and gather the next sentence as I'm ending one—right? Which is precisely what you do with a verse line. You don't stop at the end of a verse line—you start the next one. A politician will hold on to his audience by not stopping, or pausing, at a full stop, because you'll lose your audience if you do, or someone will interrupt you. These are all very practical issues that he knew from his education, his upbringing, and from his experience as an actor and an artist.

So one has to first of all recognize the practical issues of verse speaking. Then one also has to recognize that Shakespeare's language—and verse itself—operates on more profound levels than just the intellect—and that the meaning, if you like, is just the beginning of it. I was talking to somebody at lunch yesterday—a German colleague who came to see our production of *Henry VI, Part 3* in South America. And the gentleman couldn't speak English. He was rather nervous. He thought: "My God, I don't know anything about the plot!" And he was overwhelmed by the power of the piece! If you take that as an example—it's an early play by Shakespeare, end-stopped, very regular parse—you'll find in it a power, an authority, a pulse, a pounding rhythm that works on the human being in ways that have nothing to do with the meaning. But it's—it's sensuous. It's like jazz, it's like reggae music. It has bottom to it that stirs you, that affects you emotionally.

I speak no German, but I get upset and excited by hearing Adolph Hitler. I don't know what he's saying—I have no idea what he's saying at all, but I understand what happened at those rallies at Nuremberg, because this man had a cadence in his voice that was terrifying—and for some people exciting. And verse works like that on so many levels at different times. As an artist working as a director or an actor, you have to work simultaneously on all these things, recognizing the practical, allowing yourself to have a sensuous response to the words, and allow yourself to—if you like—be possessed by the language in a kind of a more Dionysiac way.

SC: But isn't it true that Shakespeare was assuming an acuity of listening skills that our audiences don't have?

AN: Yes, undoubtedly true, and that is the main reason, I believe, for public support of classical theater—because we are losing those skills. We are losing skills of articulacy; our vocabulary is shrinking. We are becoming an entirely visual nation. An idea needs to be expressed. If you cannot express an idea, you cannot master that idea. If you can't master ideas, you can't as a nation control your destiny, you know? I think it's a major, major issue in our schools. And classical theater sharpens up the ear. It's a challenge.

You're absolutely right in focusing on this, but the best way of overcoming that difficulty is to do it—to say to kids "Listen. Sit down. What's it like?" To say to actors "Don't just work on the mind. Work on their senses. Work on their emotions, as well, so they get excited by language!" Shakespeare came out of that highly rhythmic, alliterative tradition that's exciting—all those wonderful Middle English poems. They have a terrific pulse—really highly alliterative, highly assonant. Give the audiences a sensuous piece as well as an intellectual piece. And make the audiences listen. Don't assume they're gonna listen, because they're not. Make them listen! And you can make them listen, and use every device he's given you to make them listen. It isn't just a clever Shakespearean trick that you will suddenly go contrapuntal in a line, and the rhythm will change. You know, you're not conscious of it, but it keeps your ears *hot*.

SC: It sounds like you want to motivate the audience to do a certain amount of work themselves. I mean, they have to sit forward in their seats and listen. What does it take to get them to do that? Are they willing to do that?

AN: Well, the act of buying a ticket, for most people, means they are willing to do that. Some people go to the theater for other reasons, of course—modish, or they've been dragged there by their teacher or their wife or whatever—there's a lot of reasons. So therefore you have to work a little bit harder.

I believe we should, in Stratford, be trying to create a theater that is, of course, language-based but does have strong physical presence to the performances, that has an exciting visual side. I don't think we should neglect that. I love fine design. I love actors who have great bodies and can move, and can excite the audience with their bodies as well as the language. And I love bold musical scores. If you look back at the great Aristotelian virtues—dance, music, character, story-telling—it's a very bold collection of virtues, and I believe we should be playing to the full to all that. And classical theater usually gives you the opportunity to explore all of those. So you do a Greek play. Greek plays were acted; they were sung; they were danced. We *know* all those things. And so let's have music in our theaters; let's have dancing in our theaters; let's have singing in our theaters, as well as declaiming.

SC: I'm very interested in the modern classics and the problems they present. Isn't it true that Ibsen and Shaw were using shock value, to a certain extent—when Nora walks out, in *A Doll's House*,[3] or when Mrs. Warren talks about her profession?[4] How do we overcome the fact that nothing shocks us now?

AN: To a degree that's true. Having directed a production of *Doll's House*,[5] which was in its time quite celebrated, the provocative issue at the end of *A Doll's House* isn't Nora walking out. It's Nora walking out on her children. That still shocks people. Daddies can walk out on children; Mummies can't walk out on children. And people still say, "She can't leave her kids. She should have taken her kids with her." No, no, no. She says, "I'm walking out on the kids, as well." That's why, in my production, we made a big deal of the kids. We expanded that scene; she was very loving with them; they were happy children. The kids were out and around—and she walked out on her kids. People still find that totally unacceptable. A lot of men do—a lot of women do, as well, actually. I find it difficult.

SC: As I understand it, the ending was changed in its time.

AN: Absolutely—it absolutely was. Very often, one will find that things one believes have lost their shock value still have it a little bit. But a play that is only an issue play ultimately won't last. We'll stay with *Doll's House* as an example, all right? The subject of *Doll's House* isn't her walking out. It's freedom; it's liberty. Or, putting it another way, the subject is imprisonment. And the principal character of *A Doll's House* isn't just Nora. Torvald is just as imprisoned—in his upbringing, in his emotional inarticulacy. Christine is imprisoned from her inability to make a connection with somebody for fifteen years. Krogstad is imprisoned by society because he made a mistake—one mistake. Rank is imprisoned because he has a congenital disease, and his body's failing him, and his mind. Every single person in that play is imprisoned, not just her. And that's why it will last—because it's about human beings who want to be liberated. And the solution is different for everybody. You must recognize the subject in a classic. And if it turns out to be just a temporary issue play, then it probably won't last. Television usually does that better than the theater these days.

SC: And how do you respond to people who say that a play should have some involvement in current issues? People on the fringe often turn away from the classics, because they think they don't.

AN: Yeah, well, I don't know about current issues. It has to be about current life—about the human condition, and certain things about the human condition don't change that much.

Why do we do this? What are we talking about, here? We're talking about human beings trying to live together—men and women—men and men—women and children—trying to actually make life together, bring children into the world. I think that's important! Trying to balance in society individual freedom with collective responsibility. That's an issue—that's difficult to do. The rights of expression—whether it's in the newspapers or the media—over a person's freedom and privacy—these are issues! Classics deal with all of those, in different ways. *The Duchess of Malfi*[6] is about the right to dissent, and the contest in it is about what responsibilities go with certain positions. That's an issue! I think it's a universal issue—do you see?

If people say that the classics aren't about current life, it's because they've misread them—it's as simple as that. They've misread them. Or they think theater's something it isn't.

I don't want people to leave my theater—any of my theaters—and want to take to the barricades. Theatre doesn't work like that. The very act of making theater is in itself beneficial, because it's to do with bringing people together. You go somewhere together—you very rarely do that. You sit in a movie house and you're on your own—it's very private. You sit there silently—occasionally you laugh, but otherwise you're silent. People don't go to church anymore—not so much as they used to in the 1940s. When people go to the theater, when they go to pop concerts, they come together.

In pop concerts, that's the kind of a thing that's cathartic in a way that completely overwhelms you. In the theater, you're invited to open your intellect and your emotions—to take part in a fantasy—to take part in a fiction. And taking part in a fiction, I believe, is a liberating, an educative experience in itself. It's storytelling, right? A child will learn by playing. A child will play *Wolf*, and he or she will deliberately frighten himself. I'm just as frightened as if it's a real wolf, but I know it's my friend Mark, or it's Daddy. Now, in the theater, I can go in there, and I can be frightened—or I can cry—or I can laugh. And through that fiction, I can live all sorts of other things, and I can know myself more, or I can learn things about myself, or I can tackle things, like jealousy, things that one shuts off—difficult things. As well as the wonderful things, like fantasy and fiction.

SC: How can theater keep its traditional role, in light of the fact that there are television and film in the world?

AN: Well, theater will be there as long as man is there, I believe—because it supplies a need. I don't feel we're being swamped. I think television provides practical problems—like how does theater compete for the talent? You can ask any theater director in Los Angeles—it's a bloody nightmare getting actors. If something falls through, that's about your only chance of getting an actor. It's not that bad here, but you know, the writing's on the wall—which is horrific! With the explosion of television channels around the world, they must be fed, and they must be fed by more and more material that will require more and more actors. And there aren't that many good actors around, believe you me. Therefore, you know, the quality will go down.

In terms of television, I have to say I'm a pessimist. I think our television will end up like your television, if we're not careful.

Notes

1. The Royal Shakespeare Company, London, Stratford-upon-Avon, Newcastle.
2. "O for a muse of fire": this is the opening line of *Henry V*.
3. *A Doll's House*, by Henrik Ibsen, was first produced in 1879.
4. *Mrs. Warren's Profession*, by George Bernard Shaw, was first produced in 1905.
5. Mr. Noble is referring to the 1981 Royal Shakespeare Company production of *A Doll's House*.
6. *The Duchess of Malfi*, by John Webster, was first produced in 1614.

Uta Hagen
New York, November 23, 1994

7

As long as people think of theater as a commercial venture, it'll remain "show biz." A meaningful theater must be a necessary offering.

UTA HAGEN WON THREE Tony Awards—two were for her performances in *The Country Girl* and in the original production of *Who's Afraid of Virginia Woolf*, and one was a special Tony Award for lifetime achievement. Among her other honors are two Drama Critics Awards, the London Critics Award, and the National Medal of the Arts. She taught acting extensively at her studio in New York, Herbert Berghof Studio, and she wrote two hugely influential books on acting, *Respect for the Acting*, and *A Challenge for the Actor*.

Ms. Hagen died in January 2004 at the age of eighty-four.

SC: You've criticized Actors' Equity.[1] Could you say something about the union? What's the problem?

UH: There are no artistic guidelines or standards for entering the union! Anyone can be a member. You only have to be cast in a show. If you're a friend of the producer, you can join. Nor is Equity acting as a trade union—it doesn't try to develop work. It also restricts you with rules, such as the one that if you rehearse for an hour, you must take a break, whether you want to or not. Arbitrary laws about a creative process are appalling.

SC: In your book,[2] you say that actors have relinquished their responsibility to the theater. Could you say something about that?

UH: Actors depend on being "hired"—on others to provide their work. They should create their own opportunities in garages, living rooms, attics, et cetera. They must claim their rightful, essential importance to the theater.

SC: If anything could make that happen, it would be your book. Is it happening?

UH: Yes, in a very small way. For instance, I've been teaching a workshop in Detroit[3] for the past six years, and now the actors have formed a company and are producing plays for themselves.

SC: In your book,[4] you mention the McCarthy era and blacklisting. What's the feeling today among artists, considering the censorship movement?

UH: Artists have always rebelled against censorship.

SC: In every period?

UH: Yes.

SC: I spoke with Nicholas Barter, the principal of the Royal Academy of Dramatic Art. He told me that the only books he'd recommend to his students were your books. In light of what he said, is there any real difference between American and British acting?

UH: That's a broad question. There are some British actors who work externally and others who don't. And there are many American actors who lack voice, body, and speech technique.

SC: In your book, you write: "It should always be our aim to serve the playwright."[5] Is there no place for theater that is not script-oriented?

UH: Of course there is. The improvisational theater of Sills[6] in Chicago, for one. In my book, I'm assuming that we're working with traditional scripts.

SC: Are the same acting techniques appropriate for non-traditional theater?

UH: A well-trained actor has the techniques to deal with any role, in any style.

SC: Would it be fair to say that the theater is created for and by the upper middle class?

UH: No, that's not fair at all. In my experience, it's been the middle class who have been buying tickets. When we sold out *Who's Afraid of Virginia Woolf*,[7] it was the middle class who bought tickets, not the upper middle class. And in the '30s, we had the WPA[8]—a true people's theater, which should always exist, ideally. The present Broadway scene has simply priced itself out of existence.

SC: Can the theater ever regain the importance it had, in terms of influencing the public, in Ibsen's theater? Or Chekhov's?

UH: It has to! It has to! But before it can, it has to remember that it's not there to earn money! It's not something to be bought and sold! And everyone has to recognize that. As long as people think of theater as a commercial venture, it'll remain "show biz." A meaningful theater must be a necessary offering.

Notes

1. Uta Hagen, *A Challenge for the Actor* (New York: Scribner's, 1991).

2. Hagen, *A Challenge for the Actor*.

3. Ms. Hagen taught in Detroit at the Heartland Theater.

4. Hagen, *A Challenge for the Actor*.

5. Hagen, *A Challenge for the Actor*.

6. Paul Sills, founder of the Second City Company, Chicago.

7. *Who's Afraid of Virginia Woolf*, by Edward Albee, opened on Broadway in 1962, with Ms. Hagen.

8. The WPA: the Works Progress Administration Theater, a.k.a. the Federal Theater Project, was established in 1935 by the U.S. government and dissolved in 1939.

John Lahr
New York, October 4, 1995

Nobody ever went poor in American society underestimating the intelligence of the American public.

JOHN LAHR HAS BEEN A THEATER CRITIC for the *Village Voice* and the *Evergreen Review*. Since 1992, he's been writing for the *New Yorker*. His many books on the theater include *Astonish Me*, *Adventures in Contemporary Theater*, *Show and Tell*, *Automatic Vaudeville: Essays on Star Turns*, and *Coward the Playwright*. He's been given the George Jean Nathan award for dramatic criticism twice and has also received the Roger Machell Prize for theater writing and the Yale Writing Prize.

SC: If I could ask you about something you wrote in April—you wrote: "The musical has been instrumental in defining the nation's sense of abundance. In its irresistible spectacle of well-being, the musical is America's most persuasive political theater: its message is not revolution but acquisition, not change but stasis."[1]

JL: That's right.

SC: Could you expand on that? What political message is the musical giving us?

JL: Well, generally, the political message is that something's good—"Something's coming, something good, if you can wait"—that "Everything's coming up roses." It's comforting. It's enchanting. It doesn't inspire thought. It inspires a faith in the status quo, in the goodness of the society, in the righteousness of the people, and in the notion of the sense of blessing of the culture—which is why it's such a powerful form.

From its earliest beginnings, the musical has always given America the backbeat of promise, really. It's the songs and the stars of the musical first, before cinema established itself as the popular art form in the culture. It was really the Broadway theater that developed the notion of show business, and it also developed the notion of the star system.

So this whole ideology of individualism comes out of Broadway, and what Broadway sings about, what its neon signs reinforce visually, the whole idea of making your name above the title. All of that is all part and parcel of what I consider a political notion—to enhance, explore, hymn individualism in all its manifestations—aggrandizement, making a killing—

which is a happy ending in most musicals, prior to Stephen Sondheim. Singing about the city, the metropolis, the blessings, the wealth, the triumph of individuals—that's what the musical is about, and that is an ideology. That is why, in the last two wars, lyricists have special dispensations. Governments know, even if the citizens don't, that—as Plato said—songs are spells for souls, for the creation of concord. That Plato understood, and indeed, we have experienced it in this culture—that concord, that sense of well-being, that sense of comfort and credulity comes out of this great and interesting and celebratory form.

SC: When modern theater has been at its best, for Ibsen and Shaw, it wasn't assenting to the status quo. It was critical.

JL: Yes, but you're talking about drama; I'm talking about musicals, which is sung drama—only recently, only since 1942. Prior to that, it was musical comedy, and it was much more an assembly of songs and turns—which had, in a certain way, more iconic power in the culture than great plays. I mean, a star, a really great performer, lives in the mind of a culture much more than the debate of a play.

So they provided a lot for Broadway. Broadway entertainment, Broadway musicals provided a lot. It's a different thing. I mean, a play of Shaw or Ibsen wanted to have a debate with society. The musical is a business art that wants to entertain the culture. It's a con trick, in the sense that it gives confidence—that's what con tricks are—to the public. While it's winning its heart, it's picking its pocket.

SC: So would it be fair to say that it does not stand as a great art form—the way the best straight drama does?

JL: It's different. It is a great art form; it's just they're doing largely different things. I don't think—and this is one of my arguments with a lot of the more advanced musicals of Stephen Sondheim—I don't actually think that you can have a debate, as Auden[2] pointed out, in song, musicals that are just through sung, as they say. Because you don't hear words in the same way sung as you do when they're spoken in prose. And therefore, I feel that prose inhabits a moral universe, and song doesn't. Song is a sort of enchantment. By the beauty of the sound of music, which is persuasive, you can make anybody feel anything—say anything. Auden makes the point that you can say "Thirty days hast September, April, June, and November," and you can change those words around and it'll still seem to be sensible. It's a different kind of dialogue that the musical drama wants to have than the prose dramatists.

SC: If you could speak for a minute about the levels in American drama. Is there a dialogue between Broadway and off-off-Broadway?

JL: Let's get something real straight, here. In 1927–28, in that Broadway season, there were 286 plays on Broadway. Last year, there were twenty-seven. Now, there's no doubt, by just looking at those figures, that Broadway, as a sort of producing institution, is more or less dead. Seventy percent of the people who come to Broadway now are tourists. The top dollar is seventy-five dollars a seat, so you can see that there's no way that Broadway can easily attract young people. It doesn't often and easily attract people of color for the same reason. As a producing institution, on the other hand, when Broadway shows are taken on the road, they tend to gross around a billion dollars a year. So that, on the one hand, Broadway as a producing institution is declining, and on the other hand, it's still a very solid business, doing what it does, which is putting out very popular commercial entertainment.

From the early '60s, you can point to individual fine evenings of intelligent theater—serious theater. I mean Arthur Kopit's *Indians*,[3] or Tony Kushner's *Angels in America*,[4] or S. J. Perelman's *The Beauty Part*,[5] which my father[6] was in. All these plays are really extremely interesting, but they're isolated. It's very hard now. It's too expensive. The climate and the expectation for serious discussion—it's just not there. That's been for about thirty years. There really isn't a lot of real debate of the culture on Broadway. That's not to say that the musicals, in their kind of craven attempt to capture a market, aren't in some way interesting or significant. But it's not in a sort of direct, intellectual way.

The effect of off-off-Broadway, therefore, on Broadway is nil. There is no relationship. I was the drama critic in an earlier life, in the '60s, for the *Village Voice* and *Evergreen Review*, and I was lucky enough to catch the wave when the new off-Broadway movement happened. That off-Broadway movement lasted all of four years. Of course, it generated a lot of energy, and some of that energy has spilled over, over the years, to writers like John Guare and Sam Shepard and Terence McNally, who have stayed the course. Terence McNally now is a Broadway writer, but he was an off-Broadway, not an off-off-Broadway writer. Insofar as that most of things that get done on Broadway are musicals, the only things that I can say that for sure had any influence on Broadway were a few scenic effects by Tom O'Horgan and Joe Chaikin, in the '60s, which were then absorbed into musicals like *Kiss of the Spider Woman*,[7] and *Hair*,[8] and shows like that. Some gargantuan effects, some things with placards, some spatial discoveries—but there was not much. There's hardly any exchange, no.

SC: Then where is the strength of the American theater? Off-off-Broadway? In the regions?

JL: Playwrights are writing. It's burgeoning in the regions, a bit, and off-Broadway, a bit. It's odd—it goes through a cyclical series. At the moment, there are some wonderful playwrights—I mean, Tony Kushner and David Mamet are, in their own way, as ambitious and poetic and accomplished as Arthur Miller and Tennessee Williams. These are good writers, writing really brave plays. Whether or not they have the environment and the luck to keep working for a lifetime . . .

One of the nice things about this job is that theater culture is sort of dying—not that it doesn't exist, but that, on the whole, people aren't as interested in theater as they are in film, or in rock music, or in other forms—in television—and theatrical figures don't hold the imagination quite the same way. That doesn't mean that theater is not important, or less good. It just means that the public have other interests vying for their attention. But the theater culture has to be worked at—it has to be sustained. It's not as easy. It does mean that these new writers don't expect to have the kind of commercial life that writers might have expected before, and that they have to be a little more cunning, and that they have to be more peripatetic and seek out different venues for their plays—repertory venues.

And I can tell you, because I live in London, the most vivacious theater that's done in London is almost entirely American. There are a lot of new American writers being done over there. And that's very promising. That's also a trend, because it's hard to get decent technical productions over here. A lot of the better writers—Wally Shawn, David Mamet, Sam Shepard, John Guare, Edward Albee—have all had extremely good productions in England, and often go to England first to have their plays done, and then bring them over here.

SC: How do we explain why the English theater . . .

JL: Costs. It's cheaper.

SC: In the West End?

JL: They do it at the National Theatre,[9] or at the Royal.[10] Richard Nelson, another good American playwright, has no audience here, has a big audience in England, and his plays are done at the Royal Shakespeare Company. So he gets a good production with good actors in repertory system, where he's guaranteed a certain number of performances, and he can actually learn, and grow. In our system—which is not funded, has no way of really sustaining talent—the free market notion of talent is that the winners in a free market economy win big, but the actual art form isn't sustained, because there's no way of generating a whole theatrical climate. You can only put money into specific individuals.

SC: So it's an economic issue, then.

JL: I think so.

SC: Can the theater regain the importance that it had for Ibsen's audience, for Shaw's audience, in light of the fact that there are film and television in the world?

JL: Well, to me, theater is much more important in certain ways. The debate that I see in television movies or Hollywood movies is minimal. The use of language, the issues, are rarely explored. Although the numbers of the audiences certainly don't bear any relationship to film or television, the actual quality of the discussion is much higher.

And perhaps it's a very good thing that theater has to get used to being, as it were, a minority art form. In a sense, theater is where the language is renewed and chronicled, and also where the sense of community, such as it is in this culture, is also renewed—and I think that's always important. To say whether it will ever again be equally important, I think, is to miss the point. It's always important, and only if you're talking numbers is there any sort of disparity. I can't find too many American films that are comparable to Tennessee Williams or Eugene O'Neill, or Arthur Miller—or, for that matter, David Mamet or Edward Albee. They are really exploring a terrain of the spiritual, not the terrain of the commercial. Their inquiry is not a business inquiry, but an intellectual, emotional, moral inquiry.

It means that the quality of the discussion, the intention of the work, is completely different. One is to explore a truth—the other is to get a pay day. And so the value of the one is infinitely greater, although it may or may not be as commercially successful as the distractions of a film.

Nobody ever went poor in American society underestimating the intelligence of the American public. And the culture wants distraction. It's the heroine in the culture. They want jokes—they want make-believe—they want escape. Of course theater is, in its own way, trying to entertain, instruct by pleasing. It wants to disenchant, and of course disenchantment is where freedom lies—but also to a certain extent where poverty lies, because people don't want that—they want to live in some sort of cocoon of pleasure and escape. And so that's always the trade-off.

And so in answer to your question, I think the theater has always been more important than film in certain ways—has always led film, even though film is an incredibly attractive medium, and lots of fun. That doesn't mean that the theater as a generating force in the society is any less important.

SC: So would you say the theater is accepting its responsibility to have a social effect?

JL: I'm sorry—I don't understand the question, because it always has a social effect.

SC: Is there a political effect of American theater aside from the Theater of Assent, the musical, the theater that acquiesces to the status quo?

JL: Sure. Any good piece of theater changes people. And insofar as it changes people, it's political, because it makes you accept the unacceptable—or heretofore unknown—ideas. And in that sense, it's political. That's why nation-states always want to ban theater, or control theater, because it does speak directly to the people and reflect people's ideas in the moment. Also because its goal is to let the voice say illiberal, outrageous, strange things that can't be controlled. Television is controlled. It's controlled by censors—it's controlled by advertisers. The audience is finally the product that the networks sell to the advertisers. So you're manipulated. The theater is an experience of freedom, in its own way—intellectual freedom. So the very act of theater is an act of politics.

Notes

1. John Lahr, "Song of the Suits," *New Yorker*, April 24, 1995.

2. W. H. Auden: English poet (1907–1973).

3. *Indians*, by Arthur Kopit, opened on Broadway in 1969.

4. *Angels in America: A Gay Fantasia on National Themes*, by Tony Kushner. Part I, *Millennium Approaches*, opened in London at the Royal National Theater in 1992. It opened on Broadway in 1993. Part 2, *Perestroika*, opened on both Broadway and at the Royal National in 1993.

5. *The Beauty Part*, by S. J. Perelman, opened on Broadway in 1962.

6. Bert Lahr (1895–1967).

7. *The Kiss of the Spider Woman*, music by John Kander, lyrics by Fred Ebb, book by Terence McNally, opened on Broadway in 1993.

8. *Hair*, music by Galt MacDermot, book and lyrics by James Rado and Gerome Ragni, opened on Broadway in 1968.

9. The Royal National Theatre, London.

10. The Royal Shakespeare Company, London, Stratford-upon-Avon, Newcastle.

Michael Shurtleff
Boston, Massachusetts, January 4, 1993

9

Equity is the enemy of the actor. I don't know why they allow their officials of that union to run it that way. They should all get up and revolt and throw them all out.

MICHAEL SHURTLEFF HAS BEEN casting director for such directors as David Merrick, Bob Fosse, and Gower Champion, casting for many Broadway shows, including *Beckett, The Odd Couple,* and *Chicago.* He's the author of the universally praised book on acting *Audition,* as well as several plays, including *Call Me by My Rightful Name, A Day in the Life of . . .* , and plays collected in *Come to the Palace of Sin: Plays about Ladies and Love.* He's taught acting extensively across the country.

SC: I'm interested in knowing your assessment of the American theater. I'm interested in knowing what you think its strengths and weaknesses are, and what we should do, artistically.

MS: Broadway is clearly dying fast. There are nineteen theaters empty at this very moment, with nothing in sight. And it seems to me the only hope for American theater is in regional theater.

SC: Do you mean funded, nonprofit theater?

MS: Yes, because we have raised a new generation who have no interest in the theater whatsoever. When you go to the theater, you will see that most of the audience is over fifty, and until we can get young people interested in going to the theater, who's going to support it? They're not interested. They have their television and those games they play on television and these terrible movies to go to. So they have no interest in theater. And so theater has to try to develop a younger audience. That means funding, so that younger people can afford to come.

On the other hand, young people keep telling me they don't have money to go to the theater, but then they go to see a seven-fifty movie and buy fifteen dollars worth of popcorn.

But you see, theater is not part of young people's lives anymore, except for the actor, and so it seems to me that something's going to have to be done to woo the young audience into the theater.

SC: Could you compare American theater to English theater artistically?

MS: At least until recently, serious plays were given serious consideration on the West End, and some of the best plays have come from the English theater. Those same plays, if written by Americans, would never get produced. If Harold Pinter were an American, he would never get produced anywhere. It's just that we have this kind of awe of what is English, and what is English is good, and what is American is not. Unfortunately, it doesn't encourage American playwriting to be very good either.

I guess the American theater-goer now—when you consider that it costs sixty dollars to see a musical on Broadway, that's a hundred and twenty dollars for a couple to go—well, they're not going to be interested in anything except some spectacle, which is what they get.

SC: So the industry deteriorating, and artistically standards are being lowered as well.

MS: Absolutely. Absolutely. When you think that Wendy Wasserstein's play *The Sisters Rosenzweig*[1] is the big and only hit of the season. It is a very funny play, but it's superficial and non-rewarding. It's like eating Chinese food—after you get out of the theater, you haven't had anything.

SC: What changes would you like to see in American theater, artistically.

MS: Robert Brustein, at the American Repertory Theater,[2] has just received two million dollars to do new plays. It seems to me that we need to do more and more of new plays, and the only place that it's happening is in regional theater, because they can't afford to do them on Broadway. It costs two million dollars to put on a straight play on Broadway—two to three million dollars. That means it has to run for two years, so it can only be a popular appeal play. A play like Harold Pinter's is not going to run for two years; there's no audience that bright for that long. It seems to me that, along with cultivating a younger audience, we've got to do something to stimulate playwriting here, and it's only going to come through regional theater.

SC: And do you think that's a good thing—for theater to become less centralized than New York?

MS: Absolutely. Unfortunately, we still have this idea that you don't make it unless you're on Broadway, which is a shame, because I see more good theater in regional theaters than I do on Broadway.

SC: I'm very interested in what you said about developing young audiences. I'd like to see funding for theater as a whole, and not for specific companies.

MS: It seems to me that each theater should have at least one or two evenings in the run in which they bus in older high school and young college people, so they get a taste of theater and see if it would interest them. They're not going to get them to come and pay—so they've got to pay to bring them in. Funding is needed for that. Of course, you can't get funding for anything out of the government anymore. Rich people used to be philanthropists with their money. These people just accumulate more and more and more money, and never spend any of it on the arts.

SC: I was wondering if you have anything to say about the unions.

MS: Equity is the enemy of the actor. I don't know why they allow their officials of that union to run it that way. They should all get up and revolt and throw them all out. If the actor wants to perform in a play without compensation, that's the actor's choice. And for Equity to forbid them to do it is absolutely revolting and destructive.

SC: Do you have any advice for the young actor or director just starting out? Is it necessary to go to New York? How would you compare his chances of working in New York to, say, Los Angeles?

MS: Well, it depends on what he's interested in. If he's interested in theater, Los Angeles is hopeless. They're all vanity productions, and the only reason actors do them there is to be seen by agents in the hope of getting a television series. So they're not doing it for love of theater.

SC: And by "vanity production" you mean they're funded by . . .

MS: They're funded by somebody's rich father because nobody produces plays for the sake of plays anymore in Los Angeles. It costs so much. It costs eighty thousand dollars to put on an off-off-Broadway play in Los Angeles. Now, who's got eighty thousand dollars? It used to be I produced plays there—for eight years. Then I gave up because I couldn't afford to. I haven't got eighty thousand dollars! So plays are done by somebody with a rich father or a rich sugar daddy or somebody of that sort. It's totally ridiculous, the theater there!

Now, in New York, although fewer plays are done than used to be, there still is some health in the off-Broadway movement. Equity has done everything to kill off-off-Broadway and off-Broadway. And that is the only hope we have of the American theater—certainly not Broadway.

I spent my life working on Broadway and I left it fourteen years ago because I saw it was dying. So I moved to California—not to work in the industry there, because I loathe the movie industry. It is compounded entirely of greed and desire for celebrity and no desire for creativity whatsoever. There are some creative people there, but they're trampled on and they have to fight like hell to get anything decent done, so there are about five good American movies a year and all the rest is this *Home Alone*[3] crap. I still think that if theater's what interests you, there are two places to go. One is New York and one is Chicago. Chicago is a very, very strong theater town now. It produces some of the best theater in America.

The other thing is that a young director or a young actor should try to apprentice himself to some regional theater, because that's where he's going to get the right training and the right kind of environment. I mean like the Washington Arena Stage[4] and Seattle[5] and so forth—go and apprentice yourself there. Many actors come to me and say, "I want to go to graduate school." And I say, "Why?" Graduate school is not for someone who wants to be an actor. Graduate school is for someone who wants to become a teacher of actors or a technician. It's absolutely hopeless; it does nothing for actors whatsoever. It costs a fortune. Take that same money and spend it to support yourself being an apprentice in a regional theater. If you can support yourself, are they going to turn down your services? You learn much more.

Notes

1. *The Sisters Rosenzweig*, by Wendy Wasserstein, opened on Broadway in 1992.

2. Robert Brustein founded the American Repertory Theater and at the time of this interview was its artistic director.

3. *Home Alone*, a film directed by Chris Columbus, 1990.

4. Washington Arena Stage, Washington, D.C.

5. The Seattle Repertory Theater, Seattle, Washington.

Alan Ayckbourn
Scarborough, March 14, 1995

Acting's a wonderful art, but don't let me catch you doing it!

SIR ALAN AYCKBOURN IS NOT only one of our most prominent playwrights but also a most prolific. Aside from the works mentioned here, his plays include the trilogy *The Norman Conquests*, *Absurd Person Singular*, *Woman in Mind*, and *A Chorus of Disapproval*. He's won many honors, including seven London Evening Standard Awards and the Writer's Guild of Great Britain Lifetime Achievement Award. He is the artistic director of the Stephen Joseph Theatre, Scarborough, where he premiers his work. He's been decorated Commander, Order of the British Empire; he was knighted in 1977.

SC: I've been told that there's a distinct style to northern England theater.

AA: I would hate to make a generalization. I think we all, in the end, attempt to do the same thing, if it's Alan Bleasdale or John Godber or the other people who tend to write up here. We all write for our audiences. We all attempt to walk that tightrope in some way or other between what we believe in as writers and theater people—which may be esoteric—but we also know that the audience we address is necessarily a wide-based one. The people I want to talk to are not necessarily people who would take on board all the views I propose. So the more I can woo them in by good narrative, good stories, interesting characters, the more they can be confronted occasionally with thoughts and ideas which perhaps they would not give house room to in their own homes. It makes it sound as if one's trying to alter society from the inside—it isn't quite true. I think what I'm saying is that I like people to come to theater because of a certain thing, and discover more when they get there.

SC: Would it be fair to say that, like Shaw, you're "coating the pill with sugar"?

AA: A little bit—a little bit! I think I tend to write naturally that way. There was a point in my life when I tried to exclude comedy because I mistakenly thought it sort of belittled what I was writing about, and then I realized, in fact, it extended what I was writing about. Comic dramatists have inferiority complexes, probably because they're always being told—not by their audiences, but by their critics quite a lot—that they're less important than serious dramatists. Press people often start their interviews with me with things like "Have you ever considered writing a serious play?"—which is sort of as back-handed a compliment as you can get! And you say "Ah—you mean a play with no jokes! No, No! It would be like tying a hand behind your back, or running with one leg."

SC: Speaking of critics: do you attend to them otherwise? Do you look to them as dramaturges in shaping future work?

AA: I very rarely read them immediately after the event, because I tend to work on the much more general criticism of my own audiences, whom I watch a great deal. This theater in the round is a wonderful place for a dramatist to watch his or her own work—not just through the rehearsal period or technical period, but through the period of the run, which is when one gets, in the end, the most information back.

I am reasonably adroit now at putting plays together, and I can get them from page to stage fairly easily. Where the unknown comes in is when you start actually sitting and watching a play in front of an audience, because if you have tried new things, floated new ideas, and new approaches to character, and new narrative forms, that's when the information comes back. Are they following it? Are they understanding it? Are they empathizing with the right thing or are they disliking your sympathetic characters and loving your villains? That is very, very important.

So I think the critics come sometime later. I will sometimes read them on a play of mine when the first defensive flush has dropped away. I'm not alone, I'm sure, with most writers in being fiercely protective of one's new children. If you've just written a novel or a play, you tend to bridle rather badly if people criticize them or—worse still—are very rude about them. Later on, you can see what they're worth. I've gone through criticisms of plays of mine in the past and been mildly amused when they've been totally wrong. The local critic here said of *Bedroom Farce*,[1] when it was first produced, that it was a hopeless case. It's not a play that they thought would ever be done again. It went to the National[2] and was its first huge success—and it's being done today.

But, on the other hand, there have been other plays where they've probably been about right. And I think as one gets older—or the plays get older, perhaps one should say—you get a little bit more objective about them. I'm able to be reasonably coolheaded about my older work now. I say to people, "Yeah—but be careful because that doesn't really work quite as well as it should."

SC: I'm very interested in your working in the round. Is that why you're here at the Stephen Joseph Theatre?

AA: When I started, the round—or, indeed, practically any open stage in this country—was unheard of. They were all proscenium arches. And Stephen Joseph had just come back from working in the States, and he brought back with him this notion of theater in the round—which of course had been prevalent here at one point, but had disappeared, but had been rediscovered in the States. About the year I joined the theater, he started the theater up here—about '56. I was finishing a job at Leatherhead, which was a conventional proscenium arch, where I was an assistant stage manager and an actor—working my way through the ranks. The stage manager said to me, "Would you like a job in Scarborough, because there's one going and I'm about to go up there and run it." And I said, "Where the hell's Scarborough?" He said, "Oh, it's a theater in the round," and I said, "What is a theater in the round?" He said, "It's like a theater with the audience all around," and I said,

"Oh, there's no scenery. It sounds very attractive. Less work than ever!" So he said, "Well, why don't you come and see a show in London?"

They were doing, at the Mahatma Gandhi Hall, which is an Indian Youth Hostel in Fitzroy Square,[3] they were doing Sartre's *Huis Clos—In Camera*.[4] And I went there. I'd never seen that play before, which was fairly electrifying. It was done well, and it was done in the round, so I was, for the first time in my life, really, within inches of live acting. All my other theater visits had been restricted to the upper circle. You had their word for it that it was Laurence Olivier down there. "Yeah. He looks good."

SC: Two blocks away . . .

AA: That's right! And so suddenly you were there, and there's this very highly charged sexual play of great passion. I was hooked. And I came up to Scarborough—did the summer here—and began to enjoy the freedoms of theater in the round. People often point only to the limitations of theater in the round. They're usually theoretical rather than actual limitations: "Well, there's backs and things like that." Well, all those backs mean all those fronts as well. I was saying to the new company today—actors were saying, "What's the trick of theater in the round?" I said, "Well, there isn't any, really. It's just: behave as you would normally. I'll tidy it up for you, and I'll tell you where the best to be is, but for now just relate to each other, and let the scene develop." Also, it allows us to explore levels of acting that are most suitable for my work, which are the smaller levels. You can work with eyebrows and tiny hand movements, whereas in the big theater, you're talking about big gestures and big placement. Good actors can make that appear subtle, but nonetheless, it's an oil painting rather than an etching. And I love an etching.

SC: Speaking of the acting, are you hoping that actors take the characters utterly seriously and be emotionally involved, or do you want them to have the type of distance one might have in, say, Feydeau?

AA: Oh, no, I like them more involved than that! Some directors wrongly put on a totally different hat when they start producing what they see as a comedy. I prefer my plays not to be described as "comedies." I don't want them to be misled by the word. They get going: "It says 'comedy.' Let's play it very, very fast. Let's play it very, very loud. Let's get it much broader. Let's get the jokes in."

I was over in Chicago, using a play Steppenwolf[5] have just done, *Time of My Life*,[6] as a master class, taking excerpts from scenes. Because it's a series of duologues, it's very handy for master classes. I said, "You do it, and I'll watch it, and then we'll talk about it." They did it—and they did it as I feared they might, very broad. The mother was signaling everything. The invited audience that was there was very quiet and just stared at them. I said, "Now, why don't you play it like you mean it?"—I said it a little politer than that—"Just play the scene." The actress thought it was an exercise—but when she did it, the audience started to laugh. You could see her thinking: "What's happening here?" I said, "That is all there is to it."

You've got to be good enough to be able to choose the right things for the scene, but nonetheless—stop giving the play a hand. Stop getting off the vehicle and pushing it up the hill, when any decent play will get up that hill on its own. That's what it's built to do. And your job is to become very important within that. I always say, "Acting's a wonderful art, but don't let me catch you doing it! Won't have any of that sort of thing!"

SC: Yes! I'm interested in the process by which you develop the script. Do you work with actors in script development, or is it done and scripted before you give it to actors?

AA: Yes. They get very much a finished product. I don't work with them at all on the development of it. Changes do take place, occasionally, but I'm sort of a running joke in the British theater that I never change anything. If I do, it's a sort of huge earthquake. Tiny things happen, usually long after the run's started. Nothing much will happen in the initial production period.

Without false modesty: I know what I'm doing in that department. The work that used to be done on my very early plays, in rehearsal, was to put them right technically. Where it doesn't work is if you've made some technical mistake—your exposition's too long; you've not set it in the right place; you've not placed it right. After a bit, you get all that right, because you've done it for long enough, and so you should. What you get wrong is the whole damn play. I'm known for churning out plays year after year, but there are several that just get quietly put away. They work okay; they don't disgrace us. And at the end of the day, both the actors and the audience say, "Well, that was nice, but maybe it wasn't as good as the last one, and we hope it isn't as good as the next one." So I just throw the whole thing away.

SC: Some of your plays have less stress on plot and less stress on onstage action than others. And some of them use new conventions, and others don't. Have the ones that use new conventions—say, *Time of My Life*—been accepted more reluctantly than more conventional ones, like *Man of the Moment*?[7]

AA: Well, it's difficult to tell. *How the Other Half Loves*[8]—the idea of the superimposed sets and the split time that went on in that early play were really quite unfriendly, in a sense, towards a popular audience. At least I feared they would be. In fact, I think it's more to do with the tone of the play. In the end, *Time of My Life* is a fairly bleak piece. I think it should be very funny. The fact is that it is a play about the loss of love, although all the women in the play, in their various ways, manage to find their way through. *Man of the Moment*, although it says quite serious things about the media and the representation of people, is a much funnier play: it had men falling into swimming pools.

I don't set out to find a convention. What tends to happen is: I get an idea for a play, and I then start to look around for the *how* of telling the story. "How do I tell this story? How do I make this story stageworthy?" When I did *Time of My Life*, I was very interested in our ability—or our inability—to enjoy the present—how we look forward and we look back, not *enjoy*. There are some people who do very much live in the present, and they're very enviable people, but for the majority of people, the day they should have enjoyed in their life—their wedding day—is something that passed by in a sort of terror of arrangements. People always say to you, "That first night must have been so thrilling for you, when it all worked." And you say, "No, it wasn't, because I didn't know it was working, and I was drunk by the end of the show because I was frightened that it wouldn't be working." And then six weeks later I wake up and say, "My God, I've got a really successful play here, and I never really celebrated it."

That dictated the way the story was told. So I began to look at perceiving it from receding time points of view. But I often have—it's crude to say it—I often have a sort of bag of devices—things you say: "That'll be fun to do one day—have a play where you have three different floors, but they're all on the same floor—as in *Taking Steps*."[9] And you put it away, because you say: "I can't write a play like that until I have a play that asks for that sort of device." You really forget about it, but then one day out pops a farce, and the narrative suggests you need all this. Suddenly you remember that old idea about the three floors, and you say: "Wait a minute! This would actually tell that story awfully well."

I always insist that any play is idea led, not device led. You start with what you want to write about. Because I love all bits of theater, lighting, sound, stage effects—I love to employ these. Some of my plays—I come into the theater and say to the lighting guy, "It's just a straight up and a straight down. I'm sorry. That's all it is." And he looks very disappointed. With one play, I said, "It's a railway station." And the designer went, "Great! I haven't done a real railway station before!" And I said to the lighting designer, "It goes into the surreal." And he said, "Wonderful!" Everybody gets excited!

SC: Yes, yes! Your direction of *Conversations with My Father*[10] was so marvelous, so *vital*. I saw it two nights ago. I was very impressed by it. It must be difficult to direct other people's scripts, though, is it not?

AA: It's a different experience. It's much harder work, funnily enough. You have another artist to bear in mind. Because I'm a writer, I'm probably hyper-sensitive towards the other writer. But I try and deliver what they seem to want delivered. I'm very much a writer-director. There are concept directors who I think quite honestly would be happier being writers—but they aren't, so they rewrite, they redesign. I have nothing against them, except I always say I get my ego trips from my own writing.

SC: I think my favorite play of yours is *Henceforward*[11]—but the ending seems so despairing. The artist abandons life for art, and then he's disappointed in art. That's disturbing.

AA: It is disturbing. It's the most—if I say it's autobiographical, it sounds as if I'm as bleak as that man. It's very hard to write about creative artists without it becoming very boring. They're not very interesting people to write about. Watching Beethoven compose is very boring because he sits there—for hours. For the first time, I was able to write about the creative act, but I was also able to link with the idea that they are aware that practically every thing that happens to them in life—particularly their personal lives—is somewhere being recorded in their head and will later be used as evidence against, if not themselves, other people. And it's a very chilling thought. I suppose it is the guilt in oneself that one uses. Things that were said in anger or love or despair or whatever—and you just refine them and reuse them. I've had reproachful looks from people who said, "I thought that was between us."

Jerome just goes a stage further. He's looking for love, and it's right under his nose. It's a sort of fable, really. But in the end he loses his whole family, trying to find it. I defy anybody who's genuinely creative to finish their masterwork without this enormous sense of anticlimax coming over them. You never reach that height you set out for off the blank sheet of paper. It's just impossible, which is why you carry on. "Next time, the next one . . . "

But the other side of that—the play when you do finally lay down the pen and say "That is a masterpiece"—that's the time you give up, because you've either gone completely barking crazy, or you're actually finished. You've finished with your writing; you've reached your limit.

SC: About a year ago, at the Actor's Centre in London, there was a course on the language of Ayckbourn's plays. I was very struck by that.

AA: Yeah, there are people who are quite interested in it. I think it's probably actors who've played it enough times often begin to talk about it and thus generate interest in it. For many years, nobody would publish my plays, apart from Samuel French, because they had no literary content to them—that's what the editors would say. I suspect that (a) they were rather snobbish, but (b) it was to do with the fact that they were not dramatic people, and my writing is very much to be spoken—it's not to be read. It can be read, silently, but even people who know my work, when they come to a rehearsal and it's read out for the first time, they say: "Oh! I see!"

SC: And very Chekhovian.

AA: Yes! And there is another element, because when you hear it, it makes a form, but when you see it, then you suddenly see that there is a fifth character on the stage that is not there, apparently, in the script, because she hasn't spoken in five pages, who makes all the difference in the world to the rest of the scene.

And then there's the other thing, which of course is good old subtext. In most of my plays—again, like Chekhov's—it's not what they're saying but what they're meaning that's very important. Some of the dialogue in Chekhov is positively trite, but then you know why it's trite once you start to explore it. We've all been warned by Chekhov, now, that immediately you see something that looks terribly bland, you think: "What's going on under here. Why is he doing this? Something's happening!" And then you'll often have to wait until you've got all the characters there, and you go: "Oh, yeah. That's happening."

Similarly with my plays, people are becoming more interested as they realize that there's more to the lines than is immediately apparent. I suppose I've developed over the years quite an ear for dialogue, and I have to be careful with myself. There are undoubtedly things you can do in dialogue which are picked up by actors very quickly—the short sentence, the—

SC: The repetition, the talking past people, yes—

AA:—All those things, which they read, like musicians. Sometimes it's very dangerous to tell them. They will read them, and they'll do them, but they'll never ask you why, and you never ask them. And later on, people say, "That was wonderful, how uncertain you sounded in that speech." And they say, "Did I?"

SC: We mentioned the media a couple of times. In light of film and television, can the theater regain the importance in society as a disseminator of ideas that it had for Ibsen?

AA: Well, I would like to think it would, yes. That's why I'm in it. I think it's starting in regional areas like this where the new technology is e-mail, and it's slowly separating us as a society. We're talking to each other by keyboard! Human beings were never meant to do this. They were meant, in the end, whether they like it or not, to meet up and talk face to face, and to share space together, not just as a family but as a community. With the decline of the church and such, where communities met, the theater is becoming more and more the new meeting place.

People come to the theater for nothing but spiritual reasons. They don't come to make money. They don't come to exercise their bodies very much. They come to exercise their spirits, and their minds, and their brains. And in that sense it's completely unique. Although you may be so involved in the play you are totally convinced that what's happening is happening, you're still totally aware that there are other people perceiving it. You never really forget that. That is the whole point of it, really.

For me—for many people coming to this theater—the joy of it is in the shared experience, the common affirmation of a humanity. Many people like me find the same thing funny—are moved by the same thing—are involved by the same thing. That's why I love plays that are human based, rather than purely mechanical or abstract plays—someone they can recognize and relate with, even though they may be going through experiences that they don't particularly have.

It could be that one's totally wrong, the theater dies out, and we all finish up in fifty years' time with computer terminals producing completely idealized images of one other. But I can't see that happening. Where the vacuum is occurring, that is also where the social friction is occurring. In our inner-city areas, one has got to begin to recreate things other than pubs, where people just go to drink. We're going to bring six hundred people in every night, if we're lucky, into the town center, who will come in with a positive purpose. They're not here to cause anyone any harm, or to break windows—they're here to enjoy and to share in something together. This has got to be a positive thing.

Notes

1. *Bedroom Farce*, by Alan Ayckbourn, opened in Scarborough in 1975, and opened at the Royal National Theatre in 1977.

2. Royal National Theatre, London.

3. *Fitzroy Square*, London.

4. *Huis Clos—In Camera*, a.k.a. *No Exit*, by Jean-Paul Sartre, was first produced in 1944.

5. The Steppenwolf Theater Company, Chicago.

6. *Time of My Life*, by Alan Ayckbourn, opened in Scarborough in 1992, and in the West End in 1993.

7. *Man of the Moment*, by Alan Ayckbourn, opened in Scarborough in 1988, and opened in the West End in 1990.

8. *How the Other Half Loves*, by Alan Ayckbourn, opened in Scarborough in 1969, and opened in the West End in 1970.

9. *Taking Steps*, by Alan Ayckbourn, opened in Scarborough in 1979, and opened in the West End in 1980.

10. *Conversations with My Father*, by Herb Gardner, opened on Broadway in 1992. I'm speaking of the production that transferred to the West End, from the Stephen Joseph Theatre, in 1995, directed by Mr. Ayckbourn.

11. *Henceforward*, by Alan Ayckbourn, opened in Scarborough in 1987, and opened in the West End in 1988.

Fred Silver
Sarasota, Florida, April 30, 1996

The big problem is that producers and writers today are trying to capture a large market—a market that's grown up listening to Sesame Street, and grown up listening to rock, or soft rock. And so they've tried to incorporate that into their musicals.

FRED SILVER IS THE AUTHOR of the highly authoritative and successful book *Auditioning for the Musical Theatre*. He's been in great demand as a musical theater/cabaret teacher and coach for some time. He's a prolific songwriter whose songs are published in *The Fred Silver Songbook* and other collections. His musical scores for shows such as *In Gay Company* have won several ASCAP Awards. For several years, he wrote the *Audition Doctor* column for New York's *Back Stage* magazine.

SC: How has the musical theater changed in the past twenty-five years?

FS: When I was starting out, I was a crack accompanist and pianist. I'd go from theater to theater, playing a good fifteen auditions a day. I'd run from the Royale[1] to the Majestic[2]— and that began to change. When I first started out, in the mid '60s, they were begging actors to audition. Then business began to change for the worse, largely for economic reasons. The music of the musical theater was no longer the pop music of its day. Until the '60s, the music you heard on the juke boxes was written by the same people who wrote Broadway shows. The hits were by Jule Styne, or by Rodgers and Hammerstein,[3] or Frank Loesser, or Lerner and Loewe.[4] Movie musicals were certainly very, very big. And with the advent of the Beatles, things began to change—with the advent of Elvis.[5]

Hair[6] was the handwriting on the wall. The musical theater no longer represented the music of America. The musical theater was like opera. It was a relic of a bygone day that had its aficionados, but not enough to support it.

SC: That happened quite suddenly.

FS: Well, it coincided with the move to the suburbs of the affluent people that did go to the theater. Now it was too much trouble to get into town, unless it was an anniversary or a birthday or something special. Today we have the situation where a show like *City of Angels*,[7] which won a Tony—I thought was a good show, a fun show—ran less than a season. And it closed! I couldn't believe my eyes! It's because it lost its audience. The bridge and tunnel crowd were not coming in to see that. The businessmen, or convention people, they wanted to see *Cats*.[8] They wanted to see spectacle. They didn't want to see content. They didn't want to have to think.

SC: But if Broadway is producing less, certainly regional theaters are producing more.

FS: Correct.

SC: Doesn't that broaden the range of audience for American theater?

FS: It does up to a point—up to a point. Your younger generation is not going to the theater *en masse*. It's mostly people over forty-five. When you look at the audiences, you'll see that the age range has changed.

There are so many less opportunities for actors and directors to get experience. When I was starting out, if you just came into town, within three days you got yourself a job in some dinner theater out in the sticks, and then you graduated to bus and truck tours. And then you might get a national company, and then you'd get a chorus part off-Broadway, and then you'd work your way up to principal. Each time you did this you got more and more experience. And today there's no chance you get that experience.

Actors Equity helped to kill that. The way they did that was this: until the early '70s or the late '60s, agents could audition talent and sign promising people and get them a job in the chorus. Then Equity said that agents could no longer collect commission on minimum salaries. And so, all of a sudden, Equity had to open auditions and have a lottery, where a lot of unqualified people—just because they draw a number—have a chance to be seen. Producers still can't cast their shows, and they still have to have auditions, which are very, very expensive. It costs a lot of money to rent a studio, to rent a pianist. And all the people who cast shows aren't paid a penny until the show goes into rehearsal. Their salaries don't start until the first day of rehearsal. They're giving freebies all this time, so there's a limit to how much talent they want to see.

SC: So I should have a heart for agents, then.

FS: Yes. I think agents perform a valuable service. They're not greedy. They have a right to earn a living. They get 10 percent—but they're a good judge of talent, and they know how to nurture it. They know what producers are gonna buy. Without them nurturing talent, who else is gonna nurture it?

SC: And there are more actors now.

FS: Many, many more. They don't have the training, and they don't have the skills. And what can they do? Get into a showcase? Spend a fortune studying—usually with the wrong people? They see a trade ad in *Back Stage*, and they'll go to these people that they can afford.

SC: If the industry's in a decline economically, what can we say about it artistically?

FS: Artistically . . . I really don't know. About the past four years, I've been out of New York. *Crazy for You*[9] was wonderful. I think it was the last American-created show that I really saw on Broadway. Everything else is coming from London. The legitimate theater's doing better, with *Master Class*[10] and shows like that. But even the Tony's now are going to include off-Broadway shows in their categories because there's not enough to nominate.

SC: But don't regional theaters—like the one you work with—work to develop talent all over the country? And isn't that better than centralizing it?

FS: New York is still the clearing house. It has to open in New York to be reviewed before they can market or merchandise it anywhere else—whether it's the Globe in San Diego or the Goodman in Chicago. It has to come to New York to be reviewed before they can market it. Tams-Witmark and the other licensing companies are not going to pick up anything unless it's played in New York.

SC: Is the finished work that comes out of regional theater as good as the Broadway work?

FS: Oh, definitely, definitely. The Broadway work may be a little bit slicker. The problem is they change the charm, the things that worked in regional. And that's why sometimes those shows do not make it in New York—because they figure: "We gotta be bigger and better. We have to put in a production number here." So they make that mistake, instead of leaving it alone. Off-Broadway is the answer, not Broadway. If a show works off-Broadway, they can always move it to Broadway, to a small house.

SC: How well does an actor have to be able to sing to put across a song on the musical stage?

FS: It requires training. They have to work on their voice. They have to learn how to act a song. When actors sing, everything they know about acting goes out of their mind completely, and so you have to teach them to act all over again in the confines of the musical form. There are very few people who know how to teach that—luckily, I do, and that's what I work on with them.

The big problem is that producers and writers today are trying to capture a large market—a market that's grown up listening to *Sesame Street*,[11] and grown up listening to rock, or soft rock. And so they've tried to incorporate that into their musicals. Big hullabaloo about *Rent*.[12] I saw a special on it, and I heard some cuts from the cast album. I was not overly impressed. I think it's just people jumping on something new. New York is so jaded that anything new that comes along they're gonna make a big fuss over.

SC: I saw *Stomp*[13] recently.

FS: Oh, yes—they came here. That's a musical experience, and that's kind of special, because it really has to be done by the people that created it.

SC: I see the same thing in the Times Square subway station—literally. And even there it draws crowds—that's what I find so interesting.

FS: Well, because it's different. Most of the stuff you hear on the radio today, rap music—the musical theater has always used minority groups, and they've all had their turn, starting with the Irish, with Harrigan and Hart,[14] and George M. Cohan. Then, because of an accident of fate—World War I and the anti-German sentiment—Viennese opera was no longer popular, or permitted. Luckily, people like Gershwin[15] and Irving Berlin got their chance, because they were a product of America. They were Russian Jewish immigrants, but they had a lyrical gift, and anybody who's new to something usually tries to do it better. It's no accident that Jews dominated the musical theater as writers. Ninety-nine percent of the writers of Broadway in its heyday were Jewish. Cole Porter was the only gentile.

What's happened is that Motown and the blacks, about ten years ago, became the mainstay of popular music, which is fine—it was their turn. Before them, it was the Italians—the Italian singers and writers. Now what's happening—it's already happened in classical music—are the oriental, the Asians. The great conductors of so many symphony orchestra are Japanese or Chinese or Korean or Indian—Zubin Mehta, Seiji Ozawa—or the great string players, Yoyo Ma, Midori—you can see the wave of the future. It's now the turn of the Vietnamese and the Japanese who have come over to this country.

SC: And that will influence pop music . . .

FS: I really believe that's the next wave. Your articulate writers who have something to say are going to be Asian. Minorities take their turns.

SC: It's the way the country works.

FS: It's the way the country works. And it's gonna be interesting. It hasn't happened yet, but I think that any year now, you're going to see it.

SC: You pointed out that older people are the people who go to the theater. Can the theater ever regain the popularity it had for Shaw's audience, in the '20s, or Ibsen's audience, considering that film and television exist?

FS: No, because there was no film and there was no television then. It has to do with accessibility. In Shaw's time, you stayed home. If you wanted to go out, you went to the theater. Same thing was true on Broadway. If you lived in a tenement, your only escape was going to see vaudeville, or going to see a Broadway show and sitting up in the balcony with low-price tickets. Opera didn't do it because, unfortunately, opera in this country was never what it should have been. In every other country in the world, it's sung in the vernacular language of the country it's done in.

I got turned off opera a long time ago. I went when I was at Juilliard.[16] I got score desks,[17] in my twenties. Even my thirties, I went to see everything. But I got very tired of it. I found it tedious, because it just seemed to me to be an archaic art form, and the plot was so convoluted.

SC: Can a musical be as important, be as significant, as a play by Ibsen?

FS: Oh, definitely. What a musical does that a straight play can't is to involve the audience, because you're not a voyeur. You're a participant. When you're doing a play by Ibsen, there's an imaginary fourth wall which the actor cannot play through. The audience, a voyeur, is looking at these actors react to each other as they would in ordinary, everyday life. But in a musical, that fourth wall isn't there.

To give you an example: when Robert Preston was doing *Music Man*,[18] he was having a lot of trouble. DeCosta[19] kept on saying, "Come downstage and play out there!" And he couldn't understand why he had to do that, because he wasn't trained to do that as an actor. Until finally he woke up at three o'clock in the morning, woke his wife up, and said, "I got it! River City is not just back there, but it's out there also! And there's the grocer, and there's the—" He created different places in the audience where all these different people were. And once he was able to make that change, he loved doing musicals. He became a ham!

Every actor that does a musical and finally learns how to make it work would rather do a musical than a straight play any day, because of that excitement of reaching your audience and being part of them. It's very hard for a playwright to stop time, whereas a song can do that. A song, in two-and-a-half minutes, can do what it might take twenty-five pages of dialogue to do. A perfect example: in *Annie, Get Your Gun*,[20] Frank Butler meets Annie. They have a couple of sparring things. They sing a song, "They Say That Falling in Love Is Wonderful," and the next thing you know—they're in love! And you believe it! You could never do that in a play—it would never work!

SC: There's something very emotional about all of that. Can musicals discuss social problems?

FS: Oh, definitely they do. Look at *West Side Story*.[21] I saw that in 1957, and I sat there *bowled over*, because I had never seen such violence on stage before that—between the Jets and the Sharks. That had never been done in a musical before. And for dancers to do that! Talk about social statements! "Gee Officer Krupke"[22] talked about the whole psychological impact of crime and how it's generated—the fact that nobody cares. The musical theater has always done that. Look at *Show Boat*[23]—the first show to evoke sympathy for the black man. That did more than any sermons could do! Everybody was singing "Ol' Man River,"[24] and everybody was feeling this guilt for the oppression of black people, because of a show written by non-black people.

SC: I'm concerned with the size of the theater, the size of the production. I have a very different experience in an intimate fringe theater than I do in a Broadway theater, just because of the size of the theater. Do you think that that's underestimated, overlooked?

FS: Well, size has to do with the type of venue. For instance, *The Fantasticks*[25] worked marvelously at the Sullivan Street Theater.[26] Now you see tours where it's playing for an audience of two thousand people. It's ridiculous! When I go to a huge concert hall, and there's a string quartet, I walk out, because it doesn't work for me. It has to be in an intimate chamber—that's what the music was written for. There's definitely something wrong there. They're cheating their audience because they want to make megabucks. The right show has to be in the right size house. *Chorus Line* opened at the Public Theater[27]—and it was *so exciting!* And when I saw it on Broadway, it lost so much, because the intimacy wasn't there anymore.

But it did run for twenty years, which shows how much I know. But there were a lot of people that were disappointed; they wouldn't have been disappointed had they seen it at the Public Theater.

SC: If the trend is toward regional theaters across the country, instead of on Broadway, is the trend also toward smaller theaters?

FS: Yes. Because these things are designed for smaller theaters. The only way they can make the transition is if they open off-Broadway and they're so successful that they move to a small Broadway house.

SC: At the American Theater Critics Convention recently, Betty Buckley talked about "the *Chorus Line* phenomenon." She said that it was a new phenomenon that there were shows that were more important than the stars in them.

FS: I agree. If the show is wonderful, and it gets rave reviews, then you can market it. But the star system is still important because that's what makes audiences come.

SC: This phenomenon has not overcome the star system, then. It's . . .

FS: No. Take a show like *City of Angels*, which had no stars—I mean, nobody that was really well known. It had a short run. If it had stars, it may have run longer. Then the out-of-towners would have gone to see it, because they want to see this person that they've seen on television. *The Mystery of Edwin Drood*,[28] for example. Loretta Switt went into it—you know, from *M.A.S.H.*[29]—after Cleo Laine left. And all of a sudden, it had a whole resurgence of energy. All of a sudden, new audiences started coming into town to see it. And it ran for a couple of years, where normally, it would have only run for maybe five or six months.

SC: The star system is certainly helpful economically. But is it helpful artistically?

FS: Once a show has opened, and it's already proven itself, it no longer matters, because the people that you need artistically have already seen it. For instance: Merman decides to leave *Gypsy*[30] after two or three years. The next person that comes in may not be Ethel Merman, but the show is still gonna work, because it's a powerful show.

SC: But when people come to see stars, don't they bring with them a set of associations and expectations that color their perception of the performance?

FS: Think of Elizabeth Taylor in *Private Lives*.[31] The show would never have been revived—it would never have drawn an audience—if it wasn't for her. A star is very, very important if it brings people to the theater. If *Good Little Girls*[32] is ever done, I would love to see three good TV personalities.

Let's face it, most TV personalities were successful actor-singer-dancers before Hollywood picked them up. Hollywood has always raped New York for talent. This has happened from the '20s on. Bette Davis was a New York actress before she was brought out to the coast. Van Johnson was a chorus boy in Broadway musicals—so was Gene Kelly. Everybody started there. So if they started there, there's no reason why they can't come back.

SC: How about the relationship between non-profit theater and Broadway? Without commercial restrictions, is non-profit theater free to create more progressive work?

FS: They're free to create more progressive work, but they also have to fill their houses. They have to have an audience. There's a lot of stuff that's developed by regional theater that's crap. And there are some things that turn out to be marvelous gems. You don't know until you go see it.

Notes

1. The Royale Theatre, New York City.
2. The Majestic Theatre, New York City.
3. Richard Rodgers and Oscar Hammerstein II.
4. Alan J. Lerner (1918–1986) and Frederick Loewe (1904–1988).
5. Elvis Presley (1935–1977).
6. *Hair*, music by Galt MacDermot, book and lyrics by James Rado and Gerome Ragni, opened on Broadway in 1968.
7. *City of Angels*, music by Cy Coleman, lyrics by David Zippel, book by Larry Gelbart, opened on Broadway in 1989.
8. *Cats*, music by Andrew Lloyd Webber, lyrics by T. S. Eliot (based on his collection of poems *Old Possum's Book of Practical Cats*), opened in the West End in 1981.
9. *Crazy for You*, music by George Gershwin, lyrics by Ira Gershwin, book by Ken Ludwig, opened on Broadway in 1992. It was adapted from the musical *Girl Crazy*, music by George Gershwin, lyrics by Ira Gershwin, book by Guy Bolton and Jack McGowan, which opened on Broadway in 1930.
10. *Master Class*, by Terence McNally, opened on Broadway in 1995.
11. *Sesame Street*, a PBS children's series, 1969 to present.
12. *Rent*, music, lyrics, and book by Jonathan Larson, opened on Broadway in 1995.
13. *Stomp*, created by Luke Cresswell and Steve McNicholas, was first produced in 1991.
14. Edward Harrigan (1844–1911) and Tony Hart (1855–1891), comedy team.

15. George Gershwin (1898–1937).

16. The Juilliard School of Music, New York.

17. Score desks: inexpensive seats in the upper balcony of a theater.

18. *The Music Man*, music, lyrics, and book by Meredith Willson, opened on Broadway in 1957.

19. Morton DaCosta (1914–1989): director of the original Broadway production of *The Music Man*, 1957.

20. *Annie, Get Your Gun*, music and lyrics by Irving Berlin, book by Herbert and Dorothy Fields, opened on Broadway in 1946.

21. *West Side Story*, music by Leonard Bernstein, lyrics by Stephen Sondheim, book by Arthur Laurents, opened on Broadway in 1957.

22. "Gee, Officer Krupke," a song from *West Side Story*.

23. *Show Boat*, music by Jerome Kern, lyrics and book by Oscar Hammerstein II, opened on Broadway in 1927.

24. "Old Man River," a song from *Show Boat*, by Jerome Kern and Oscar Hammerstein II.

25. *The Fantasticks*, music by Harvey Schmidt, lyrics and book by Tom Jones, was first produced in 1960.

26. The Sullivan Street Theater, an off-Broadway theater, New York.

27. *A Chorus Line*, music by Marvin Hamlisch, lyrics by Edward Kleban, book by James Kirkwood and Nicholas Dante, was first produced in 1975 at the Public Theater, a theater of the New York Shakespeare Festival. It opened on Broadway that same year.

28. *The Mystery of Edwin Drood*, music, lyrics, and book by Rupert Holmes, based on the novel by Charles Dickens, opened on Broadway in 1985.

29. *M.A.S.H.*, a CBS television series, 1972–1983.

30. *Gypsy*, music by Jule Styne, lyrics by Stephen Sondheim, and book by Arthur Laurents, opened on Broadway in 1959.

31. *Private Lives*, by Noel Coward, opened in the West End in 1930. The production to which Mr. Silver is referring opened on Broadway in 1983.

32. *Good Little Girls* was Mr. Silver's latest musical at the time.

Harold Prince
New York, September 20, 1995

I2

I actually think that there's an Armageddon facing all of us—in art, as well as everything else.

HAROLD PRINCE IS ONE OF the most prominent directors ever on Broadway or the West End. His many honors include twenty Tony Awards and the 1994 Kennedy Center Honors. The Broadway productions that he's directed or produced have included *Fiddler on the Roof, Fiorello, West Side Story, Damn Yankees, Pajama Game, Cabaret, Sweeney Todd, Evita, The Phantom of the Opera,* and *Show Boat.* His work has also encompassed opera and film, and the off-Broadway production of his own script, *Grandchild of Kings.*

SC: In *Contradictions,*[1] you criticize the unions.

HP: Oh, I criticize everything—the unions and the people who negotiate with the unions. You know, it's always very dangerous when the dominant thought is commerce. If you think predominantly about commerce, when you're dealing with an art form, you're going to have problems. I know that people have to eat, but featherbedding, and unfair costs that are illogical and have infiltrated the whole business of doing commercial theater—they're inhibiting and, ultimately, very dangerous to the future of the art form.

I'm always reminded of restrictions on the creative input of union members. The musicians have been the most dangerous and difficult, over the years. I do find other unions have been using their heads. The actors' union has worked out a whole plan whereby their people can join non-Equity members in working on a show where they can be paid far below the Equity minimum if the production isn't earning or is not-for-profit or is a losing proposition, so that shows get to keep running. But everybody has been in varying degrees slow to recognize the realities, and so what you've come up with ultimately is a hit-or-flop commercial theater, and one that in no way nurtures non-musicals.

But our audiences are responsible, as well. I've come to feel less angry or frustrated with unions, with management. I think that what we're suffering from is a national—and in some instances international—malaise.

I would put the largest responsibility at the feet of television. Television has, in fact, destroyed the quality of films—feature films—and it hasn't helped the quality of theater.

Because right now you can get on television first-rate, serious theater. What used to be the foundation of popular theater, the well-made play, the naturalistic play, the stuff that Sidney Kingsley, and Elmer Rice, and Lillian Hellman wrote, is now available to you on television all the time. When you watch *ER*,[2] or *NYPD*[3]—you're watching good realistic drama. Perhaps you know, Sidney Kingsley's *Detective Story*[4] was a huge Broadway success and then equally successful with Kirk Douglas on film. *Detective Story*, or versions thereof, are on television every single week, beautifully written, beautifully acted—usually by Broadway actors who have moved out to California—directed well. So why would you go into a theater to see a well-made, realistic play? You would not have anyone writing *Dead End*,[5] *Street Scene*,[6] *Detective Story*, *Men in White*[7] for the theater today.

SC: What can we expect of an audience, in terms of their taking responsibility in the theater.

HP: Well, they don't want to take responsibility. Now, mind you, they're out there. There are very intelligent, inquisitive people out there, but they've turned away from the theater.

You rarely encounter writing in films today because there's so little room in film for genuine dramas or comedies. The aforementioned Sidney Kingsley, Philip Barry, Robert Sherwood, Moss Hart, Brackett and Wilder[8] wrote for the stage and the screen.

And what of the performers? Jean Arthur, Claudette Colbert, Rosalind Russell, Bette Davis, Irene Dunne—all worked on Broadway and moved to Hollywood. Their male counterparts—a long list which includes Humphrey Bogart, Spencer Tracy, and Clark Gable—all started on Broadway as well, and all brought their brand of charisma, intelligence, and sophistication to films.

What Broadway celebrates today are musicals, but they are infrequently of the quality of the lyric writing of Oscar Hammerstein, Lorenz Hart, Cole Porter, E. Y. Harburg, and Ira Gershwin. Yes, there are Sondheim[9] and Fred Ebb, and there are first-class composers, but the Broadway musical today specializes in events, spectacles—something you can't get on television. And film, too, delivers something you can't get on television—Stallone,[10] Schwarzenegger,[11] and incredible visual effects. All these megalithic entertainments neglect classy, sophisticated, intellectual material.

So I think television's at the base of it. Now, along with television, and instant gratification, and a shorter time span, you've certainly seen a diminution in the intelligence of audiences. You have a wide spectrum of people in the audience, but you don't have the elite peak that you had. I happen to agree that "elitism" is not a dirty word. It started to be a dirty word with the Nixon administration, and it's continued to be a dirty word. It's a very dirty word now that we have Newt Gingrich[12] in power. So, increasingly, I find myself railing against the sheer mediocritization of art and the nature of audiences.

SC: Is this forever?

HP: I hope not. I just returned from London, and with very few exceptions, their theater emulates ours. The big difference is that they have a National Theatre,[13] and their National Theatre is the House of Hits.

SC: Doesn't regional non-profit theater function as the English National Theatre does?

HP: No, it doesn't, because it isn't of the same quality. I served on the NEA's[14] National Council of the Arts for six years. As important as it is to have encouraged the proliferation of not-for-profit theaters all over the country, we have been unable to extend the quality that was Broadway's hallmark during its golden days.

The quality of new playwrights—of playwriting—isn't as high because the nature of not-for-profit theater is to feed off a nucleus of talented people that could never be large enough to accommodate four or five hundred theaters. The thing about Broadway was it was central. There were thirty good playwrights, thirty great producers, thirty excellent directors, and probably a hundred wonderful actors.

What you see today are pockets of achievement. There are instances of first-rate productions in Chicago, Hartford, Los Angeles, New Haven, Minneapolis, St. Louis—all over the place. There are wonderful directors out there, but not the concentrated achievement that was Broadway's.

The not-for-profit theater movement has accepted certain dangerous compromises. There are too few second acts off-Broadway and in the field. To demand those was imperative when Broadway was flourishing.

There is an agenda espoused by New York's newspaper of note and popularized across the country that a not-for-profit effort is somehow loftier than a commercial one. Picasso didn't die poor, and as artists get older, they seek a measure of security and comfort.

SC: Tell me about *The Petrified Prince*[15] and *Grandchild of Kings.*[16]

HP: I did *The Petrified Prince* at the Public,[17] and *Grandchild of Kings* down at the Irish Repertory Company.[18] It was swell, and it was subject to all the hobbling restrictions of the commercial theater: too short a rehearsal schedule, therefore a need to have everything in place before we begin. We rehearsed three weeks and then we invited audiences.

There is an indulgence in the not-for-profit theater. A musical commissioned may be coddled for years. I can't afford that. When I start to work on a musical, I want it written. We're not gonna just keep coddling and say, "Oh, we missed your deadline by a year," and "Well, I'll see you next year," and so on. That happens all the time in the musical theater, off-Broadway. I don't approve of it. In the commercial theater, rehearsal time is limited, so you must be prepared. Get as much of it right as you can the first time. Just nice, pragmatic, no-nonsense stuff.

SC: You must have had your vision totally formed when you approached it.

HP: I think I'd better! *Petrified Prince* was a really interesting piece. I think it was flawed, but exciting. I'd hoped it would do better than it did. I'd hoped it would do well enough to generate the next step. What's interesting about it: it did, almost. The American Music Theater Festival in Philadelphia said they loved it and offered to present it this season. The composer went away for the summer to work. His reviews were savage and he got discouraged, and I fear that's the end of it. What happened to Kander and Ebb[19] with *The Kiss of the Spider Woman*[20] was just as savage, but they are Broadway babies and that rewrite came up with a long run on Broadway, and productions in London, Buenos Aires, and Tokyo.

SC: And what about New Musicals?[21]

HP: The SUNY Purchase[22] experiment—you followed that on the papers—went down the drain, but it proved itself subsequently, with *Kiss of the Spider Woman.* The next two shows that were going to be offered in the same season made it to New York without the SUNY process. One was *Secret Garden,*[23] which wasn't ready to open on Broadway, and would have benefited by eight weeks on New Musicals. The second was *My Favorite Year*,[24] which opened at the Beaumont[25] and wasn't remotely ready to open on Broadway. But both did. Is there a lesson to be learned from that? There should be, but I don't know who's in the business of learning lessons anymore.

SC: You mention in *Contradictions* that the presence of conventional elements make a show comfortable for its audience. Is it fair to say that you balance your aesthetic impulses with an eye for convention?

HP: No, I think that I'm just more mainstream. I don't want to be considered less of an artist for it. I just happen to have that kind of taste. I'm not Antonin Artaud. If I were, my audience would be limited—much more limited. That's just the luck of the draw. You know, I have staggering respect for the likes of—in the musical theater—Steve,[26] the Gershwin's,[27] Mr. Hammerstein,[28] and Mr. Kern.[29]

SC: Of course.

HP: They were popular—all of them, in different degrees. So—fine! The *avant-garde*—some of it I like; some of it *bores the bejesus* out of me. A great deal of what is celebrated bores the bejesus out of me because it would appear to be okay to be boring. I've bored some people in my lifetime, let me tell you. But not by choice, by indulging myself.

I'm just lucky. I figure more than half of what I've done has interested people. The other half surely hasn't. They're head-scratchers: "Why did he do that?" I did it because I love it as much as they love the things they love.

SC: It's wonderful that you did them, yes.

HP: It's a really good position to be in. I don't regret those moves. If anything, I've learned from them. I can look at something and say: "This success owes itself, in large part, to that failure."

SC: Could you say something about the critics, and the contribution they make?

HP: They don't make much, anymore, because they are influenced by an excessive publicity mill. There have always been certain critics who were personalities, and certain critics who were not. In this day of instant celebrity, it's hard to avoid wanting to be more famous than the plays you review. The critic as a celeb—dangerous.

I don't know how you counter any of it. I actually think that there's an Armageddon facing all of us—in art, as well as everything else. I think, basically, we have to hit rock bottom before we get in touch with humanism again. I'm much more concerned with the loss of the National Endowment for the Humanities than I am the Arts. Of course, we can't afford to lose the arts, but in preserving "the arts," we've so totally lost track of what the humanities represent—which is education, respect for knowledge, and respect for the peak of intellectual elitism.

As long as the elite are our enemy, our society is in trouble.

Notes

1. Harold Prince, *Contradictions* (New York: Dodd, Mead, 1974).
2. *ER*, an NBC televisions series from 1996 to present.
3. *NYPD Blue*, an ABC televisions series, from 1993 to present.
4. *Detective Story*, by Sidney Kingsley, opened on Broadway in 1949.

5. *Dead End*, by Sidney Kingsley, opened on Broadway in 1935.

6. *Street Scene*, by Elmer Rice, opened on Broadway in 1929.

7. *Men in White*, by Sidney Kingsley, opened on Broadway in 1933.

8. Charles Brackett and Billy Wilder.

9. Stephen Sondheim.

10. Sylvester Stallone.

11. Arnold Schwarzenegger.

12. Newt Gingrich, Speaker of the U.S. House of Representatives 1995–1999.

13. The Royal National Theatre, London.

14. The National Endowment for the Arts.

15. *The Petrified Prince*, music and lyrics by Michael John LaChiusa, book by Edward Gallardo, was produced by the New York Shakespeare Festival in 1994.

16. *Grandchild of Kings*, by Harold Prince, was produced in New York by the Irish Repertory Company in 1991.

17. The Public Theater, New York Shakespeare Festival, New York.

18. The Irish Repertory Company, New York.

19. John Kander and Fred Ebb.

20. *The Kiss of the Spider Woman*, music by John Kander, lyrics by Fred Ebb, book by Terence McNally, opened on Broadway in 1993.

21. New Musicals, a musical theater laboratory established in 1990.

22. State University of New York at Purchase, which sponsored the New Musicals Project.

23. *The Secret Garden*, music by Lucy Simon, book and lyrics by Marsha Norman, opened on Broadway in 1991.

24. *My Favorite Year*, music by Stephen Flaherty, lyrics by Lynn Ahrens, and book by Joseph Dougherty, opened in New York at Lincoln's Center's Vivian Beaumont Theatre in 1992.

25. The Vivian Beaumont Theatre, Lincoln Center, New York.

26. Stephen Sondheim.

27. George Gershwin (1898–1937) and Ira Gershwin (1896–1983).

28. Oscar Hammerstein II (1895–1960).

29. Jerome Kern (1885–1945).

Robert Brustein

13

Cambridge, Massachusetts, January 19, 1995

It's just that audiences have been disappointed so often that they've given up—very reluctantly—their hopes for the theater in certain areas.

ROBERT BRUSTEIN WAS DEAN of the Yale School of Drama for several years; he founded and directed the Yale Repertory Theatre. He later founded the American Repertory Theatre in Cambridge, Massachusetts, and remained its artistic director until 2000. He's the drama critic for he *New Republic*, and his several honors include two George Jean Nathan Awards, for his dramatic criticism, and the Elliot Norton Award for Sustained Excellence. His many books include *The Theatre of Revolt* and *Dumbocracy in America*.

SC: In *Dumbocracy in America*,[1] you talk about the Theater of Guilt. In *The Theatre of Revolt*,[2] you wrote that propaganda plays and problem dramas are offshoots of social revolt and should be judged by social and not literary standards. Can we not also say that of the Theater of Guilt—that it's an offshoot of social revolt?

RB: Absolutely.

SC: And should we not judge it then by the social standards that you talk about?

RB: By its social efficacy, by how effective it is in effectuating change—sure.

SC: Are you not judging it by aesthetic standards in the book, though?

RB: Well, I'm saying, in effect, that by aesthetic standards, it's probably second rate, but by the standards of whether it effectuates change, I think it can probably be said, without too much objection, that art has never changed anything.

SC: In "Lighten Up, America,"[3] it seems you say that racist and sexist slurs are not damaging.

RB: Well, what I say is they're not as damaging as they're made out to be, that Lenny Bruce liberated us from the notion that words were weapons of some kind that would pierce skins. He *demythologized* language in that way, and we were eternally grateful to him. But, unfortunately, progress in this country goes backwards instead of forwards, and we are now in a state where people are so sensitive to the slightest slight that it's becoming virtually impossible to speak any longer. So that's why I called on us to lighten up a little.

SC: I get the impression you're saying that Arthur Miller's plays, and Brecht's plays, and Shaw's plays are not *art*.

RB: I wouldn't say that about Brecht. I think Brecht is a poet and an artist, and I think the ideologist in Brecht occasionally muffled—or tried to muffle—his poetry, but the poetry always found a way to seep through, in subterranean ways. I think Arthur Miller doesn't have a poetic bone in his body. I think he's essentially a prose mind, and not very good prose at that. Bernard Shaw, to quote T. S. Eliot, was a poet, but the poet in him was stillborn. So it was suppressed, as it were, and it was very rarely able to break the skin of the consciousness of these plays. It does in a play like *Heartbreak House*. So my point of view toward each of these playwrights is different.

SC: But aren't you limiting the definition of theater so intensely that you're cutting out a great deal of what Western tradition has considered theater?

RB: Well, I don't mean to "cut out" anything. I'm not suppressing these plays; I don't think they should be banned or abolished. I'm just trying to be discriminating about quality, and to say that on a level of judging quality, they're very rarely of very high quality. But they can have a very important function at a given moment, but once that moment is over, we will see them, really, aesthetically, and aesthetically they'll be wanting.

SC: In your review of Bergman's plays, you write that there is a market for good theater. I think you were talking about the crowd at the Brooklyn Academy of Music.[4] That's very interesting—very optimistic. How much of a market is there?

RB: A lot! I mean, we have it here—we see it here every day. They flock to our productions, no matter how controversial or difficult they are, and there's a very alert and lively audience in this area, and we don't have enough days in the year to provide theater for them, or enough productions to satisfy them. There's an insatiable appetite here, and I think, if it's here, it's elsewhere. It's just that audiences have been disappointed so often that they've given up—very reluctantly—their hopes for the theater in certain areas. I think New York is one of those areas, which is a shame because New York had the liveliest theater audience in the world at one time, and now, I think, the liveliest theater audience is in Cambridge.

SC: It seems possible! So you're saying then that it's a failure of the market that Broadway hasn't responded to this appetite.

RB: It's a failure of the market. Broadway, because of the incredible amount of money that it now requires to produce a show there, has gotten very cautious, and instead of venturing into new areas and new territories and new realms, it tries to clone successes of the past. And the audience quickly catches on to this. I mean, they'll go along with it for a certain amount of time—if there's a helicopter in one play, there's got to be a chandelier in the next one, or a flying saucer in the next one, and after a while, outside of expense account executives, no one's going to be paying for these things any longer. They'll consider it a waste of money.

SC: You've made contributions both as a critic and as a creative artist. Can you say something about the relationship of the critic to the theater? Does the A.R.T, for example, have a relationship—your contribution aside—with a critic like the one you described in your welcome to Critics and Criticism,[5] where the critic helps the company understand the nature of drama and the nature of roles?

RB: Well, we have on the grounds here a dramaturgy program at the Institute—you know, we have an Institute for Training here—and our actors and directors rub shoulders with dramaturges and special students who are deeply interested in the intellectual aspects of a play. And, of course, we have our own resident dramaturge in Robert Scanlan, and I suppose you could consider me a resident dramaturge as well. Dramaturges are essentially internal critics who not only contribute scholarly material and background to actors and directors and playwrights that request it, but who keep a kind of impartial eye on the production as well.

SC: I notice that you don't mention external critics—print critics. Is the A.R.T.—or are there any theaters—lucky enough to have a relationship with a journalist critic that's helpful?

RB: Well, I think you can't have a relationship with a journalist critic because you can be accused of influencing the impartiality of that critic if you have a close working relationship with a journalist or a critic. I'm very fond of John Lahr,[6] for example. I admire his criticism a great deal, but I really can't pal around with him. This is ironic because I've been accused by Bill Marx, for example, in the current *Theatre Week*—when he's supposed to be reviewing my book—but he's really accusing me of conflict of interest because I "bed down," as he says, with people in the theater. And I think it would be much worse to bed down with a critic, if you're running a theater.

Notes

1. Robert Brustein, *Dumbocracy in America: Studies in the Theater of Guilt, 1987–1994* (Chicago: Dee, 1994).

2. Robert Brustein, *The Theatre of Revolt* (Boston: Little, Brown, 1964).

3. Robert Brustein, "Lighten Up, America," in *Reimagining American Theatre* (New York: Hill and Wang, 1991).

4. Brooklyn Academy of Music, New York.

5. Critic and Criticism, a 1992 conference over which Mr. Brustein presided.

6. John Lahr, theater critic for the *New Yorker*.

Edward Albee
New York, May 22, 1996

14

I don't understand why people have to go to a play with a scorecard. I think they should be told "This is a fucking good play which advances the theater, and it's going to be a disturbing and marvelous experience for you. Go see it!"

E DWARD ALBEE HAS WON three Pulitzer Prizes, for his plays *A Delicate Balance*, *Seascape*, and *Three Tall Women*, as well as two Tony Awards, for his plays *Who's Afraid of Virginia Woolf* and *The Goat*. His other honors include the Gold Medal in Drama from the American Academy and Institute of Arts and Letters, the Kennedy Center Honors, and the National Medal of Arts. Aside from the works discussed here, his many other plays include *The American Dream*, *The Zoo Story*, *Tiny Alice*, and *The Play about the Baby*.

SC: You've expressed impatience with critics who—you use the term *hunt the symbol*. How can a critic help us to discuss drama without inappropriately *stressing* things? What contributions should critics be making?

EA: Well, the first question that comes up is "What is the basic function of criticism?" Are you talking about reviewing, or are you talking about scholarly criticism here? Let's take an analogy of classical music rather than drama for a moment. I wanted to be a composer when I was a kid, having studied Bach and Mozart and all those types, but I didn't make it because I was incompetent, and it wasn't what I was supposed to be doing. I know a great deal about classical music. I have on my shelves lots of books on composers and their music—a very, very good book on Beethoven's string quartets, which analyzes each one, goes through it page by page.

And I know the Beethoven string quartets backwards and forwards, both, very well. I know their intellectual and emotional content. Those books are of very minor importance to me. I don't need them. I'm not convinced the equivalent scholarly work on a play is of any more value than that. A play is a piece of literature to begin with, which has the added virtue of being able to be performed, and so people can experience it one of two ways. Either on the page, read, as a literary experience, or the other way, as a performed piece. The folly is to think that a play exists completely only in performance. That's absurd. A

Beethoven string quartet—to somebody who knows how to read music—can be heard by reading it. A play can be heard and seen by reading it. But most people don't know how to read music, and most people don't bother to read plays—or even know how to read a play intelligibly—so it would seem.

The scholarly work that is done is of interest to other scholars, I think. Not to anybody else. The black magic that makes any work of art any good escapes the careful analysis of any scholar. An engine of a car works—you can find exactly how it works—*exactly* how it works—every mechanical thing that makes the whole thing work. That has nothing to do with why an automobile engine exists. An automobile engine exists because somebody saw the need for the automobile engine to exist, and found a way to make that necessity occur. Same thing with a piece of literature, with a play. How the person puts it together— how the playwright puts it together—all the structure, and the rest of it—is minor compared to the need and the urgency in that which created the piece in the first place.

But, of course, most critics are not scholars. Most critics are there, unfortunately, to make the theater safe for the audience, rather than the dangerous experience it should be. Also, everybody should always keep in mind that no critic is ever maintained on the staff of any magazine or newspaper unless the owner or the publisher wants him to be there. I don't think that any critic would—oh, except somebody like John Simon, who is kept on *New York* magazine because he is sniggeringly scandalous. He's kept there for that reason, because he's an offense to common decency. No critic is kept unless he or she reflects the taste and needs of the organ for which this critic works. You have to keep *that* in mind. So what used to be my attack on critics—I've come to realize—really shouldn't be. They are hired hands, for the most part. And they will not keep their jobs unless, consciously or unconsciously, they cotton to the attitude that the owners want them to.

SC: But certainly the theater needs all the help it can get . . .

EA: It needs all the help it can get, yes, but it certainly doesn't need the supposed help of a bunch of critics who are trying to make it safe, who are trying to do—as Walter Kerr[1] once said, in a radio interview years ago—quote—"I consider it my function as a drama critic to reflect what I consider to be the tastes of the readers of the newspaper for which I work"—unquote. The critic who's there, supposedly creating taste, considering it his responsibility to reflect the existing taste. Of course theater needs all the help it can possibly get, but a lot of the supposed help it receives is killing it—just really killing it.

I have never seen a straight play on the Broadway theater in New York that has ever gotten the money reviews that a musical has gotten—ever. This is simply because the musicals are what everybody seems to want to be popular. They bring in more advertising dollars to the newspapers. They bring in much more money to the Broadway community— restaurants and hotels and all the rest of them. So there's so many unfairnesses and so many things going on—this particular help doesn't help much. Serious drama just doesn't do well in the commercial theater anymore. Unfortunately, the audiences at commercial theater are for the most part upper-middle-class, wealthy whites—which really has nothing to do with what theater should be all about in this country.

SC: You've also said that you write so intuitively that you don't always understand intellectually every point of your work.

EA: That's a slight misstatement of what I said. There is the conscious mind and the unconscious mind. The play moves from the unconscious to the conscious mind. By the time a play has moved completely to the conscious mind and I put it down on paper, I'm pretty much aware of what metaphors and symbols people will find in the piece. There are occasionally some things that I learn, but I've never learned anything accurate about a play of mine that I wasn't able to say when I learned it, "Well, of course, that's what I intended." I never learned anything contradictory to what I, in my gut, knew was my intention.

SC: Do critics at least help to articulate these points so that most people can recognize them?

EA: I don't understand why people have to go to a play with a scorecard. I think they should be told "This is a fucking good play which advances the theater, and it's going to be a disturbing and marvelous experience for you. Go see it!" I don't think the thing should be analyzed. I don't think the plot should be told. Nobody reviewing a new piece of music gives us the tunes. They don't do that.

SC: But most people think so much drama is inaccessible.

EA: It's not inaccessible. It's totally accessible! Sometimes it's a little different in form from what people expect. If *Waiting for Godot*[2] had been set in a living room, nobody would have had any trouble with it. It's this fucking blasted *heath* that got in everybody's way. They see a strange setting—they see something that is not naturalistic—automatically the warning flags go up. They say, "I'm not going to be able to understand this." And therefore, they can't understand it, because they're determined they're not going to. There's nothing in any Beckett play that I've ever experienced that is inaccessible to anybody with a reasonable mind.

SC: Certain plays of yours have been more successful, critically, and in terms of popularity, than others. Can we generalize . . .

EA: The most naturalistic ones have been—yes—of course, because American theater—as opposed to European theater—is based on naturalism. We don't like the political, intellectual theater of Brecht; we don't like the stylized theater of the European *avant-garde* much. We like good, old-fashioned, naturalistic plays. Any play that wanders far from those boundaries is in trouble. And the plays of mine that have been most successful have all been naturalistic ones. *The Zoo Story*,[3] for what it's worth, is a naturalistic play—so's *Who's Afraid of Virginia Woolf*[4]—so's *A Delicate Balance*.[5]

SC: *Seascape*[6] . . .

EA: So's *Seascape*—sure—that's a naturalistic play.

SC: Do European audiences—in Vienna, London . . .

EA: They respond more equally to the stylized as well as naturalistic plays—yes. Well, some of the influence of the American theater is beginning to hit London now—the West End is not quite as adventuresome as it should be. Thank heavens for the fringe theaters and the RSC,[7] and the Almeida,[8] and the National,[9] and the Royal Court.[10] Without those, the West End would look just like Broadway, unfortunately.

SC: Some time ago, you said: "I get criticized for not having the catharsis in the body of the play. I don't think that's where the catharsis should be. I think it should take place in the mind of the spectator sometimes afterwards—maybe a year after experiencing the play."[11]

EA: I think that's one of the interesting things that happened with twentieth-century drama—that it moved the catharsis out of the body of the play.

SC: But up to a year after seeing the play?

EA: Well, it depends. Sometimes you get things quick—sometimes you don't. You can't comprehend anything unless you can relate it somehow to the limitations and parameters of your own experience. I just don't think everything should be tied up in a nice bundle so you don't have to worry about it after you leave the theater.

SC: In light of the fact that there are film and television, can theater regain the popularity it had for Ibsen's audience, or its importance as a disseminator of ideas?

EA: Well, for a time in this country, before there was television and there really was serious film, there was a short period there where people saw American plays—up to about 1910. Then film started coming in and people started going to film, and then television, sound film, and all the rest of it. No, I don't think it ever will have the popularity it did, for a whole variety of reasons—price, for one. Television—my God! You just sit there and it comes to you! Plays don't come to you—you have to go to them. Movies are preposterously expensive—I think seven-fifty or eight dollars a ticket to see something that is not a real experience, but a photograph of a past experience, and a fantasy experience.

SC: And very naturalistic.

EA: Plays of course are ridiculously expensive, but even when they're not ridiculously expensive, people don't want to go see them because they are real experience. They're not safe fantasy experience. There's something about the reality of a play experience that's disturbing to a lot of people. You go to a movie, and you sit there with your popcorn and your coke, and you watch people shooting people's heads off, and brains splashing against walls and things like that. It has no effect on you whatever. You try any kind of physical violence onstage, if you duplicate something like that, people would run vomiting out of the theater, because it's a real experience. It is happening at the time. The reality of the theater experience is the one thing that makes it—for me—far more exciting than most filmed experiences ever could be—because it is happening at the moment. And our suspension of disbelief is a totally different kind.

SC: I understand you're saying that the American public is very hooked on naturalism. It's always difficult to educate an audience to a new form. Is there something about naturalism that is more seductive than . . .

EA: Well, it doesn't demand that we use our imaginations. "Oh, that, yes—my family, my friends live there—in that living room, in that kitchen. Yes, that's the way my friends talk. Yes, of course."

SC: So drama has reached a point—or chanced upon a form—that it would be more difficult to move away from than . . .

EA: Well, we always had naturalistic plays in the United States. Some of them were more fantastic than others, I thought—but you look at American drama around the turn of the century. With the possible exception of *The Scarecrow*,[12] Percy McKaye's play, most of them are really quite naturalistic. Some of them fairly melodramatic, but, I mean, the first people who made serious experiments in America were Sophie Treadwell and Elmer Rice—the late '20s. There were some experiments that were made—*The Machinal*[13] is a good experimental play. Elmer Rice's *The Adding Machine*,[14] around 1930—an experimental play. We don't have very many.

SC: If a play changes the spectator unconsciously, you've also said that it will be translated into social action—political action.

EA: Indirectly, sometimes. Because how we vote, how we respond to the world around us, socially and politically, is determined by our concept of ourselves. And our concept of ourselves *can* be formulated by the arts. And should be. And so if a play can make us realize that we're skimming along, we're really not grabbing—participating—in our own lives, and we're letting other people do all the stuff we should do—if that nagging thought can be put in us, then maybe we'll change a little bit. Maybe we'll start being more socially and politically responsible animals.

SC: But can we translate into political terms what that means?

EA: Well, aside from some agitprop plays which are very highly specifically political, agitprop plays have turned out not to be terribly good, as opposed to, in Germany, Brecht and other people. Their agitprop plays were better than agitprop. They were deeply political, socially involved plays. In this country most agitprop plays weren't terribly good . . . But, if a play can make us more aware of our failings, our responsibilities, to ourselves and others, then it may be able to change us into better people. Movies won't do this, generally. Because movies are a fantasy experience and we know we're not supposed to pay any attention.

SC: But people do pay attention, at least in terms of going to them. They're so much more accessible.

EA: Going to them, but I don't know that they necessarily learn much. Maybe the people who went to see *Burnt by the Sun*.[15] Did you see it? Maybe the people who went to see *Burnt by the Sun* learned something. Maybe they did. But not many people went to see it. It's the Russian film about Stalin's execution of the final Bolsheviks in the middle '30s. Glorious film. One of the finest films of the past ten or fifteen years.

SC: I'll remember it. I think you addressed an Outwrite Conference[16] several years ago, and you criticized gay writers for becoming ghettoized, is that right?

EA: Yes. My point was that everybody belongs to many minorities—many. I pointed out that I belong to a number of minorities. There are more women than men in the world, the minority being the male. I'm a minority by having white skin; I'm a minority by being educated—even a smaller minority by being a creative writer—and also sorts of minorities, and down there at the end, I happen to be gay—another minority. My identity is created by all of them, not by any one of them, and my objection was to those gay writers who felt that their identity was created by the fact that they were gay. Therefore I made a distinction between gay writers and writers who were gay.

I pointed out that if you were gonna take some of the most important gay writers of the twentieth century—writers who happened to be gay, by the way—who were not activists, so to speak—you start with Proust, and Stein, and you work your way right up through to the present—with a lot, including Tennessee Williams, and many, many, modern writers, poets—you'll find that the majority of them did not find their identity in being gay. They found their identity in being writers, one of whose shaping forces was the fact that they were gay. I made a lot of friends, and some enemies, at the Outwrite Conference. I remember that

Paul Monette[17] quite agreed with me, and some others did, too. My only objection was the fact there is the ghettoization, and the assumption that we're valued only because we are gay—and that therefore that must be our only subject—leads to ghettoization, and I thought that the whole thing was supposed to be an attempt toward assimilation.

SC: But aren't these gay writers motivated by a concern to create work that has an immediate political effect, in the sense that Shaw would have liked it?

EA: Political effect, fine, but you could be a writer who is gay and accomplish the same thing without writing about gay themes. You must not let the gayness become a limitation, and I find this happening a lot. There's an awful lot of good writing done by gay writers, but there's also a lot of *shit* being published, because there's a gay audience that will read it because it's by gay writers, and it's pushed by gay publishers. And that's the kind of thing that I don't like. I've never—never ever—made a secret about my sexual predilections. It seems to be one of the many, many things that I am. I'm a liberal Democrat, I live in the United States. I'm many things, and being gay is one of them. But it's not the defining thing in my life.

SC: Certainly. At the risk of jumping around, topically—

EA: Mmm, why not?

SC: I wanted to point to a couple of passages from Aristotle. Most of your work, and so much of modern drama, is very concerned with language. Aristotle is very clear when he says that language is secondary: "Plot is the heart and soul of drama." "The dramatist must construct action before words."[18] What are we to make of the fact that drama seems to have gone through such a basic change?

EA: Well, I don't agree with your premise. Words are a conveyer of the emotional, intellectual message of the piece. Words are what is used to communicate. I don't find any worthwhile drama that has become about words. I've never put a speech in a play of mine just because I liked the sound of the language. I keep telling my students: "Anything you put in a play—any speech—has got to do one of two things: either define character or push the action of the play along. Otherwise, it should leave—it should go away."

SC: There's been a lot of concern about content restrictions in NEA[19] grants, and several people have called for the abolition of the NEA. Would you prefer to see no public funding of the arts, or public funding that restricts content?

EA: I would rather have no public funding than censorship. But the whole question, after what's happened with the NEA, is so corrupt in its logic, and so corrupt in its reporting. What is being attempted is stripping the American people of aesthetic education. We're supposed to give people a twelfth-grade education in this country. I say that unless you give people an aesthetic education, you run the risk of raising highly educated barbarians. It's our responsibility to give them an aesthetic education at the same time, and that's one of the things that the NEA does—gives people an aesthetic education.

Approximately 5 percent of the money of the NEA ever goes to individual grants, by the way—individual creative people. Ninety-five percent of it goes to organizations which supply the forum for the intellectual argument to take place. People never think about *that*, either. There have been twenty-six thousand grants given by the NEA up to this point, of which I believe eleven or twelve have raised any question.

It has nothing to do with three Mapplethorpe[20] photos of erect penises. It has nothing to do with that whatever. I saw that exhibition in Cincinnati, by the way. You could barely even see them because they were face up on a high table, and you had to lean over and you had to *look* at them. And they were tiny—and they were in a small room which said—you know—"Abandon all hope, ye who enter here."[21] But then again, I have similar attitudes about people who feel that the flag should not be burned. I think this particular kind of *jingoism* is intolerable.

But the people who want to destroy the National Endowment for the Arts, and therefore destroy the aesthetic education of the people, are afraid of an aesthetically informed people. They're afraid of the kind of intelligent voting that might take place. They're afraid of the kind of rational discourse that might result from aesthetically educated people. They're *terrified* of the intellectual. They're terrified of the life of the mind, because they know that they're gonna end up out of office. It's pretty appalling, what's going on.

SC: It's very frightening, yes. You've talked about aesthetic education. People need a specific type of education to appreciate certain art.

EA: Well, it certainly helps, yes . . .

SC: How did the American public respond to *Box*?[22]

EA: Well, you must remember that *Box* was done in context with *Quotations from Chairman Mao Tse-Tung*,[23] though I have directed it myself, separately. Audiences who have experienced various kinds of theater are not put off by seeing a play in which there is nobody onstage, just a voice. They listen, and then they're quite interested in it.

SC: But don't they need to be prepared for it by having seen works like it?

EA: It would help, I suppose. I always go back and remember the report that when Beckett's play *Waiting for Godot* was done in San Quentin prison, in front of people who'd never seen a play before, the audience responded with comprehension and enthusiasm.

SC: But you can appreciate *Waiting for Godot* in naturalistic terms. Could people accept *Box* on its own terms, or did they need to have been prepared for it?

EA: I don't think you can ever be fully prepared for that which is startlingly new, nor should you expect to be. That's what television is based on, and most movies are based on—the redoing of the familiar. The best drama doesn't do that. *Box* was based, as far as I'm concerned, on a lot of Beckett's work. I thought it was a perfectly comprehensible experience to anybody who was willing to say: "This is the way this wants to be. Let's approach it on it terms rather than my preconditioning." Anybody who's unwilling to take that risk is not going to enjoy much theater at all.

SC: That's very tough, though. It's very tough to learn how to accept a work of art on its own terms. I don't know where we start.

EA: Well, I try to do it every time I look at a painting, every time I go to a play, an opera, a concert. Every time I go to a play, I say to myself: "All right. This is the first play I've ever seen." I'm not bringing any preconditions. I try to avoid any comparative stuff. I say: "Let it happen."

SC: But didn't the playwright stem from work that he'd seen in order to create that play?

EA: Well, I think most playwrights do a trick on themselves. The *have to* do a trick on themselves. We should be enormously informed as to the history of the art form we're looking at—completely informed. We should have done our homework. But at the same time, we should also, every time we sit down to write a play, write the first pay that's ever been written. We are writing the first play that's ever been written. The audience should be seeing the first play that it has ever seen. If you have that particular kind of communication, then I think you have a fair chance.

Notes

1. Walter Kerr (1913–1996): theater critic for the *New York Times* from 1966 to 1983.
2. *Waiting for Godot*, by Samuel Beckett, was first produced in 1953.
3. *The Zoo Story*, by Edward Albee, was first produced in 1959, in Berlin. It was first produced in the United States in 1960, and it opened on Broadway in 1968.
4. *Who's Afraid of Virginia Woolf*, by Edward Albee, was first produced in 1962, on Broadway.
5. *A Delicate Balance*, by Edward Albee, was first produced in 1966, on Broadway.
6. *Seascape*, by Edward Albee, was first produced in 1975, on Broadway.
7. Royal Shakespeare Company, London, Stratford-upon-Avon, Newcastle.
8. The Almeida Theatre, London.
9. The Royal National Theatre, London.
10. The Royal Court Theatre, London.
11. Irving Wardle, "Albee Looks at Himself and at His Plays," in *Conversations with Edward Albee* (Jackson: University Press of Mississippi, 1988), 99.
12. *The Scarecrow*, by Percy MacKaye, was first produced in 1914.
13. *The Machinal*, by Sophie Treadwell, was first produced in 1928.
14. *The Adding Machine*, by Elmer Rice, was first produced in 1923.
15. *Burnt by the Sun*, a film directed by Nikita Mikhalkov, 1994.
16. Outwrite Conference: a national conference of lesbian and gay writers.
17. Paul Monette: author of *Taking Care of Mrs. Carroll* and *Becoming a Man: Half a Life Story*.
18. Aristotle, *Poetics* (Ann Arbor: University of Michigan Press, 1970).
19. The National Endowment for the Arts.
20. Robert Mapplethorpe (1946–1989): photographer. His graphic photos caused a sensation in the United States in 1990, largely because their exhibition was funded by the National Endowment for the Arts.
21. "Abandon all hope, ye who enter here": the inscription on the gates to Hell in Dante's *Inferno*.
22. *Box*, together with *Quotations from Chairman Mao Tse-Tung*, both by Edward Albee, opened in 1968, on Broadway.
23. *Quotations from Chairman Mao Tse-Tung*, together with *Box*, both by Edward Albee, opened in 1968, on Broadway.

Zerka Moreno

Beacon, New York, September 25, 1995

15

The major concern Moreno had—he said it's the problem of the human being—is spontaneity and creativity—twin principles. They go together.

ZERKA MORENO WORKED for many years with her husband, the late Jacob Moreno, in developing psychodrama, and she is the foremost authority in the field. She is a fellow of the International Society of Group Psychotherapy and honorary president of the American Society of Group Psychotherapy and Psychodrama; she is known internationally as a teacher, therapist, and lecturer. The several books that she's written or edited include *Psychodrama: Action, Theory, and Principles* and *Psychodrama: Foundations of Psychotherapy.*

SC: Why does psychodrama work as well as it does?

ZM: Well, it's built into the human organism. Children do it all the time, and they don't know they're doing it, but they're playing different roles. They're playing roles of the heroes, heroines, their mom, their dad—their dreams. It's really a way of people learning about the world in a comfortable setting, without actually having to go into the world.

SC: And it works particularly well in a group setting.

ZM: Yes, because drama is actually a group phenomenon. In fact, drama probably started first at Dionysian festivals, which were played in the streets of the cities—they weren't in a closed space. They were in the streets, and all the citizens became actors and actresses in it. Later on, the creators of the festival sat and became audience—they became witnesses. Moreno[1] turned the clock around and said the witnesses should become actors, rather than sit and watch other people perform.

SC: But even for the people who only watch—they're also affected therapeutically.

ZM: Oh, very much. That's a phenomenon that's already described by Aristotle, in *The Poetica.* Drama probably started first as comedy. It's much easier to improvise in comedy than it is in tragedy. "Tragedy" actually means "goat song," which comes from the Dionysian festival.

All the so-called primitive people we know have a form of drama. Their rituals are a form of drama, but they live it. Instead of having an artificial setting, they do it in life itself, which is what children do, and which is, by the way, what psychotics do. The difference between children doing it and psychotics doing it is that when psychotics do it, they become very threatening. When children do it, it's just fun. One of the things my husband was most fascinated by was spontaneity and creativity in children, and spontaneity and creativity in psychotics.

What happens with psychotics is they lose their audience. We have an audience. You and I are each other's audience. That's the smallest unit of social interaction, a pair. Psychotics don't have that. People don't believe who they present, and so, from their perspective, you're ill and they're well, because you don't know what they're experiencing, and you don't trust what they're experiencing. One of the things that psychodrama does is build *trust* between people. You trust who I am—*why* I am—because I show you, nakedly, who I am. So it's a trust-building phenomenon.

SC: Then the presence of the audience is also therapeutic for the subject.

ZM: Yes, that's what I want to talk about. Aristotle described how—in tragedy, especially—there are two emotions that are aroused through watching: pity and fear.

So Aristotle believed that people watching these tragedies evoking pity and fear in them, or pity and terror—*terror* is very profound—he described it as a catharsis of these emotions, a *purging* of these emotions. When Moreno began to study that phenomenon, he said, "Yes, it may be a catharsis, it may be a purging, but I don't think it's an emotional one; I think it's an aesthetic one. You can appreciate the beauty of this play, the beauty of the actors, the great genius of this playwright." I've seen *Hamlet* performed dozens of times in London, by the greatest British actors, and I always have an aesthetic catharsis. But I can't say I have an emotional catharsis when I see a dozen dead bodies lying down on the floor. There's nothing I can do for them, right?

SC: But, certainly, aren't people reduced to tears in a theater?

ZM: Yes. St. Augustine has described that in *The Confessions*. There's something very interesting. He really has an absolutely perfect description of what Moreno called *spectator catharsis*. It is removed, in a sense, because these are not real people. You're supposed to feel misery and mercy for people who are not real? St. Augustine calls this an absolute madness. What about the reality of the people sitting next to you who have pain and fear? Should you not be commiserating with them, rather than with someone who is either dead or a fictional character? Psychodrama is the Theater of Mercy. Mercy is the essence. In the Judeo-Christian tradition, at least, mercy is something that is very significantly aroused in us—to be careful of other people's feelings, to be merciful. Moreno said, "You know these actors are not the real people, so even the catharsis you are getting is a secondary one. What if we took away the script, and we have the real people there. Then the catharsis that you as a spectator are experiencing is a genuine one—an emotional one, not merely an aesthetic one." I think that's a very profound and true observation.

SC: That would be, then, the difference between being a spectator in a psychodramatic presentation and a spectator at a conventional theater.

ZM: Exactly. That's the difference.

SC: Did psychodrama grow out of the Theater of Spontaneity, and did that theater start as a dramatic presentation and not as therapy?

ZM: That's correct. The major concern Moreno had—he said it's *the* problem of the human being—is spontaneity and creativity—twin principles. They always go together.

He began to do theater with children, in the gardens of Vienna, and he noticed that when they rehearsed, the first time, they were fresh, they were creative, they were wonderful. The more often they repeated that performance, the less spontaneous they became. So he defined *spontaneity* as a new response to an old situation, or an adequate response to a new situation. By "adequate" he meant "integrative," intrapersonally and interpersonally. Now, when he began to look at the theater, he realized that spontaneity had been completely deadened in the actor. The actor has to submit him- or herself totally to the creativity of a director, of the playwright. He said, "What would happen if we threw away the script?" He wanted to start a Theater of Spontaneity—that's what it's called—to show that all art emerges out of spontaneity and creativity, and that it is possible to have a theater based only on spontaneity and creativity.

Now, there were some problems with that. When it worked well, the drama critics who came said it was rehearsed—they didn't believe it was spontaneous! It was so polished! When it didn't go well, they said it didn't work!

He had to find a happy medium to prove to them that it worked. What he did was— he turned his actors and actresses into reporters. He sent them out into the city to get the news of the day. You could go then in the evening and see the *Living Newspaper*. For instance, in 1923, there was the business with Mussolini and the rally—you know? They performed that in the theater that night. Or a murder of—a murder of a prostitute in the red light district. You know who acted that? Peter Lorre was the pimp. Peter Lorre always told the story about how Moreno discovered him. He came from Budapest, as an eighteen-year-old, homeless young man. He'd been kicked out of his father's house.

SC: This was before the Berliner Ensemble, then.

SC: This was all before everything else! I'm talking about the '20s. And what came out of that! He used to have that mysterious look about him, Peter Lorre. The first movie he ever made for Ufa Film became a world classic—*M*.[2] It's the story of a child-murderer. He learned that leer in the Theater of Spontaneity. He had no drama training.

Another was Elisabeth Bergner,[3] one of the greatest actresses in the Reinhardt theater.[4] She wrote her autobiography.[5] It's not been translated into English; it was written in German. She credits Moreno. I translated that whole chapter—about her working with Moreno—in our journal.[6]

One night, one of the actresses who always portrayed the Virgin Mary in the Passion plays—all she had to do was to look pure—you know, pure womanhood. She didn't have to move in the Passion play, she just had to *embody*, in a tableaux. Well, she was engaged to a poet who came up to Moreno one night and said, "Moreno, that angel, that pure image of womanhood that you all know—she's a hellion at home. She uses the most outrageous speech from the streets, and it's unbearable to me. You said you can do something." Now, poets in those days were very lofty, right? They were *up there* somewhere. Not like the modern poets, who deal with the dirt of the earth. This poet said to Moreno, "Do you think you could do something about Barbara? She's becoming unbearable to live with."

So Moreno began to see that this image of pure womanhood had frozen her—had not allowed her spontaneity to come out. He said, "Let me try something."

Well, it just happened that that night, the report came in about a prostitute having been murdered by her pimp over money—they had an argument over money. He claimed she hadn't turned all her money that she'd earned over to him, and she claimed she did. And he killed her. That was one of their stories that they brought from the city.

That evening, when Barbara came to the theater, Moreno said, "You know, Barbara, I've been thinking about you and your acting career. I really don't think you're getting enough opportunities to play different roles. How would you like to have an entirely different role tonight?" She said, "What? Yes, yes—I've been thinking the same thing." He said, "Well, how would you like to play a prostitute tonight?" She said, "Do you think I can?" He said, "I have great faith in you." She was superb! What happened? She was now legitimately able to use the flip side of her pure womanhood, that of the prostitute, to create some beautiful art piece out of it, and be applauded for it rather than rejected. That was the beginning of her cure.

SC: And the beginning of using the drama as therapy.

ZM: Yeah! That is how the Theater of Spontaneity began to emerge as a theater of therapy.

SC: That theater in Vienna, and the early work in New York, must have been so seminal to the theater that occurred for decades.

ZM: Absolutely! There was, in 1924, a theater exhibit sponsored by the city of Vienna, and a man named Fred Kiesler[7] came, who Moreno claimed copied some of his ideas of the design of his theater. They are exactly the same, it's true. Kiesler had seen Moreno's theater. They actually had a case in court, in which he was his own advocate. What he was defending was anonymity. He didn't put his name on the stage. Kiesler put his name on his stage. The whole idea is that creativity is an anonymous factor. He said name is a form of capital. It's something that Marx never talked about, but you can sell your name. It revolted him—that people would sell their name. All his German books were published anonymously. The result was they were not burnt during the Holocaust. There was no name on them. Some of his students after the Second World War found some of them in antique bookstores. Fascinating . . .

SC: What about the relationship of this work to Stanislavski's?[8] It's . . .

ZM: Yes, Moreno describes that. They never met, but a man named Meyerhold[9] came from Russia, and he was, of course, involved with the design of the theater. The difference was this: Stanislavski wanted to use emotional memory to create a more perfect actor. Moreno wanted to use emotional memory to create a more perfect person. He didn't care how you acted, artificially, as an actor. He wanted you to be better integrated in life. Now, that's a great difference!

SC: Oh yes! The Vienna theater influenced guerrilla theater—and the Living Theater[10]— and he had a direct influence on a number of actors. You've said that Dustin Hoffman came to watch your work in New York City?

ZM: Yes. We used to have psychodrama sessions open to the public. He used to come in late and leave early. Late, because it was dark—nobody would see him. He'd sit in the back, stay for about half an hour. Many, many people from the American Academy of Dramatic Art used to come regularly.

We treated a lot of actors and actresses, because they became disturbed. He said that they suffered from what he called "the histrionic neurosis." I have a theory about that, knowing what I know now about how the personality develops. Here you have these young people who are not formed yet. They started at fifteen, sixteen, seventeen—come on!—it takes us about thirty years before we begin to feel that we have a core within us, or our own being!

SC: As an adult . . .

ZM: And stable . . .

SC: Yes, if we're lucky enough to reach that point!

ZM: Exactly! Some people a little earlier, some people later, but certainly not at seventeen or eighteen! You think you know everything at seventeen or eighteen. Then you begin to find out . . . Well, so they're not formed yet. Superimposed on them are pieces of other personalities, creatures they have never met, except they have to meet them intimately. They have to absorb all this stuff. So instead of becoming more integrated, they become disintegrated. How many of them have terrible lives? They become alcohol addicted, drug addicted, gamblers, sexually addicted—you name it. And if not they, their children—ending in violent deaths, or living violent lives. Very, very few people knew who Laurence Olivier was. I understand that Hitchcock[11] always said it's very difficult to like actors, because you don't know who they are. What piece of them is coming out right now? You look at their lives—they're really very disturbed people, most of them, a large majority. There are a few of them—Lunt and Fontanne[12]—but how many are there?

SC: And so you developed techniques that deal with these problems, specifically?

ZM: Yeah, right! We worked with them—and they became better actors. They became more natural. Their behavior actually changed.

SC: So being helped personally helped them artistically.

ZM: Being helped personally makes us better actors in life.

SC: Can you tell me why role-playing is often not healing for an actor onstage but is so healing for the subject in a psychodrama?

ZM: It is healing for an actor when the role parallels his own or her own experience. To the extent that it deviates, and most of them deviate . . . Look at *Waiting for Godot*.[13] It's a wonderful *play*! The symbolism's wonderful! But you play that night after night, you begin to feel desperate. I mean, if you're really in the role, you can go crazy!

SC: I would think so!

ZM: I wrote about that from the point of view of the warm-up. You see, here it is . . . here: [*reading from the* Journal of Group Psychotherapy, Psychodrama, and Sociometry] "Striking example of actorial catharsis . . . If you've acted in *Waiting for Godot* for two weeks, your warm-up is established: *Oh, my God. I'm going to have to do this scene again!*" This is how they become disturbed. Long before they actually go onstage.

Here's—here is something: [*reading*] "Moreno discovered early in his work with the children in the gardens of Vienna that even a *role conserve*"—like, a finished role—"can be catharsis-producing for the actor, provided the role dynamics parallel those of the actor, that they are the right fit, do not crush his spontaneous creative function, and help him to expand and intensify this function."

SC: Stanislavski asks us just to make substitutions from our lives, but that's not enough . . .

ZM: Well, Moreno's asking you to role reverse, or to think of other alternatives, and so on. He would work that out first, with you, in action. If you explore it in action, you could find out: "Is this really a suitable substitution? Am I going again in the wrong direction? What other substitutions are possible?" So, *alternatives*—and then explore that in action. What are your expectations of this substitution? It's not just a substitution—that's only the warm-up. What do you expect to come out of this, and is that likely to happen in life itself? How are the other actors going to interact with you on this basis?

Do you know that Eleonora Duse[14] hated the playwrights? Moreno met her through Elisabeth Bergner, and he asked her, "How do you feel about playwrights?" She said, "I hate them. They put *words* in my head. I don't want words. I want emotions."

SC: So some actors have the ability to live each performance as if it were the first time.

ZM: Exactly. That's spontaneity and creativity.

SC: And warm-ups will help her do that.

ZM: The right warm-ups, yes, could help her do that. Eleanora Duse wanted to forget the words, so that she could tap into the roots of emotion in herself.

SC: And relaxation is a lot of it, isn't it?

ZM: Right, right. But relaxation also here in the head. Physical relaxation helps, but also the emotional—the two have to fit. Together, the body and the mind. You may think you've relaxed your body and some crazy notion suddenly pops into your head. And the fear—performance fear—is tremendous.

SC: And the associations people have with the theater, it puts so much pressure on the actor.

ZM: And the competition is so fierce . . . destructive . . .

SC: I see so many therapeutic and artistic overtones to all of your work, but there's a religious component to all of it for you and your late husband also, isn't there?

ZM: Yes, definitely. When I talk about the Theater of Mercy . . . Moreno had a group he called the encounter group—young philosophers and doctors and so on—people who followed him and his ideas, and they talked. They walked the streets of Vienna. They started a home for refugees. They decided that the best thing for a human being to be was good. I remember a young woman saying to me, "You know, I'm supposed to go to church and feel so much love for my fellow beings. I love my fellow beings so much better after psychodrama. I feel much more humanhood, here, than anywhere else."

Notes

1. Mrs. Moreno is speaking of her late husband, Jacob Moreno (1889–1974).

2. *M*, a film directed by Fritz Lang, 1931.

3. Elisabeth Bergner (1900–1986), Austrian actress.

4. The Deutsches Theater, Berlin.

5. Elisabeth Bergner, *Bewundert viel und viel gescholten: Unordentliche erinnerungen* (Munich: Bertelsmann Verlag, 1978).

6. *Journal of Group Psychotherapy, Psychodrama, and Sociometry.*

7. Frederick Kiesler (1890–1965), Austrian designer and architect.

8. Konstantin Stanislavski (1863–1938), Russian director and actor, a founder of the Moscow Art Theater.

9. Vsevolod Meyerhold (1974–1940), Russian director and actor associated with the Moscow Art Theater.

10. The Living Theatre, American theater company that helped to launch the off-off-Broadway movement.

11. Alfred Hitchcock (1899–1980), film director.

12. Alfred Lunt (1892–1977) and Lynn Fontanne (1887–1983).

13. *Waiting for Godot*, by Samuel Beckett, was first produced in 1953.

14. Eleonora Duse (1858–1924), Italian actress.

Stephen Daldry

16

London, August 27, 1997

It would be wrong to view theater that doesn't deal directly with a political issue as being nonpolitical, because it's about perception and reality, and imagining. That can be a very strong political act, even if you're not dealing with politics in a very direct way.

STEPHEN DALDRY WAS THE director of London's off–West End Gate Theatre, and then, from 1992 to 1998, director of the Royal Court Theatre. He's received two Olivier Awards for his directing, as well as Critics' Circle, Drama Desk, and London Fringe Awards, a Tony Award, and a Peter Brook Empty Space Award, among other honors. Aside from *An Inspector Calls*, his most noted work includes *Machinal*, *The Kitchen*, and *Search and Destiny*. He's also highly acclaimed as a film director.

SC: *An Inspector Calls*[1] is such a social statement. Is the experience of other audiences—say, the Americans or the Japanese—the same as the experience of Londoners, in watching the play?

SD: I wouldn't like to speak on behalf of the Japanese. It's very difficult to know how they respond, because they have a very more reserved response in the theater generally. They're very polite, so you don't really know what they're thinking.

In New York, the audience response was rather similar, on the whole. The audience base is very different, so it's difficult to know whether the differences are to do with ticket prices, or the sort of audience it is, or whether it's actually to do with differences of nationhood.

SC: Since it opened on the West End, the Labor government was reelected. Is the experience of the audience now different than it was a year ago?

SD: The play's a romantic play. It believes in the possibility of a better world. In that sense, it's romantic. I think that people were yearning for that aspiration, right the way through for the last five years. I think that there is still a moment now that people feel something might happen, although that little honeymoon period that Labor government had might well be rapidly falling apart. Certainly that yearning for something else, which was so evident in that landslide victory that Labor finally got, was very present when the audience watched the play. They wanted something better. They wanted something else.

SC: It speaks so eloquently about the Labor government. Does the theater have a political effect?

SD: Direct?

SC: In any way. Does art have a political effect, for that matter?

SD: It depends on what you believe the definition of political is.

SC: Can we talk about the short run and the long run, or is it more complex than that?

SD: It's about whether you believe the human aspiration to art and culture are political acts in themselves, or what you believe the role of aesthetics are, or what you believe the role of imagination is, or the politics of imagination, or transformation within the imaginative sphere. Whether those are political acts in the way that "Let's go lay the government in" is a political act . . . It would be wrong to view theater that doesn't deal directly with a political issue as being nonpolitical, because it's about perception and reality, and imagining. That can be a very strong political act, even if you're not dealing with politics in a very direct way.

SC: To speak of the form of the production: it's quite bold. It opened, I think, at the National.[2] Were you worried about its reception?

SD: I think we all were. Richard Eyre[3] was particularly worried about its reception—on two counts, really. One, it was a play that is very well known in this country. It's a very strong, stable fare for the amateur groups. So when we toured with it to Bradford, you could sort of guarantee that 40 percent of the audience had been in it—out of those, maybe 20 percent had actually played the Inspector. So they have a very strong knowledge of this piece. The idea of doing *something else* with the play—investigating the play in a different way than currently people had always imagined it—meant that they might react very strongly against it. Even in previews we were very unsure whether we would get away with it. If you know something and then you see it again, do you believe that's the play, or do you think that it's just a conceit that's been ladled on top of it? We were very careful to argue that the play as it's been handed down to us was, in fact, not meant to be traditionally staged.

SC: You're noted for bold stagings of traditional plays. Do you have to temper your vision with an eye for its reception? Do you modify what you do because of a concern that the audience won't accept anything that's too bold?

SD: Certainly not. I don't do that.

SC: Do you worry, then, about the specific makeup of the audience—whether it's regional, or the National, or the West End, or Japanese?

SD: I've been heavily involved in producing, running the Royal Court.[4] One is constantly concerned with who's coming. Who are these folk? How do you expand the audience base?

SC: In light of the fact that there are film and television, can theater be important as a disseminator of ideas, the way it was for Shaw and Ibsen?

SD: Theater is still central to our culture in a way that perhaps it isn't in America, where the movies are more central to the culture. You feel it at customs. You go through customs in New York and you say you're in the theater—they think it has something to do with pornography, and they search your bags. But if you say you're involved in the movie business, they wish you good will in your enterprise. You go to parties in New York, and you say I'm involved in theater, and it's sort of *peculiar*. Whereas in England, it still has a status.

Plays at the Royal Court can start in the little theater upstairs and have a huge political impact, a social impact that's very fast and very acute. We did a play called *Blasted*,[5] which was about violence in Bosnia. This was front-page news for a week. In a sixty-seat theater, it's phenomenal that you can still do that.

We've just got a play that's coming up in the autumn about kids raping each other[6]—which we'll play with kids. That was front-page news in the *Times* yesterday. It's remarkable, the impact that theater still has, socially and politically, in our consciousness in this country.

SC: If we could talk about casting, and the rehearsal process—do you always get the actors you want?

SD: You never get the actors you want—and then sometimes you do get the actors you want. But it's very difficult, because it's a hugely competitive market—both in terms of other theaters, and in terms of an expanding film industry. A lot of actors at the moment are busy making films. There are more films being made in this country now than there have been for the last thirty years. So it's difficult to get the actors.

SC: So if can't have the actors that you want theoretically, do you have to modify the result that you're working toward?

SD: No, we're still blessed in this country with rather a large number of good actors. I think any director would say a lot of the time you're lucky, and you get actors that you want, but sometimes you're not lucky.

SC: Well, it's not only a question of quality but a question, as well, of fitting the character, and also of acting style. Do you have to work with the actor to get a particular style of acting—for example, a style that's not naturalistic?

SD: I don't know what naturalism is, so that's difficult to answer. It does depend on the play entirely, on what you're trying to achieve, or what the language, the linguistics, of the play is.

SC: How do you know that your actor can work in the style you want?

SD: You usually know the actor. You've usually seen him.

SC: Could you describe British theater in the '90s?

SD: I think the biggest thing that's happened in the last seven years or so has been the emergence of a new wave of British writing—a generation of writers who are speaking very differently, who are changing form, some attacking political issues, some just based on language—and wildly imaginative. I think that's a huge boost.

Having said that, I think there's a real problem with Shakespeare. We haven't reinvented the language for a new generation, so the language itself seems stultified. There's no uniformity in it. There's no training for it. There's no understanding anymore. We're *losing* it. We're losing the *reason* for it—except for heritage purposes. That's a problem.

There is a lack of fluidity, at the moment, in our production of plays generally. It comes in stops and starts—a little bit here and a little bit there. There is not a groundswell of confident productions in the way that there's a groundswell of confident new plays.

SC: When I lived in London, I saw a lot of pub theater, and a lot of off–West End theater, and although I thought a lot of it was superior to off-Broadway and off-off-Broadway, I didn't see new forms, the way I do in the East Village. There are probably twenty theaters in the East Village that are throwing things up that are exciting in concept, not necessarily polished. Can you explain that?

SD: Expressionism arrived at the end of the First World War, because they didn't feel that art could talk to that generation about what had just happened. They needed a new form of expression. In some senses that's true now—there needs to be a new form of expression.

It can quickly become decadent, because to have the right form, you need to be engaged in another exploration. A lot of the forms are for form's sake, so it becomes a veneer. It becomes useless. It becomes an irrelevant investigation, a decorative art—so you get decorative design. New, spurious terms come up, like "total theater" or "physical theater." People talk in silly tongues, for the sake of it, as far as I can see. It's experimentation for experimentation's sake—which is not true experimentation.

Notes

1. *An Inspector Calls*, by J. B. Priestley, was first produced in 1945. I'm speaking of the Royal National Theatre's production of the play, which opened at the Royal National Theatre in 1992, and in the West End in 1993, under Mr. Daldry's direction.

2. The Royal National Theatre, London.

3. Richard Eyre: director of the Royal National Theatre from 1988 to 1997.

4. Royal Court Theatre, London.

5. *Blasted*, by Sarah Kane, was first produced in 1995, at the Royal Court Theatre.

6. *Fair Game*, by Rebecca Prichard, was first produced in 1997, at the Royal Court Theatre.

Quentin Crisp
New York, April 1, 1996

17

It will to cease to exist, the theater, because it's a large space in which you could get a television audience.

QUENTIN CRISP FIRST BECAME known for his autobiographical book *The Naked Civil Servant*. He wrote several other books, including *Quentin Crisp's Book of Quotations: 1,000 Observations on Life and Love, by, for, and about Gay Men and Women* and *Resident Alien*. He wrote and starred in his solo stage piece *An Evening with Quentin Crisp*, which won a special Drama Desk Award for Unique Theatrical Experience.

Mr. Crisp died in 1999, at the age of ninety.

SC: Some years ago, you did *An Evening with Quentin Crisp*[1] . . .

QC: That's right.

SC: You were the only actor, and there was no plot, no dramatic action.

QC: There was no dramatic action. I simply told people how to be happy. In my opinion, whatever we *seem* to be speaking about, we are always speaking about happiness. Whether we say we're speaking about religion, or politics, or whatever, it really means "Are we happy?" San Francisco is the only city where I've had totally bad notices.

SC: Isn't that odd?

QC: That's because they thought I was somebody who went throughout the length and breadth of the land delivering a manifesto. And, of course, I never mentioned homosexuality. In my opinion, a theater-goer, throughout the world, is a middle-class, middle-aged woman with a broken heart. So it was to them I spoke. Someone in the audience said, "You didn't mention homosexuality!" And I said, "What did you hope I would say?" Well, the house went up!

SC: Aside from the message in your play, I'm very interested in knowing how a play works with no plot, no dramatic action. What holds the audience?

QC: Well, I asked Miss Stritch[2] what the business was of controlling your audience, and she said, "Don't bother with any of that, honey. Get 'em to like you." And that's what you do. You stand on the stage and you try and get them to like you. Originally I was the only person in the world who went on the stage without bothering to act or sing or dance, but now . . . Mr. Mason[3] goes on the stage, in a large theater, in front of twelve hundred people, and says what he thinks. And there's Spalding Gray—he goes on the stage, and he speaks, on the radio or on the television. On television, I would say it was harder, because you're more removed. You don't know who your audience is.

In the second half of the show I did on the stage, people found within their programs a card on which they would write a question. That's in case they felt embarrassed to stand up and say, "Yes, I have something"—especially with your husband beside you, tugging at your skirt, saying, "Sit down. Don't make a fool of yourself." I know they don't want to be identified, because if I can't read all the question, I read a bit of it and I say, "What was this word?"—and nobody answers.

They asked me all sorts of questions. The extraordinary thing was that every evening they asked me under what sign of the zodiac was I born. I said I was born on Christmas Day and an argument broke out as to whether I was a *something* or a *something*. I said, "Is it good?" And they said, "Possibly." You see, astrology is like fortune-telling. If you can't get it right, you say, "Well, if Venus was doing something peculiar in the background, that would alter your prognostication"—because, of course, astrology is rubbish.

SC: Of course.

QC: They also asked what would I like to have written on my tombstone, did I believe in reincarnation, and I explained to them that I would be dead, and it wouldn't matter what was written on my tombstone. But you can't get people to accept death. They will believe in reincarnation. I can't think of anything more terrible than to fall out of your mother's womb with the words "Here again?" But Miss MacLaine[4] never expresses any weariness, and she's been born into various Cecil B. DeMille productions throughout her life. She's been a slave and been abducted and all that. Well, she never says, "And now I'm here again!"

I think she hasn't come to the end of herself. But I have come to the end of myself. I cannot think of anything new to say or do. Well, I find that I repeat myself.

SC: Well, then, your listeners are new.

QC: That's right. We hope the listeners are new, because otherwise, it's impossible. When I did it in England, there were people in the front row, and when I looked down, they were going [*mugs*]. And I said, "You've been here before." And they said, "Yes." And they knew it all.

But some people don't mind. Some people will see a film twice, which I find *weird* unless it's a musical. At a musical, the enjoyment is at part sensual. It's the sound of the music and the sight of the dancing. But when you've seen a film with a plot, you know what happens. I couldn't bear to see *Hamlet* twice. I know what happened. I know who won.

SC: What do you think of the direction theater is going in? You've been reviewing for some time. You've been working for some time. Is it getting better? Is it getting worse?

QC: Oh, it's getting worse, because it's getting more technical. There are very few plays which are dominated by people. They're dominated by machines. My niece said of *Evita*,[5] "It doesn't matter whether they sing correctly. What matters is seeing one scene change into another." And even with *Victor Victoria*[6]—it is a sort of technical triumph, rather than a triumph for Miss Andrews[7]—she is indestructible. I've seen one or two plays which are about people. I saw *The Heiress*[8] by Mr. James,[9] without a single mention of Mr. James on the program. It was about people, which was nice. It had one set, which was realistic.

SC: Do you see much English theater?

QC: No, I live here now, and I don't go to England. Americans say, "Oh, we go into London as often as possible for the acting." And I say, "They're not acting. That's the way they are."

SC: Is there a difference between British and American acting?

QC: There is, and it starts when they're in training. Now when I was only English, I met a woman from Miami, and she admitted that she'd been to a drama school. And I pounced forward, because I hold that you cannot teach people to act. She said, "They taught me to be a candle burning in an empty room." Well. I'm happy to say she was laughing when she said it, but she meant it. In England, you do not learn to be a candle burning in an empty room. You learn to make a huge noise for a long time without getting tired.

Elsie Fogarty, who was a great teacher, made all her students learn to say the first four lines of one of Shakespeare's sonnets without taking a breath, because that's what you can learn. That's the unnatural part of acting. All American actresses, when they are called upon to amplify their voices—they scream. A woman who had to speak to someone in the fourth window when she was standing in the street would scream. And she'd be right, because the quality of her voice would cut through the sound of the traffic. But on the stage, you cannot scream. All English actresses have their voices artificially amplified and artificially lowered.

The prime example of English teaching was a woman called Miss Greenwood.[10] If she'd been American there would have been "the Greenwood part"—and she would have played it forever. Instead of which she was only English and had to play juvenile leads and all sorts of silly things. But she triumphed because very late, when she was much too old to play the part, she was given the part of Gwendolyn Fairfax.[11] She said, "You have filled my cup with sugar, and when I asked for bread and butter, [*in a descending pitch*] you give me *cake*." And the note was so low you couldn't believe you'd heard it! And she was a triumph! She was wonderful, because she was mannered, and the theater is mannered, and we do not want naturalism.

SC: The British just don't want it. But in America . . .

QC: In America . . . well, you know the famous situation in which Mr. Hoffman[12] ran about the set in order to be out of breath when he had to play a part, and Mr. Olivier[13] said, "Try acting, dear boy." Why not act tired? Why not act sad? It's so *weird*! And in the movies, they do it. They told Miss Temple[14] various terrible things to make her cry and then photographed her, instead of saying, "Cry!"

SC: That is extraordinary! Do you think that awards to individuals—like the Oscars, and the Tonys, the Obies—are helpful to the art, or are they only helpful to the individual?

QC: I think they do affect the popularity of a film. I wouldn't go to see a film because it won an Oscar, but people *do*—they do go. They do watch the Oscars, whatever happens. It's the most boring show program ever, because it lasts so long.

SC: I wonder if stardom gets in the way of the art, or if stardom attracts people to the theater who would otherwise not go.

QC: Well, everyone in America is absolutely besotted with the idea of fame in the world of entertainment. If you brought up a symposium with all the great generals in the world, and the highest preachers in the church, and the great teachers, and Elizabeth Taylor, the press would repeat everything Miss Taylor had said, and describe her clothes, and count her emeralds, and they wouldn't mention anybody else.

SC: Does a star still have to work to entertain, or can a star get away with anything? Or is it more difficult for a star to entertain an audience—because of their expectations?

QC: No. You see, she entertains in a different way. If you're an actress—if you're Meryl Streep—you *act*. And if you're a star, you don't act—you're yourself. You have to establish a relationship with the audience. When Gertrude Lawrence and Noel Coward appeared on the stage in England, the audience went not to see a play, but to see a party given by Mr. Coward and Miss Lawrence. When he walked back up the stage, she stood up and she scratched her bottom. And he heard the laughter, and he turned—and she wasn't doing anything. It had nothing to do with the play, but that's what people went to see. They went to see their friends, Miss Lawrence and Mr. Coward, and not to see a play.

SC: Do you think that that undermines the art, in the long run?

QC: Well, it's another art. It's the art of expanding your personality over a whole group of people. You do for a whole theater what you would do for one person. You need certain characteristics. You need to be big, with a big head and a big face, and big eyes—so that they can see what you're thinking and doing. And you need a huge voice, preferably a magnetic voice.

But there's something else that you do. They said of Henry Irving that he would neither impersonate nor declare. So what was he doing? People were content just to see him walk across the stage. There's something that all stars *are*, over and above what they're doing. There was, when I was young, a pianist called Harriet Cohen. She had a profile in which her nose was in a straight line with her forehead—she looked like the head on an Assyrian coin. So she approached the audience in profile. She came on and went straight forward to where the conductor was, and she bowed, as though music were a friend who was dead. And then she realized that all that noise was for her, and she bowed. And she sat down on her seat so that her dress went *like that* [*gestures*]—she wore dresses that clawed the stage behind her. And that was not all. Then she had to prepare her hands! By that time, it didn't matter *what* note she played—the audience was totally convinced that she was wonderful!

SC: I imagine that theater was much more important to people in general decades ago.

QC: Yes.

SC: Can that happen again? In light of the fact that there are film and television, can theater become that important again?

QC: No. It will cease to exist, the theater, because it's a large space in which you could get a television audience. You see, television speaks to millions of people. I saw an interview on television with Miss Lansbury,[15] in which some wretched girl asked if she liked being famous, after being so obscure. I watched Miss Lansbury's face, and she said, "I've always been in work"—because she's always been famous, to us. But people who don't go to the theater, and who don't watch the movies, who only watch television, have now seen her in a serial called *Murder, She Wrote.*[16] They never saw *The Manchurian Candidate,*[17] which is a wonderful film.

That shows you that a world has sprung up of people who live through television. They prefer television not only to the movies, and to theater, but to real life. Barry Humphries was having a meal with a lot of women who'd invited him. So he sat at the table and entertained them. And after a bit, he said, "Oh, I'm on television now." They rose up, left him, went into the other room, and watched the television set!

Notes

1. *An Evening with Quentin Crisp*, by Quentin Crisp, was first produced in 1978.
2. Elaine Stritch.
3. Jackie Mason.
4. Shirley MacLaine.
5. *Evita*, music by Andrew Lloyd Webber, lyrics by Tim Rice, opened in the West End in 1978.
6. *Victor Victoria*, book by Blake Edwards, music by Henry Mancini with lyrics by Leslie Bricusse, with additional songs by Frank Wildhorn, opened on Broadway in 1995.
7. Julie Andrews.
8. *The Heiress*, by Ruth Goetz and Augustus Goetz, opened on Broadway in 1947. The script is based on Henry James's novel *Washington Square*. Mr. Crisp is speaking of the 1995 Broadway production.
9. Henry James (1843–1916).
10. Joan Greenwood (1921–1987).
11. Gwendolyn Fairfax, a character in *The Importance of Being Ernest*, by Oscar Wilde, which was first produced in 1895. Mr. Crisp is speaking of the 1952 film directed by Oliver Parker.
12. Dustin Hoffman.
13. Laurence Olivier (1907–1989).
14. Shirley Temple.
15. Angela Lansbury.
16. *Murder, She Wrote*, a CBS television series, 1984–1996.
17. *The Manchurian Candidate*, a film directed by John Frankenheimer, 1962.

Martin Sherman

18

London, August 20, 1997

I suppose that always was my problem with the American theater, something that's built into American culture—that something has to be extraordinary or not, it has to be event or not. It has to be what's perceived as a huge success, and if it's not perceived as a huge success, it's perceived as a failure.

MARTIN SHERMAN IS AN AMERICAN living in London. He won the Dramatists Guild's Hull-Warriner Award for his ground-breaking play *Bent*, which was also nominated for a Tony Award. He wrote the film adaptation of the play, which won the International Critics Award at the Cannes Film Festival. His play *Rose* was nominated for an Olivier Award. His many other plays include *A Passage to India . . .*, *A Madhouse in Goa*, and *Some Sunny Day*. He's also written for the BBC.

SC: You live in London and introduce your shows here. Is that just because you like the city, or does it have to do with the theater community here?

MS: I do love the theater community—and London is my home. In that sense I'm very out of touch with New York, and I don't think I can talk that knowledgeably about the community there. There is a very strong one here, very nurturing. It's extremely bitchy in a very nice way, in that everyone does bitch everyone else, but there is also a subtext of enormous support here. I think in New York, on the surface, there's a great deal of support, and the subtext is bitchery. Here, it's the other way around. I suppose I prefer it that way.

SC: Are your plays received as well in both countries?

MS: I'm virtually unknown in America.

SC: I don't think that's true!

MS: Well, I'm not—I'm not terribly known, and if I am, it's just for *Bent*,[1] nothing else, really.

SC: So, your plays are—

MS: —Better received here, and throughout Europe.

SC: Can you say something about how plays can be received equally well in such different cultures, across Europe. You're an American, and one would expect that your plays would reflect that upbringing and that culture. How can they be received the same way in other cultures?

MS: Well, a lot of European countries thrive on plays from outside their own culture. England probably has the widest and most considerable group of people writing for the theater anywhere in the world. America might come second. For instance, there are an enormous amount of British plays, certainly, done in Germany. British plays are constantly done in Germany, and I would suspect that American plays are as well. There are relatively few new German plays done.

So basically what we're doing is filling a void that exists within that culture. And different plays have different receptions in different European cultures. My two plays that are most popular throughout Europe, away from England, are *Bent* and *When She Danced*.[2] Other plays of mine are not as popular. My latest play, *Some Sunny Day*,[3] hasn't been done at all in Europe, because, ironically, they say it's far too British. It actually doesn't make any sense at all. Also, in some countries it depends very, very much on the quality of the first production. If you have a good first production, you're off and running; you can be done throughout the country. If you have a bad first production, you're dead in your tracks, and that play won't get done again. In that sense, it's a bit of a crap shoot.

SC: Speaking of *Bent*, it's generally your most popular play, is it?

MS: I'd say that and *When She Danced*.

SC: Is *Bent* your best, the one you are most satisfied with?

MS: No. I would say now that I think my last play, *Some Sunny Day*, is my best, but perhaps one always says that about one's last play. It's hard to ask a writer what he thinks is his best, because that's something that changes. It's like children—it's like asking, "Which child do you prefer?"

SC: How was *Some Sunny Day* received? Was it difficult for people?

MS: It was a very odd experience, because I got the best reviews I've ever had in my life, and it was virtually sold out before we opened. You couldn't get into it! The audience reaction was terrific. And, for the first four weeks, it wasn't playing to an audience that would seem to me to be right for it. It was quite a conservative audience. It was only when the advance sales began to peter out that it became more eclectic.

The audience reaction was always extraordinarily strong. It was hugely shocking to everybody concerned that it didn't move on to the West End, because it was in a lot of ways the most successful production I've ever had. It was a great mystery to us.

SC: How many plays have you written?

MS: I have no idea.

SC: But you've been writing since you were at Boston University . . .

MS: I wrote my first play when I was twelve. It was better than a lot of stuff I wrote later, for my respective ages. That's why I don't know how many plays I've written, because I wrote a lot of stuff when I was a kid.

SC: In *When She Danced*, you write about artists. There's a wonderful line when Mary says to Isadora Duncan,[4] "People try. Not everything has to be great art." I thought that was wonderful! You parody great artists in that play, and so many of us are going to find that encouraging.

MS: Well, I think if people are attempting to express themselves through art, that's the game—that's what's wonderful. It's a bonus if it becomes extraordinary, but even if it's ordinary, there's something to admire in the fact that the person's doing it.

I suppose that always was my problem with the American theater, something that's built into American culture—that something has to be extraordinary or not, it has to be event or not. It has to be what's perceived as a huge success, and if it's not perceived as a huge success, it's perceived as a failure. There's no in between. There are a lot of people, including wonderful artists, who do things all the time that don't fall into those categories, and are worthy of attention.

SC: If a play has achieved popular success, is that necessarily an indication that it's important?

MS: Well, I'm not sure what makes a play important, but I think you probably can't tell if a play is important until about fifty years later. But popular success shouldn't be discounted. It means it's saying something to somebody at that time, and that's nothing to sneeze at. Sometimes plays are considered important that have never really reached or intrigued an audience—they're academically considered important, or intellectually considered important.

I think theater is extraordinarily intelligent, but I don't think it's necessarily intellectual—because it does have to do with something that is acted. The art of acting is a much more instinctive art than—than an intellectual one. I don't think plays exist to be read. They exist to be acted, to be played. So that's why I think it takes fifty years to see whether a play is important, because when it has been acted again and again, and has appeared in front of different audiences in different cultures in different times, you can begin to judge, really, if it's important.

SC: You mentioned that theater is at least intelligent. Can it regain the importance that it had for Ibsen's audience, Shaw's audience, in light of the fact that there are television and film in the world?

MS: Well, it has that importance here, in England, I think. We may not necessarily have an Ibsen or Shaw—maybe we do. I don't think we'll know—again—until a little bit of time has passed and we can look back. But films and television have leapt ahead, perhaps, in terms of audience numbers, but not in terms of what's discussed, what's argued about, what seems to prod the conscience of the nation, and sensitivities and emotions of people in the street. Theater does that here. And what's extraordinary right now is that there are a lot of really, really good and exciting young writers, playwrights—very, very young. Probably in any other country, they would be writing films. And they're probably going to go on to write films. But they've started out in the theater, in a way that I don't see equaled anyplace else.

This is a very strange culture, because the British are constantly negative about themselves and yearning for good rewards and the assets of other cultures. Everyone has a serious case of America-mania. They completely undervalue themselves. I think the strength of the theater here is often more appreciated abroad than it is here. It's very, very powerful.

Now, in America, the theater is not particularly talked about, other than in very small circles. It's not written about the way films are written about. It's become the pathetic child of culture, there. I don't know what's going to happen to it there. In the last three days, every newspaper's had an editorial about the Old Vic,[5] because the Old Vic is up for sale. That wouldn't happen in America.

SC: At its best, when theater has a social consciousness, does it have a political effect? Did *Bent* have any social effect?

MS: What do you mean by social?

SC: Political. Ultimately, I think a social effect is manifested as a political effect. Does it change society?

MS: I don't think it does in obvious ways. I don't think politicians are affected. I don't think laws are affected. I don't think what we think of as the more visual side of society is affected. But I've discovered, after many years, that *Bent*, for instance, has deeply affected the lives of many people who've seen it. I didn't know that at first, because you're separate from the audience, and you just don't get that kind of feedback.

Writers are very isolated. It's rare—it's very rare for anyone to write to a writer. Actors get letters all the time, and very often letters about the play. Writers don't. Even directors sometimes get letters, but writers actually don't. So you're quite isolated from what the reaction is, other than the immediate reaction, during the play. So it's taken me years and years to realize what the effect of *Bent* has been, and that's only because I've just met so many people who, in the last six or seven years, have told me how it affected their lives. Maybe they needed time to see how it did affect their lives, before they can say.

And I think lives have changed because of it. So, on an individual basis, I think theater can cause change—and if you cause change on an individual basis, that can later translate into something broader. I suspect that's how it has to be measured.

SC: Could you say something about the development of your script before it opens? Is it workshopped? Is it read? Do you work with actors?

MS: No, I'm very much against workshops—they're very destructive in America. There's a paternalistic attitude that goes hand-in-hand with workshops. It's an attitude that says: "The writer is a child and we're gonna help—we're gonna help the writer." Well, I don't think a writer needs help any more than an actor needs help, or a director needs help, or a painter needs help, or an architect needs help, or a composer needs help. I think a writer needs to grow, but that's different—that's not help.

I think a writer can only grow, and improve, by learning his or her craft, and you do that by working directly with actors in a production, in front of an audience, where you make a hell of a lot of mistakes and learn from the mistakes. I don't mean a group of people sitting around afterwards with a critique, which usually reflects what they wanted to write, rather than what you're trying to write. I've seen, through the years, plays really ruined by a workshop process.

And of course by the time, if you go through that, and you finally, finally reach New York, for instance, it's assumed that the play is gonna be perfect, because it's been through all that. I don't think there's any such thing as a perfect play. I've seen plays here, and for a moment I could think: "If they had some kind of workshop process, some of the mistakes would be gone." But then, why should they be gone? It's part of where that writer is in that writer's development. The plays were not particularly successful, but the writer's next play was successful—that's the difference.

I'm not talking about a situation in which a writer, for his or her own aid, wants to have a group of actors together and have readings which will be helpful to the writer. I'm talking about the formalized workshop situation that exists in America, and does not exist here. And you'll notice that we have more interesting young writers, here.

Now, after everything I've just said about workshops, I'm going to say that *Bent* was an exception to my rule—I wrote the screenplay in a workshop situation.[6]

I suppose that clarifies my feelings about workshops. When I think of a workshop in America, it means helping the writer, and seeing if it works. Whereas I think you can have a workshop with a group of other artists in which you're working towards a common goal, and that's it. Sean Mathias, the director, suggested that I not write a screenplay, but that we cast it and work with the actors in a workshop situation for four weeks. We would go over the text of the play, and I would go home every night and translate the play into a screenplay out of that.

I'd very much looked forward to doing that because I wrote the play in isolation—and because I wrote a screenplay of it originally when the play was on Broadway, when we were gonna do a film, I wrote that in isolation. I thought it would make a completely unique experience for me and I wouldn't have any shadows of the past one, if I did it in this kind of circumstance.

There's a huge difference between films that are made in this country and films that are made in America, and that has to do with the way a writer is treated. I adore American films—as does the entire world. But writers are fucked around a lot, by everybody in America. Much less so here, because of the tradition of the theater.

SC: Will you be focusing more on screenplays than you have in the past?

MS: I've never, ever been a prolific playwright, and I've always wanted to be able to do something in between the times that I am writing a play. So now, I have this avenue that's open to me. I really do think one can feed into the other very, very nicely. I've found that it's helped me enormously as a playwright. For one thing, I discovered how much I loved language—what a pleasure it was to have characters talk, because you can't talk at that length in a film.

SC: Will you make changes in a stage script at the request of a director, for the first production?

MS: I think you always make changes when you're rehearsing, because you discover more things. The problem is that new plays can be so individual, and uniquely their own thing, that it's often hard to really understand what it is you've written the first time. Sometimes, it takes a number of productions, a number of different actors, in front of different audiences, with different approaches from different directors, until you really understand what that play is. I didn't understand what *When She Danced* was until I saw a production in Germany. That greatly influenced a production we did here on the West End, because I finally understood exactly how it should be played. I hadn't completely understood that before, although there had been about four productions, with wonderful actors. Learning about a play takes a long time, and—again—it's not something you can do in a workshop. You can only do it by being out there.

Notes

1. *Bent*, by Martin Sherman, was first produced in 1978. It opened on Broadway and in the West End in 1979.

2. *When She Danced*, by Martin Sherman, was first produced in 1985. It ran off-Broadway in 1990, and it opened in the West End in 1991.

3. *Some Sunny Day*, by Martin Sherman, was first produced in 1996.

4. The character of Isadora Duncan appears in Mr. Sherman's play *When She Danced*, first produced in 1985.

5. The Old Vic Theatre, London.

6. The film version of *Bent* was released in 1997, directed by Robert Chetwyn.

Oskar Eustis

19

Providence, Rhode Island, July 30, 1995

We have to be fiercely local, in a way that wasn't true a hundred years ago, because that is something we can provide that television and movies can't provide—something that is of this time, of this place.

OSKAR EUSTIS HAS BEEN the artistic director of San Francisco's Eureka Theatre and Los Angeles's Mark Taper Forum. Since 1994, he's been artistic director of Providence's Trinity Repertory Company. He received the Elliot Norton Award for Outstanding Director for his direction of *Angels in America, Part I: Millennium Approaches*, among other honors. He has worked extensively with the National Endowment for the Arts, as chairman of a theater panel as well as in other capacities.

SC: I know that you do a lot of work with the NEA.[1] Could you tell me about that?

OE: This evening, as a matter of fact, I'm going to New York as a site visitor, which I've been doing for about ten years, and I've also served as a panelist on a number of occasions. Perhaps most prominently, I was chair of the playwrights panel for two years.

SC: Could you say something about Jane Alexander's[2] management of the NEA?

OE: First of all, I'm not an expert on this subject. Second, I think Jane is in an extremely difficult position. She is prohibited by law from active political lobbying, even on behalf of her own institution. She is not allowed to engage in partisan debate about the motives of the people who are attacking the NEA, which I think is the key political issue that needs to be examined right now.

I would hate to be in her position. I think she has done a marvelous job of advocacy. What I instinctually wish she would do—I'm not sure it's the smart thing, but it's just what I want—is to actually draw lines in the sand, and make absolutist stands about the First Amendment, and about what it means for a democracy to subsidize arts. I think she can't do that—there are some legal reasons she can't do that, and I think there's also probably some *realpolitik* reasons that it does not pay to aggressively and absolutely defend the rights of minorities right now in the way that I think is morally and ethically necessary. I mean, what they're trying to do with Highways at the moment—the performance space in Santa

Monica that Tim Miller runs, which is an openly gay and lesbian performance space. They are seizing on Highways, and the fact that there's been some NEA funding to Highways, as a wonderful public relations lever to try and garnish support for the destruction of the NEA as a whole.

The policy of the extreme right, from the beginning of this NEA debate, has been very simple—first separate out the faggots, and, second, then use that to tarnish the entire arts establishment. Anything that we do that allows ourselves as a community of artists to be separated, allows us to come for the gay people in the morning, is disastrous. They've been whittling away at us that way.

Now, she's been a much more principled person than Frohnmayer,[3] but, again, there's part of me that just dies for her to draw a line in the sand, saying: "We're funding everybody. The peer review panel is absolute." As soon as you allow any incursions, it's very hard to defend the basic principle as a whole.

SC: Many people have called for the abolition of the NEA—not only people on the right wing, but also freedom of speech advocates. Would you rather see no NEA than see an NEA with content restrictions?

OE: No, but that's a devil's choice. The reason I disagree so passionately with those putatively on the left side of the spectrum—Ruth Seymour, who runs KCRW in Santa Monica is a big advocate of abolishing the NEA; Brustein[4] has talked about abolishing the NEA—the reason I think they're so wrong is that I think there's a fundamental principle about art subsidy that's to be defended. Serious art has never existed primarily in the marketplace. It has always received subsidy from whichever class happens to be in power. The claim of a Western democracy is that no single class is in power, that all classes are in power through the medium of a semi-autonomous government. The debate is not "Will the arts be subsidized?" but "Will America proudly claim that it is a democracy, and that therefore the arts should be subsidized democratically?"

If the NEA's abolished, the arts will continue to be subsidized. They will be subsidized by the rich—for the rich. The operas will exist. The painting market will not collapse. The arts which specifically serve those people who have massive amounts of disposable income will continue to exist. What will cease existing is all of the serious art forms that try to reach people who don't have massive amounts of disposable income. Those are the ones that will suffer.

I just believe that fight's a fight worth fighting to the end, because we are a democracy, and we need to stand for that.

SC: If we could speak for a moment about something you said about your roles: you said you wanted to produce and develop experimental works that tell stories and engage audiences.

OE: Yes.

SC: Why that stipulation about works that tell stories?

OE: Perhaps it's a little of my own reaction to my upbringing. I was trained in the *avant-garde* theater of the '70s in New York, where, among other things, narrative was under constant attack, and the idea of storytelling was often held up to ridicule. Nonlinear ways of approaching material, non-narrative forms of theater, deconstructed stories if there were stories at all—all of this was where our emphasis was, and not on storytelling, which was seen as inherently old-fashioned.

That's a bias and a training that I've rejected as I've gotten older. I have returned to a belief that the act of telling stories is primary to the theater I want to do, because of some things that are essential to what the theater does well, and essential to any ideal of a theater that's gonna be populist. It's because drama tells stories that it does what it does better than any other art form—which is reach high and low at the same time. Stories are what hook children. Stories are what hook people at the simplest level of engagement, and yet, they don't preclude the most sophisticated and complicated and grandiose examination of everything from thematics to linguistics.

It's almost a truism that Shakespeare was the greatest writer in the English language. It's not a coincidence that he wrote in the theater. The demand on Shakespeare was that he serve all audiences simultaneously—that he tell a story that'll hold the groundlings, but tell it with a sophistication and depth that'll hold the most educated member of his public. That's what theater does at the best, and storytelling is the string that carries all of it. You take out the storytelling, and you're removing the populist strain of it. You're saying: "We don't need to reach the broadest mass of the people," and that's something that I don't want to do. I really want a theater that's committed to telling stories that anyone can walk in here and appreciate.

SC: Do you think that you can overcome the class bias of the American theater?

OE: Single-handedly? No. I do think that I am working in a theater that has overcome that bias more than almost any other in America.

SC: The Trinity.

OE: Yeah, Trinity. I think what Adrian[5] and Eugene[6] and this acting company established here thirty-one years ago is a theater that has more of a blue-collar feel to it than—more of a populist, working person's feel to it—than any other serious regional theater in America. I have not met a cab driver who at least doesn't claim to have gone to a lot of shows at Trinity, and can talk about them. Now, I expect *Christmas Carol*[7] gets attended more than most of the others—nothing wrong with that! And, of course, by no stretch of the imagination could you say that Trinity has a primarily working-class audience—no theater in America really has. But I think we've come closer to it than other theaters and I think we can continue to build on that.

One of the enormous helps there is Project Discovery, our high school performance program, because, in terms of high school students, we do reach a huge chunk of the working class. Those are working-class kids who come in here as high school students, and we reach eighteen thousand of them annually. What I hope we can do when we are fully funded again is go back to what Project Discovery was meant to be, what it was at its start—a program that brought every high school student in Rhode Island into this theater twice a year.

SC: It makes me think of something you wrote in one of your newsletters. You said, "There's no point in saying anything if no one's listening." In light of the fact that there is film, and there is television, can theater regain the importance that it had a hundred years ago as a disseminator of ideas?

OE: I doubt that it can ever regain fully the role that it had in some way up until the advent of the talkies. The nonprofit theater movement in this country was founded in the mid '60s, and I don't think it's a coincidence that it was founded a decade after television became ubiquitous in American life. One of the many forces that led to the creation of the regional theaters was a sense that we were not going to allow television to become the only thing that Americans did at night.

The entire history of this movement is, in a way, an attempt to define what is irreplaceable about theater. This whole field has been struggling with that issue, and with some remarkable success in the past thirty years. But the strengths that theater brings to bear are focused in a different way than they were a hundred years ago. We have to be fiercely local, in a way that wasn't true a hundred years ago, because that is something we can provide that television and movies can't provide—something that is of *this* time, of *this* place. The personal relationship to the storytellers, the ongoing relationship over years between the audience and the artist talking to them—that's terribly important, because it's so unique about the theater, because it separates the theater. There are ideas of certain complexity that can only be dealt with in the theater, that don't survive the commercial processes of television and film.

And even more important, the theater reaches the audience in a different state of mind than television and film reach them. There's something about the act of coming together in a building in your town that makes an audience more receptive to deeper thematic resonances than the act of sitting at home in front of the TV alone. At its best, theater brings audience into the building as customers, and has them leave as a community.

So yeah, I think there's a real role for theater—it's maybe not as grandiose as we'd hope.

SC: That's good to hear. If we can get back, for a moment, to your stated goals for the Trinity, you also said that you want to work on the development of scripts. Do you mean commissioning works, or soliciting scripts?

OE: I mean the whole gamut. Before commissioning, I want us to be able to work with young writers who are just starting in the theater, and help them develop their talent. I want to attract writers who might not otherwise work within the theater, and make the theater an exciting and viable place for them to write. I want to commission plays from writers who are already established, and I want to take plays either that we've commissioned or that we're getting in an early form, and help writers develop them further into a more polished form. All of those steps are necessary, and all of the programs to support those steps have to be in place for us to be the kind of organization I'd like us to be.

SC: Could you say something about commissioning plays? Why commission a play instead of taking a play that's had its genesis in the mind of the playwright?

OE: Let me take three projects, all of which I commissioned, all of which ended up on Broadway, all of which had a very wide scope: Emily Mann's *Execution of Justice*,[8] Tony Kushner's *Angels in America*,[9] Anna Deavere Smith's *Twilight*.[10] Each of those three projects was commissioned by the theater I was at—in two cases the Eureka Theater in San Francisco, and the third case the Taper in L.A. Each of them involved the theater going to the playwright and saying, "We want you to do a show about our town—about this place." That's how *Angels* started—going to Tony Kushner and saying, "Write something for San Francisco, about San Francisco, for our company of actors." It was the specific challenge of writing a play for San Francisco and for that company of actors that led to *Angels* being as expansive a work as it was. Same with Emily's *Execution of Justice*, and—minus the actors—with *Twilight*.

In other words, we were taking writers and giving them a set of very local, specific demands that they then had to wrestle to integrate into their vision. In each case, I think that wrestling produced work of greater scope. I'll never forget Tony just whining incessantly [*laughing*] about *how* he was gonna write this work about gay men and put three women in it! What was he gonna do with three women? Well, we had three women in our company, we needed three women in it. Part of that struggle is what opened *Angels* up to become the size of play that it became. If there had been no restrictions at all, if Tony had written this in his attic—which, by the way, he's never done with a play—he's always had actors in mind—if he had written this without any commission, without any grounding from a specific theater in a specific community, I think it would have been a very different play, and, frankly, a much smaller play, much more tightly focused, less important.

SC: So a commission, then, is an invitation to the playwright to be included in your sense of *local*.

OE: Exactly. I would say, Steve, that *that* has been the way all the great playwrights worked. Very few of the great playwrights didn't write for actors, didn't have a specific, collaborative, usually difficult relationship with a director and actors.

Even Miller[11]—he's one of my favorites. Miller essentially wrote for a theater company that he'd been an audience member for that had gone out of existence—the Group Theater. He had the Group Theater in mind when he was writing those great plays. And the Group Theater essentially reformed as a Broadway company in order to do Miller's plays. Kazan[12] and Clurman[13] and Lee J. Cobb came back together in order to present this writer's works. So even if it was a company in the mind, it was a company.

One of the only great playwrights who didn't do that was Beckett, and I think that was part and parcel of the content of Beckett's work.

SC: It's a very introspective body of work.

OE: Absolutely. So I don't think I'm saying anything that's really radical. All I'm trying to do is what I think every serious theater person's tried to do: in this time, in this place, find out how you really keep the theater art alive and exploding.

SC: You said once that the American residential theater movement was modeled on the British theater structure, and you wanted to move away from that. What characteristics of the British theater do you want to move away from?

OE: What I want to move away from is the overt anglophilia of much of American theater. I grew up in Minneapolis, where the Guthrie[14] was the theater of choice. It is no coincidence that the flagship of the American regional theater movement bears the name of a Brit, and was founded by a Brit. As I grew up, everybody on stage spoke in something that I was assured was a mid-Atlantic accent. It sounded to me an awful lot like a British accent. They didn't talk like us. They were *other*. And what makes the British theater so great is that it's a *British* theater, and the American theater movement has to define itself as an American theater with an American theater tradition that incorporates what we have learned from the English, but is by no means slavishly devoted to it. Of the six artistic directors that the Guthrie has had, only two of them have been born in America. They've had four foreigners. I'm not anti-foreign, but there is something about our obsequience to the British classical tradition that I really would like to get away from.

SC: If you could say something about your experience in Europe—you were very successful. What can you tell me about the difference between the way an American audience relates to the theater and a continental audience?

OE: It's a tough question, because we just sort of get overwhelmed with envy at the role that the theater has in Central European culture. The theater is so central to the cultural life of the country—there is simply no debate about it. My friend Stefan runs the theater in Zurich. Ninety percent of the budget—literally 90 percent—is subsidized directly from the city. There is an assumed importance that's reflected budgetarily that also gets reflected in the intensity with which the audience engages theater, in the intensity of debate that can be unleashed. You will often find productions discussed in the editorial pages. Directors are constantly looking for how to make the theater speak to the issues of their times, and that's accepted as part of their job.

What's interesting about them is that, with a couple of notable exceptions, the German-speaking world has not produced serious new drama since Brecht's day. Their theater, because of its institutionalization, has ended up focusing overwhelmingly on productions of the classic repertoire, and therefore the creativity of the theater is on directors' interpretations of the classic repertoire. Now, that's interesting and important, but it's also to a certain extent, I think, leached some of the real life force out of the theater.

One of the things about America and the American theater: there's something kind of raffish about being in the theater. There's something always a little bit on the edge of criminality—certainly on the edge of poverty. It's not quite respectable. And I don't think that marginalization is entirely a bad thing. It's part of what gives us our vitality. It's a truism to say that most of the great American art forms end up being centered in marginalized groups—whether it's the African American community or the Jewish community—whether it's the gay community. And that position of being one uncomfortably present within the culture is obviously a tremendously creative position to stand in.

So there are certain blessings that come with the struggle that we have. Another way of putting this is to say: "We will not survive unless we continuously make the case as to why this city, this state, this country can't exist without us." We have to constantly remake a case for our own—of the necessity of our own existence. If we fail to make that case, we'll be out of business in a year.

Notes

1. The National Endowment for the Arts.

2. Jane Alexander, chair of the NEA from 1993 to 1997.

3. John Frohnmayer, chair of the NEA from 1989 to 1992.

4. Robert Brustein, founder of the Yale Repertory Theatre and the American Repertory Theatre (A.R.T.) and, at the time of this interview, the A.R.T.'s artistic director.

5. Adrian Hall.

6. Eugene Lee.

7. *A Christmas Carol*, by Adrian Hall and Richard Cumming, is produced annually at the Trinity Rep.

8. *Execution of Justice*, by Emily Mann, was commissioned by the Eureka Theatre, San Francisco, in 1982, and first produced at the New Play Festival at the Actors Theater of Louisville in 1984.

9. *Angels in America: A Gay Fantasia on National Themes*, by Tony Kushner, was commissioned by the Eureka Theatre, San Francisco, and first produced there in 1991. Part 1, *Millennium Approaches*, opened in London, at the Royal National Theater, in 1992. It opened on Broadway in 1993. Part 2, *Perestroika*, opened on both Broadway and at the National in 1993.

10. *Twilight Los Angeles 1992*, by Anna Deavere Smith, was commissioned by the Mark Taper Forum in Los Angeles, and first produced there in 1993.

11. Arthur Miller.

12. Elia Kazan (1909–2003): director.

13. Harold Clurman (1901–1980): director.

14. The Guthrie Theatre, Minneapolis.

Hilary Strong
London, March 11, 1995

The funny thing is that people actually seek out a bad show. They often will say, "I want to see just one typically bad Fringe show." Then they feel quite satisfied.

HILARY STRONG WAS the director of the Edinburgh Fringe festival, the largest arts festival in the world, from 1994 to 1999. She was then appointed executive director of London's Greenwich Theatre. She was for two years on the board of the National Campaign for the Arts, and in 1998 she was appointed to the board of the Arts Council of England. She is a stage director and choreographer, and has acted as administrator for the Merlin Arts Center in Somerset and for the Natural Theatre Company.

SC: What countries have been sending shows to the Fringe?

HS: Thirty different countries last year. The world theater aspect is growing, predominantly from America and Canada, and Eastern Europe. What we don't tend to get a lot of is companies from continental Europe. Subsidy in continental Europe is so great that a typical small-scale theater company would be well funded, and when you say to them, "Yes, you can come to Edinburgh, but you have to take the risk, financially," that gets them off. So we don't tend to get very many French, German, Spanish companies. What we do get a lot of now is Russian, Hungarian, Polish, Czechoslovakian—largely because they're funded by either their own governments or by Visiting Arts in London, who are an organization that's paid to bring interesting companies over to Britain.

It's very interesting because you do see the different trends, different theater styles. There is at the moment great interest in physical theater. That's the sort of main area, really—particularly contemporary dance. I think what's happened—particularly in the United Kingdom—is that there was a great increase in interest in contemporary dance about ten years ago, and that sort of worked its way through, so that companies that were doing just dance started using their movement skills in theater productions, and broadening out, mixing actors and dancers, and generally kind of creating a physical theater style of work. A lot of Eastern European countries have a strong physical sense.

SC: How has the theater been affected by the political change in Eastern Europe?

HS: The first thing that happened, it seems to me, is that they lost their very high level of subsidy. If you talk to a Russian company, for example—they would be used to a really high-grade sponsorship from their government, to the tune of having twenty-four people in a box office running a small theater. That's gone, of course. The last five years have been an interesting transitional phase, in that many of the companies are now looking for commercial sponsorship and trying to find alternative funding to replace core government funding.

SC: It must be very tough, considering how the private sector is doing.

HS: Very tough.

SC: It hasn't burgeoned as much as people expected it to.

HS: That's absolutely right. The problem for them is that some of them are forced to tour all the time, because that is the only way they can survive. The Maly Theatre,[1] for example, in Russia, are touring constantly, because the foreign income they can earn touring supports their enterprise in Russia. That's very tragic for them, because their base is within a fairly small community. They're very, very popular, and they're having to go away from home—a very, very good company. I saw them in Glasgow—forty of them onstage—massive! Of course, those countries are used to having large-scale productions.

SC: Is there very little participation from developing countries—Latin American, African?

HS: There's not as much, but it's not bad—it's building up. South Africa is a country that came on line last year. We had three companies—from Soweto, Johannesburg, Capetown. It's curious that the countries that have perhaps got the hardest time getting here do get here, whereas perhaps the richer countries, like France, Germany, Spain, don't.

SC: I imagine that it's the Latin American and African countries that really need to present themselves to the world arena.

HS: Yes, that's right—absolutely! And I think it's great when you can encourage them to come, and help them make it possible. We do a lot of extra support for the countries that have more trouble organizing themselves—we'll maybe try and help them find the best venue for their show. Our whole way we operate is to act as an enabling service, so we don't actually contract any of the companies; we just give you the information, and then encourage you to go and sort it out yourself. I think that hands-off management approach is important because things happen in Edinburgh spontaneously and without our control, and that allows it to grow. If you look at the Canadian model of fringes, where, for example, in Edmonton,[2] the management run the venues—then, if you want to be in it, you have to go into a lottery. You sort of apply and they pull out of a hat five—fifty—companies—whatever. And so a lot of people are disappointed and can't go. Once you're accepted, you have to conform to their time slots and so on. I wouldn't favor that because I think it's too controlling. If a company comes along and says, "Look, we want to do a six-hour epic, outdoors," I don't think the Canadians would be able to accommodate that, but we could in Edinburgh. We'd say, "Go find your outdoor venue."

SC: Could you say something about the trends in the work that's been brought to the Fringe?

HS: The Fringe is an interesting mix, because it's sort of a mix of high art and commercial market forces. What you've got is, on the one hand, the very, very popular comedy—typically, comedians like Jack Dee, Joe Brown, Eddie Izzard—very well known in Britain—to tour a comedy circuit. At Edinburgh, a very important part of the Fringe is still comedy. Not just stand-up—I think, unlike America, comedy in Britain is still very diverse. It encompasses comedy theater, physical theater, all sorts of different elements, stand-up being the most well known. That's always been part of the Fringe, going back to the days of *Beyond the Fringe*,[3] with Dudley Moore and Peter Cook, Alan Bennett. It's culturally important, but it's become very commercial over the years. I think that that's fine, because the thing about the Fringe is that it's a festival that's open to everyone. So I support that, enormously. The man in the street—it may be the only thing he wants to see.

But then alongside that, you've got very interesting theater, and that's the growth area. In recent years, it's come away from the one-man shows that we used to get a lot of—still get a lot of—but it's become much more ensemble work.

SC: Important writers and directors have come out of the Fringe.

HS: Yes! If you look at the West End at the moment, there are productions that have come from the Fringe: *Killer Joe*,[4] which came from the Traverse,[5] in Edinburgh, to the Bush,[6] and then to the West End; *The Live Bed Show*,[7] which is a comedy play that was on at the Fringe. That's quite typical, really. The great thing is that there has always been a tradition of new writing. There is an award called the Scotsman Fringe First Award, which is given to good new plays. Something like three or four hundred plays are eligible, and the *Scotsman*, which is the Scottish newspaper, arranges for them all to be reviewed by a team of critics. So they get to see a lot, and then they give up to about sixteen awards during each Fringe. Some of the work is really excellent, including international work. There is a company from America that won a Fringe First last year, a company from Poland—a very broad range of work. That is crucial, because in the touring theater, and directory theater, in Britain, there's far less new work commissioned—it's too risky. Once you get to a middle or large scale, you have to get a reasonable capacity in to sell the show. You cannot risk a new writer. So one of the most significant contributions the Fringe makes is the fact that it's generating new writing, which is tested out in a marketplace that has a lot of media, a lot of foreign directors.

SC: That's important. I've found the London fringe to be very conservative, in terms of form, compared to the New York fringe, and I would hope that a place like your festival would nurture new forms and encourage people to take chances.

HS: I think that's absolutely right. It does. It comes down to the fact that it's a completely open festival; absolutely anybody can do a show on the Fringe. There is a cost implication; it doesn't come cheap, but it is within reach. I directed a play on the Fringe in 1990—now that I'm the director of the Fringe, I understand what it's like to get through it. If you work it very carefully and you do all the right things, it is possible. My point is that those kinds of finances are within reach of most people. It might take you a year to get it together, but you can do it. So it's not exclusive. What you get is a vast range of work—some of it terrible—there's no doubt. But within it, you get a gem, or several gems.

SC: Sure. It's important to have work that fails in order to have one piece of work that's successful—that's something we have to deal with.

HS: Exactly. The funny thing is that people actually seek out a bad show. They often will say, "I want to see just one typically bad Fringe show." Then they feel quite satisfied.

SC: Well, as a critic, I would rather see a bold show that fails than a conventionally successful show. It's more interesting to me, writing for the theater community.

HS: Exactly! One of the weaknesses of the Fringe is the fact that people have tended to slip into your typical Fringe production—i.e., one actor, no costume, no set, minimal resources. After a while, the audience begins to feel cheated, and that's one area that we need to address. We need to try and challenge the companies to come up with designs that are more interesting. I mean, it's very difficult because you're doing very quick get-in's and get-out's. And they overlap—for example, a typical studio will have a show at ten o'clock, twelve o'clock, two o'clock, four o'clock, and so on. So people tend to get lazy and just not bother with any set.

SC: How much of an audience can we expect, in a festival that has so many productions?

HS: The average comes out at about fifteen people per performance. That's within a situation where you've got some theaters with five hundred, eight hundred people selling out. And, equally, there are some shows that get no audience at all. But then, when you see their entry in the program, you actually know why. It's kind of obvious, either because they've done completely the wrong sort of product, or because their lack of experience just glares out at you—it's so obvious they're not going to do well.

In terms of the likely winners, new plays are always of interest to the public, and classic plays. I say to American companies: "A good bet would be to do a Sam Shepard, because people would be interested to see how an American company would do a play of their own culture." And, equally, a French company doing Molière—things like that. That's looking at it with a really hard-nosed commercial sense—those kinds of plays do well. All plays by well-known contemporary writers—Alan Bennett, Alan Ayckbourn, David Hare—so on. What's often a mistake is if companies choose a play that they know they like, but which isn't known to the public and is not new. It's an unknown writer, it's an unknown company, and it's not got the excitement of being a new piece.

SC: It sounds like that's always good advice, for the festival or otherwise! You give people a lot of help. I get your monthly support letters, which are wonderful. They really guide a new producer through every step of the production process specific to the Fringe.

HS: I think that they have a relevance for any kind of theatrical situation on the fringe, because it's about looking ahead, and thinking about all the various elements that you've got to be aware of. Obviously, it's the worst marketplace in the world, but in some respects, it's easier. The people that are wandering about actually want to see shows. You're dealing with a market that is absolutely amenable to being sold to. If you take somewhere like London, you're fighting all the time, because there's so many alternatives.

SC: Isn't the market largely people who produce fringe shows? Are we presenting shows to the theater community?

HS: No, no. I would say 40 percent of our audience is local, ordinary people, all sorts of different people—taxi drivers, housewives, doctors, nurses. And then, an awful lot of people visit from southern England, London—that's probably our next market. And then you've got foreign tourists as well.

SC: Edinburgh must be packed!

HS: Absolutely packed! It is great! It's a wonderful city, because it's a small city. If one was to create a new international festival from scratch, you have to choose your city very carefully. You have to be somewhere which is small enough that you feel the festival dominates it, and you get a great sense of occasion and of party. A lot of festivals that have failed over the years been situated in large, sprawling cities. You don't get that sense of communal enjoyment. The thing about Edinburgh is that, being on the east coast of Scotland, and being a cold city, in the winter very little happens, really, and so the locals feel enthusiastic about the summer festival because it's time to party. So there's a general good spirit towards it. And, of course, the Fringe is not the only festival. The International Festival,[8] of course, is the main one, but there's also the Film Festival,[9] the Jazz Festival,[10] the Book Festival,[11] and the Tattoo[12]—so there's a lot going on!

Notes

1. The Maly Theatre, Moscow.
2. At the Edmonton International Fringe Festival, Edmonton, Alberta, Canada.
3. *Beyond the Fringe*, music and lyrics by Dudley Moore, was first produced in 1960.
4. *Killer Joe*, by Tracy Letts, was first produced in 1993.
5. The Traverse Theatre, Edinburgh.
6. The Bush Theatre, London.
7. *The Live Bed Show*, by Arthur Smith, was first produced in 1989.
8. The Edinburgh International Theatre Festival.
9. The Edinburgh International Film Festival.
10. The Edinburgh International Jazz and Blues Festival.
11. The Edinburgh Book Festival.
12. The Edinburgh Military Tattoo.

Ellen Stewart
New York, April 2, 1996

I don't read plays. I'd much rather read the person.

ELLEN STEWART, "the Mama of La MaMa," founded La MaMa Experimental Theatre Club in New York in 1961. There she produced the early works of playwrights such as Sam Shepard, Jean-Claude van Itallie, and Lanford Wilson. La MaMa's international tours have been extensive, and Ms. Stewart has introduced many foreign directors to New York. Her many honors include the Order of Sacred Treasure, Gold Rays with Rosette, from the Emperor of Japan, as well as the Les Kurbas Award from the Ukraine and a MacArthur "Genius" Fellowship.

SC: You've been producing experimental theater for thirty-five years. How has it changed? How have the forms changed since you began, over the past three decades? Is it as exciting as it was in '61, when you began? The '60s are known for being such an exciting time for *avant-garde* theater.

ES: Well, I think we're still exciting—at least people say so.

SC: I can see that La MaMa is. I see your work all the time.

ES: So? Okay? When I started La MaMa, I didn't know anything about theater, and in fact, I didn't care anything about theater. My interest was in two young people who wanted to do theater. So things happened and made me decide: "Fine, then—we'll just *do* it." So I opened a little basement on East Ninth Street, a little bit bigger than this room, and this was our theater. We were gonna do plays, and these two persons were gonna write the plays, and whoever wanted to direct would direct them, and whoever wanted to act in them would be in them. I thought that was fine. I didn't know that you had to have lights, and I didn't know that you had to have anything technical. Music is my first love. We had music throughout the play.

I was sitting down behind the coffee bar, working the radio. We had two lights. Paul Foster—you might know him; he's a very well-known playwright now—at that time, he hadn't written a play. He was sitting on one side of the room, and I sat on the other side of the room, and we had two wall sockets, and we each had a light. When we had to have a blackout, we'd pull the lights out—but then there was long blackouts because we couldn't find the sockets!

Now, I didn't know any different than that. I'll tell you how much we knew. This director came. He was a real director. He came over from the Cafe Cino, and his name was Andy Milligan. And so he was gonna really direct a play. So then he asked Paul, did he have any jells? Now Paul and I did not know what a jell was, but we didn't want him to know we didn't. So Paul says, "Ell! Did you bring any jells today?" I always carried a big pocketbook—like this—because I worked in fashion, freelance, to support the theater. So I opened this big pocketbook. I said, "Paul, I left the jells at home." So that was that! Now, as we progressed, the people had the shiny pink paper, and they had shiny blue paper, but nobody ever used the word "jells" with the paper—so we didn't know that was jells. Six months later, somebody said, "Give this jell to . . ." That's how we finally got to know what "jell" was, you see!

Now, I didn't know how to read a résumé, so I don't read résumés today. I didn't know then, and I think I've done pretty well. And I certainly was not interested in plays talking a lot. The playwrights in those days wrote plays talking a lot, but I never read them. I've read about ten plays, I guess, in thirty-five years. I don't read plays. I'd much rather read the person. If I think that person has something, I'm really interested, and I'll try to help what I think that is. But it doesn't come from reading the plays.

So La MaMa hasn't changed. It's merely . . . I have pushed it into what I think it should be, and that is: we should be a theater of communication. I don't think that the English language is the beginning and the ending of anything. I'm Chinese, and therefore I speak Chinese. I am speaking—which I don't really, but in my mind—I am speaking Mandarin or Cantonese, and if you give me a script in English—what the hell does it mean? I can't read it. So I don't read them. It's all these words, and if it is somebody Chinese there, what is your script gonna mean to them, if you're gonna sit there and talk your English? So with that, I have tried to guide La MaMa into the path of finding ways to communicate using language, but beyond the language—so that your language, in a sense, becomes like part of an extended symphony. That I can see what you're talking about doesn't mean that I necessarily understand everything, but I get a kind of visceral connection—and I think this is very important.

Therefore, what you will see for the most part at La MaMa—and you said you've come a lot—have been plays that are not talking so much. You've seen a lot of movement; you've seen dance; you've heard a lot of music. I'm told that we do more music than any theater in the world, because I encourage every playwright to work with a composer. And the first thing I tell a playwright is: "Stop being a playwright. Be a *play-maker*. And understand that music is as important as your words, and that you shouldn't do anything without thinking of music—and understand that the composer is as important as you are." That's it!

SC: The work that you've done has been always experimental.

ES: Always.

SC: Does it get assimilated into off-Broadway, Broadway, mainstream theater? Do they pick up your techniques?

ES: Darling, have you seen *Blue Man?*[1] Well, that was made right here. Okay? Does that answer your question? Did you see *Torch Song Trilogy?*[2] That was made right here—written for me, by Harvey Fierstein. Did you see *Godspell?*[3] That play was made for me.

SC: You take American work, work that . . .

ES: Now wait a moment! I don't call my work *American*. I call my work *our work*. And our work is always work that is international—both in its feeling and in the persons that are in it. I have an artists' residence in Italy. I got the MacArthur Genius award ten years ago, and I took that money and I started building an artists' residence in Italy, which is there now. And so every year, we go there, and then kids from all over the world come. We make projects. It has to be things that they can be involved in. So *Uncle Tom's Cabin*[4] I'm not.

SC: Does England receive your work as well as America?

ES: England? I haven't been in England in years. But I'm an officer in the French Academy. I'm the first person to receive a Les Kurbas Award in the Ukraine. I've gotten a thing from the President of the Philippines for my human rights work. I am a doctor thirteen times, including being a doctor in the Philippines, and I received a doctorate from Princeton. Last year, I got the Gold Crown, which is an award from Korea for my work in Korea. And just this past—when was it? December?—the Emperor of Japan made me a Sacred Treasure. I'm the only woman in America that's ever been made that. I'm inducted into the Order of the Sacred Treasure, Gold Rays with Rosette. I'm the only person who has not ever been on Broadway, but I'm in big gold letters in the Broadway Hall of Fame, here. So . . . other countries . . . let's see . . .

SC: So all over the world, then, they love your work.

ES: Yes, that's what they tell me.

SC: More than here?

ES: Right.

SC: That's very interesting.

ES: Uh-huh.

SC: Is it easier to show an audience something new, that they've never seen before, outside this country?

ES: No, dear, because we don't go outside La MaMa. We don't get invited outside La MaMa. Nobody invites us to do anything here in America, but we get invited all over the world. I've just come back now from the Philippines. I've just come back now from Korea. I'm doing a big project in Vietnam . . . everywhere. But in America, we don't get invited.

SC: So you invite various companies here, but you're not invited to work all over America?

ES: Not invited to work anywhere in America.

SC: Why?

ES: You know, international theater, as such, hardly exists, and this so-called cross-cultural thing—it all came out of La MaMa, but we don't get any funds to do that kind of work. Rather, the funds are given to persons who are trying to do it—to encourage them.

SC: And it must be very influential in every country that you go to. In other countries . . .

ES: They like us.

SC: Their theater must be very influenced, too. Do they take the techniques that they see in your stage?

ES: Yes. But I have doubts with the South Koreans, who were invited for the first time to break the red—the barrier between the Chinese and the South Koreans. We danced there, and Mama, too[5]—I did the National Theater in Beijing. Did a lot of things.

SC: Finally, what about American theater that isn't La MaMa? What about . . .

ES: I don't know about it because, honey, I've got four stages. I got all my kids. I got my arms full. I don't got to be going see what they doing—I really don't. You know? I don't have time to go see what somebody else is doing. Not only that—I never did.

SC: So you try to get a lot of diversity within La MaMa.

ES: Try? I don't have to try.

Notes

1. Blue Man Group, a multimedia performance company founded in 1987, first produced its show *Tubes* in 1991, at La MaMa E.T.C.

2. *Torch Song Trilogy*, by Harvey Fierstein, comprises *The International Stud*, *Fugue in a Nursery*, and *Widows and Children First!* It was first produced as three separate plays in 1978 and 1979, at La MaMa E.T.C. It opened on Broadway in 1982.

3. *Godspell*, music and lyrics by Stephen Schwartz, conceived by John-Michael Tebelak, was first produced in 1971. It opened on Broadway in 1976.

4. *Uncle's Tom Cabin*, a classic American novel by Harriet Beecher Stowe, 1852.

5. "and Mama, too": Ms. Stewart is referring to herself here.

Joseph Chaikin
New York, May 21, 1999

Society has changed and assimilated the Ibsen theater as a conservative theater, and the radicalism of Ibsen has moved out into the margins where the middle class does not attend.

JOSEPH CHAIKIN FOUNDED the Open Theatre in 1963, after having worked with the Living Theatre; he was later associated with many other prominent companies. For his work with the Open Theatre, he was honored with the Vernon Rice Award. He also received six Obie Awards and the National Endowment for the Art's Distinguished Service to American Theater Award, the Edwin Booth Award, among many other honors. His book on theater is *The Presence of the Actor.*

Mr. Chaikin died in 2003 at the age of sixty-seven.

SC: You wrote, in your book,[1] that you reject all that comes before, because of your skepticism about the theater. Is that still true?

JC: I think so—because I don't like the commercial stuff. That's not for me.

SC: You also wrote: "We're willing to fail. It helps to go beyond safe limits." Can that still be true, now that there's so much attention on your work?

JC: I think it's as true now as it ever was. It may look more established, because I'm doing more formal plays, scripted works, but I've not neglected experimental work at all. I don't enjoy working within limits. I like to discover things—poor ideas and good ideas.

SC: You wrote: "An actor was to remain present in his impersonation of a character." Do you still use the approach?

JC: No.

SC: So you—since you wrote the book, then, you've developed other approaches.

JC: Yeah.

SC: Do people respond to your work in the same way in other countries?

JC: Yeah.

SC: So then, theater is universal. It's not specific to the culture.

JC: Yes.

SC: In the experimental theater of the late '60s and the early '70s, so many new techniques were developed. You must think that many off-off-Broadway theaters aren't doing their job today. We don't have that burst of energy that came twenty, twenty-five years ago. Do you think that's true?

JC: Yeah, I think so.

SC: Can the theater have the same importance for American audiences, now, that it did for Ibsen's audience? Even though film and television get so much attention, can the theater be that important again, in terms of spreading ideas?

JC: I think that theater today expresses ideas in ways that Ibsen would admire, but they're not to the Ibsen audience. For example, there are many, many types of theater devoted to marginal cultures, who never get expression in the media—and the theater is their vehicle.

SC: So it's the audience that's changed—not the theater.

JC: Society has changed and assimilated the Ibsen theater as a conservative theater, and the radicalism of Ibsen has moved out into the margins where the middle class does not attend.

Certain types of mainstream plays address issues for a middle-class audience, maybe at not the same level of quality as Ibsen did, but there are plays such as *As Is*,[2] by William Hoffman, which is a play about AIDS, *The Normal Heart*,[3] by Larry Kramer, which were mainstream hits. *As Is* won a Tony Award for best play of the year. These are groundbreaking dramas in terms of content, that bring to a middle-class audience subjects that they wouldn't ordinarily attend to. The same thing can be said of *Angels in America*.[4] It was an enormous success. So occasionally there is a kind of mainstream breakthrough *theater of ideas*.

I think that the power of *Angels in America*, for example, is that it gave a kind of legitimacy to talking about the subject of AIDS. When Ibsen staged *Ghosts*,[5] it was considered impolite in polite society to speak the word "syphilis." The play was not discussed. On the contrary, I think *Angels in America*—and the AIDS plays—made those subjects more visible, and more often discussed.

Notes

1. Joseph Chaikin, *The Presence of the Actor* (New York: Atheneum, 1977).
2. *As Is*, by William Hoffman, opened on Broadway in 1985.
3. *The Normal Heart*, by Larry Kramer, was first produced in 1985.
4. *Angels in America: A Gay Fantasia on National Themes*, by Tony Kushner. Part I, *Millennium Approaches*, opened in London, at the Royal National Theatre, in 1992. It opened on Broadway in 1993. Part 2, *Perestroika*, opened on both Broadway and at the Royal National in 1993.
5. *Ghosts*, by Henrik Ibsen, was first produced in 1882.

Spalding Gray
New York, February 9, 1999

23

I don't think theater—live theater—has a vital place in our culture right now. I don't know if it will come back. It feels antiquated.

SPALDING GRAY WAS BEST KNOWN for his many autobiographical monologues, such as *Sex and Death at the Age of 14, India and After, Interviewing the Audience,* and *Monster in a Box.* He also wrote plays such as the trilogy *Three Places in Rhode Island* and was an actor in films such as *The Killing Fields.* He was a cofounder of the New York theater company the Wooster Group. Among his honors are an Obie Award for his monologue *Swimming to Cambodia* and a Stubby Award for Literary Achievement.

Mr. Gray died in January 2004 at the age of sixty-two.

SC: How much of your performance is read? How much is memorized? How much is improvised?

SG: Well, I'm calling the new monologue I'm doing, *Morning, Noon, and Night,*[1] a work in progress, because I'm evolving it with the audience. I do a little explanation speech at the beginning about how I work—to tell the audience that I start from my memory. I'm living my life for a bit, without reflecting on it. I outline it—just a pencil outline of key words—just enough to jog my memory about a situation. After a year or two of just living, without trying to do a monologue, I begin to think through the journal: "What is a particular focus that I could take? What is the highlight of these past few years—what has been the center of that?"

For example, *Swimming to Cambodia*[2] was the making of *The Killing Fields.*[3] *Monster in a Box*[4] was trying to finish this nineteen-hundred-page novel—that was the monster in the box. *Gray's Anatomy*[5] was the loss of my sight in my left eye. *It's a Slippery Slope*[6] was breaking up with my girlfriend, and learning to ski, and having my first child—all very traumatic. Now in this one, *Morning, Noon, and Night,* I wanted to do *one day.* It was a matter of going back and looking at my journals, and outlining a typical day.

So it's a condensation of a lot of memories. It's really like collage art, because I'm cutting and pasting my memory. Everyone that has a memory is creative, because you're recreating the original event through memory. People don't realize that. They have the fantasy that they're in touch with the original event. Then you have something like *Rashomon*,[7] or the O. J. Simpson trial, when you realize the variables.

So I'm using my memory as a structure. Then I'm sitting down in front of an audience with a penciled outline and a tape recorder. When I hear it back, not only does it suggest new memories, but it also suggests editorial ideas, juxtapositions, what works for the audience and what doesn't. It's a dialogue with the audience—or, should I say, like a dancing partner. I don't think of it as *pandering* so much as *dancing with the audience*. 'Cause they're also telling me what they find funny. They could find something funny that I wouldn't even know. They're my reflector. And so, every monologue is worked out with—and for—an audience. It's never without one.

A good example: *New York Times Magazine* wanted to do a cover story on an excerpt from *Gray's Anatomy*. I said, "I don't have it yet," and they said, "When are you gonna have it?" I said, "When I do the first performance in March," and they said, "We need it before March." I actually said, "Well, another time." My agent said, "This is the *New York Times*! It may be a cover story! Make the monologue! Now!" So I had John Howell, who's an editor friend of mine, come down and sit across from me. I had the outline, and I spoke it to him, with a tape recorder. He was my audience of one, but it was an audience. It was me making contact with him and telling the story, as I'm doing with you. If I was trying to talk about my process alone in this room with a tape recorder, there just would be no boundary for me. I wouldn't have a resonance in it.

SC: I know you've said that memories were not literal fact. I didn't realize that the audience participated in the creation of the piece.

SG: I'll give you another example. In *It's a Slippery Slope*, I get into a very serious section where I say that I'm going down to see my son for the first time—born out of wedlock. And I say about how Kathie took him out of the crib to wake him, and he went right for her breast. I say, "And there was no need for a blood test, because I saw the back of my father's head in his head—the shape of it. I saw my brother Rocky's eyes in his eyes." Maybe three performances into it, in Martha's Vineyard, I said, "And he went right for Katie's breast, and I knew there was no need for a blood test." Big laugh! I couldn't even get to "I saw the back of my father's head." I said, "Oh, all right. The audience needs comic relief there—they're going for a low joke: *Oh—he's a tit man.*" It's not me, but I gave them the joke. I'm actually playing a moment in there that is not my true self. The audience is telling me that right there they need a little relief. It's been very heavy up to that point. So now that's—that's a laugh that's built in *through them*. They instructed me, you see.

I don't see it as pandering. Elizabeth LeCompte,[8] for instance, might. I mean, that was one of our breaks in the way that we worked in the Wooster Group. She felt I depended too much on the audience. She wanted to be completely free of the audience.

It's a risky thing to evolve in front of an audience, but I'm good at it now. I've been doing it nineteen years. When I start out, it feels fluid enough to hold them. That's why I don't block. I'm describing a film that I'm seeing—I'm describing my memory. I have an inner scene of that event—I'm seeing it as I tell it. It's a kind of *mind theater*. I think when the audience can tune to it is when they also begin to do their own seeing. I grew up with radio, and that influenced the way that I imagine. Television and film literalize the story. In radio, you have to imagine.

SC: That's another interesting thing about it: the audience has to work. They have to participate enough to stay with you. And I'm proud of American audiences for being able to do that!

SG: Absolutely! I'm still amazed that people have the attention span for an hour and a half. I just came from playing in Scottsdale—to a large audience, older people, very conservative, retired golfers—they were able to sit there and get into that.

Part of it has to do with the fact that I don't move from the table. That creates a steady state. Movement creates time. If you were on one side of the stage at one point, and on another the next, wandering around the room with a microphone, there's a distracting time element there. The audience is saying, "Oh, he was just *there* . . . and now he's *there*." If you're just doing the story, the room becomes a collective memory after a while. It really is *theater of the mind*. It's very subtle, but it's going on in people's heads, if they're imagining it. They have their own associations. They're not only following my story, but they're having their own story.

SC: In terms of the content, you said once that you couldn't express your depression in the monologues. Why can't you do that? Certainly not all of the monologue is light, not all of it is laughter.

SG: In *Slippery Slope*, I may not express it as much as I *talk about* it. That's where the difference between the acting and the story comes in. I am telling a story, and the story will be *about* the depression. I'm past it in order to talk about it. So I will *act*—but I also *tell* about it. I'll say: "I was acting very manic. I was letting out shouts in the street—like *Ow!*"—and I let one out in the performance. It would be illustrative, not an attempt to reenact it. I'm not real interested in impersonation. When I'm in a story, and I'm talking about meeting an Irish doctor, or whatever, I'll sketch at him rather than to try to get a perfect imitation of an Irish accent. It's much more impressionistic. I'm not interested in doing characters, say, the way Lily Tomlin and Eric Bogosian do, or Whoopie Goldberg used to do. The characters are great, but that's not my cup of tea.

SC: At Life,[9] when you were answering questions from the audience, you said that you censor.

SG: Well, yeah—I think there's some natural censorship in everything that we do. But there's also some editorial factor, where I don't want to say too much because it's too long. I mean, to some degree I censor, but not in a real conscious way—just in a normal way. I'm pretty confessional. With *It's a Slippery Slope*, I didn't think I could speak a lot of it, because a lot of it was very personal. I didn't know what belonged onstage and what didn't. So I went into a very good, intensive, therapeutic relationship with a Jungian therapist—not with the idea that we would try to filter what was appropriate for the stage, but that's what happened. In talking with her, in private, I began to understand what could be the story.

SC: Is there anything you think the audience wouldn't accept? Or is it just because you prefer to keep certain things to yourself?

SG: I'm trying to think of something that might create a negative image of me for them, something that, if it wasn't redemptive in some way in the monologue—if I didn't redeem myself in front of their eyes—they would judge me. I was heavily judged for *It's a Slippery Slope*. I got my first hate letters—and I thought that I had grown up! I thought that the work had finally matured! I would always read my fan mail at Lincoln Center[10] before going on, and it would just be pleasurable reading. During *Slippery Slope*, I got ones that were so angry that I almost couldn't go onstage—from women, about the betrayal factor, and sneaking around, and infidelities, and all of that. I thought that was interesting—that some of the audience had a negative reaction. I began to feel that the work was more complex because of that. In Chicago, at the Goodman Theater, there were a number of women that *hissed* me—the first time that's ever happened around a particular statement.

But I'm trying to think if there's some topic that I feel close to that I haven't spoken about, and I don't think so. One of the funny things that people often try to call me up on is that they just found out that I made a porn movie. The *Village Voice* harped on that. I had already talked about making the film in a monologue called *India and After*.[11] I go right into the details of it—it's a very hilarious scene. But that monologue was never published, and very few people saw it at the Performing Garage.[12] So then, all of a sudden, the muckraking press—the *New York Observer* or the *Village Voice*—thinks they have something on me. Michael Musto[13] printed: "Oh, you think Spalding Gray is Mr. *Swimming to Cambodia*. Well, you should see his X-rated film!" But I always beat the press to it. I had already talked about this, but because it's not in the public lexicon, they thought they'd jumped on me for that one.

SC: You mentioned Lincoln Center. Does the audience there have a different experience than the audience at the Performing Garage fifteen years ago, when it was a downtown, *avant-garde* thing?

SG: Well, you know—those are hard things to talk about, because how do you measure? From what point of view do you measure?

The difference is in the extraordinary intimacy that was in the original pieces, when a small audience was just being spoken to by me. It was just a very simple act of telling a story. But once you're at Lincoln Center, in your eleven-hundred-seat house, on that big stage, you have to project so much that it becomes almost like ancient Greek theater. It becomes very histrionic. Even though you're using a microphone, the gestures have to get out to the balcony. I like both.

In Scottsdale, I played a small hundred-and-twenty-seat house to test out the new monologue, and then I played *Slippery Slope* to eight hundred and fifty people. It's quite different in the tone of voice, and the energy projection. I think that's the big difference.

Also, the setting of Lincoln Center is so much more formal. What I like is that I've been able to maintain my relaxed, seedy, downtown spirit, and then place it at Lincoln Center. It's an interesting juxtaposition, because it's a very unusual and idiosyncratic stone that is set in a much more traditional setting.

SC: In terms of the variety of tone in your monologues, between the personal parts and the laughter, is there a constant structure?

SG: Well, it's an organic structure that I discover after playing it thirty or forty times. To some extant I'm a Freudian, and I think that if you, say, have a dream, and you write it down, you will see in that writing an architecture of references, symbols . . . resonances. If you tell a story enough times, a similar thing happens. I begin, through telling the monologue, to see repetition, patterns—and then I start to create the patterns.

In the new monologue, *Morning, Noon, and Night*, there's a conversation I had with my son about good and bad words—that there's no such thing as a good or bad word unless it's put in context, and then it begins to have a good or bad meaning. That little lecture that I give him plays out through the monologue, later on at dinner, and then it comes round again a little later on. And so, what's being talked about begins to have its own resonance, and takes its own form, organically.

The human consciousness has a structure. What I'm looking for is the random structure that comes through remembering over and over the same events—you know, repeating the story. It takes what I call "heightened composition." I'm talking to you now not in a heightened way. I'm looking for words. The first monologue I'd do would be like that. But the second time, I would be repeating myself more, and doing it with more dramatic elan. I would be *dramatizing* it. The fourth, fifth, twentieth time, it would be like a show.

People think: "Oh, he's just talking." I'm not. I'm really doing a heightened, rather precise conversation. I know what's coming next—my mind and body are almost programmed. In the opening of *It's a Slippery Slope*, when I was first doing it. I just would have one note: say "the first mountain." Then I'd describe the first mountain I ever remember seeing: "I saw it when I was looking out the window of my geometry class, in Maine. I was going to Fryeburg Academy at the time. I think it was around 1958. And it really wasn't a very big mountain . . ." So that's how I'd be doing it—the first time. After a hundred times, it now opens like this: "The first mountain I ever remember seeing, I saw framed in the pane of my window in geometry class, Fryeburg Academy, 1958. I couldn't stop staring out this window. It was the first relief I've ever experienced in my life. And I was in need of relief. I came from Rhode Island, the flatlands, where I was failing everything in Barrington High School." There is not any foundering there. There is no searching for the right image or the right word.

SC: And it's never been written.

SG: No, it simply is the respeaking it. The respeaking it finds its rhythm. I am an oral writer. It's as simple as that.

SC: And how far does it get from the original fact?

SG: Well, you know . . . how would you ever research that? You have no witness to the original fact. You have witness to the original memory on the tape. And the tapes vary. In the first fifteen performances, say, there really is a lot of switching around, and rejuxtaposing. And then at some point I bring in a creative consultant, Paul Spencer, and I have him listen to it and give me feedback on what he thinks could be cut, what would go better, what would be more dramatic.

SC: You and the other—quote—"performance artists" have done so much to revitalize—

SG: But I don't think of myself as a performance artist. I think of myself as an actor, because I'm a trained actor, with all of those acting techniques that I learned at Emerson College. I apply them to myself and play myself. Performance artists are not trained in acting and they don't know how to repeat well. It's difficult for them. They'll do something a couple of times, if it's a conceptual thing, and then that will be it—they'll be on to the next performance piece. I can do two hundred very alive and vital performances of a monologue, and do it just as well each time, because I'm trained to *reenact*, and have the emotional memory and those techniques. I think all actors, for whatever reason, like the ritual of repeating, and not all performance artists do. And they don't have the chance to do long runs, whereas I do.

SC: In light of the fact that there are film and television, can theater regain the importance that it had for, say, Ibsen's audience, Shaw's audience, in terms of spreading ideas?

SG: No, I don't think that's possible. There's an interesting book that was reviewed in the *New York Times* this Sunday, called *Readings*.[14] He talks about a "Farewell to Henry James" because everything is so speedy now and so *on the surface*. We're scanning a net; we're not falling into any pockets in that scan. He thinks of consciousness now as being like water striders. There's a different consciousness there, and I see it in my young fans that will watch me on a video, where they can control it, in their living room, and get stoned or whatever. They understand the video, and they find out I'm in town, and there are lots that won't come to a live show. They like it better on the video. They just don't trust the live theater experience because they have to make all the close-ups and the decisions.

The construction of a Shaw play now would feel like a museum piece, a historic piece. It would be very difficult to make it immediate because people don't relate as much to the artificiality of acting. They've gotten so used to films. When they walk into a room and see the fourth wall missing, and hear people shouting at each other, it strikes most people, me included, as being false.

That's why my farewell to theater was playing the stage manager in *Our Town*.[15] Gregory Mosher wanted me to do one of the characters in the play, and I said, "No. If you—if you want me for the stage manager, I'll do it, but I don't think I could get inside the character and pretend that I was that character. I do think I could play the stage manager; I could be that go-between, doing commentary. *That* I can do, because of my monologues." Once I started relating out to the audience, it's hard to go back. It's hard to shut them out, and not do asides, and say, "We all know this isn't a room. We all know we've memorized these words."

I don't think theater—live theater—has a vital place in our culture right now. I don't know if it will come back. It feels antiquated.

Notes

1. *Morning, Noon, and Night*, by Spalding Gray, opened on Broadway in 1999 with Mr. Gray.

2. *Swimming to Cambodia*, by Spalding Gray, was first produced in 1985 with Mr. Gray.

3. *The Killing Fields*, a film directed by Roland Joffe, 1984, with Mr. Gray.

4. *Monster in a Box*, by Spalding Gray, opened on Broadway in 1991 with Mr. Gray.

5. *Gray's Anatomy*, by Spalding Gray, opened on Broadway in 1993 with Mr. Gray.

6. *It's a Slippery Slope*, by Spalding Gray, opened on Broadway in 1996 with Mr. Gray.

7. *Rashomon*, a film directed by Akira Kurosawa, 1950.

8. Elizabeth LeCompte cofounded the New York theater company the Wooster Group, along with Mr. Gray and others.

9. Life: a Manhattan nightclub.

10. Lincoln Center: a performing arts center in New York.

11. *India and After (America)*, by Spalding Gray, was first produced in 1979.

12. The Performing Garage: the Wooster Group's theater in New York.

13. Michael Musto: columnist for the *Village Voice*.

14. Sven Birkerts, *Readings* (St. Paul, Minn.: Graywolf Press, 1999); reviewed by Brooke Allen, "You Can Kiss Henry James Goodbye," *New York Times*, February 7, 1999.

15. *Our Town*, by Thornton Wilder, was first produced on Broadway in 1938. Mr. Gray is referring to the 1988 Broadway production.

Andrei Serban
New York, April 26, 2000

At heart I'm very much a classical director.

ANDREI SERBAN IS DIRECTOR of the Oscar Hammerstein II Center for Theater Studies at Columbia University. The former director of the Romanian National Theatre, he's been associated with La MaMa E.T.C., the American Repertory Theatre, the Yale Repertory Theatre, the Guthrie Theatre and many other companies. His international work as a director of theater and opera has won many awards, including an Obie Award and the Elliot Norton Award for Sustained Excellence.

SC: You're known for being very eclectic in your work. How do you keep unity in a production if you're taking elements from different idioms?

AS: Theater should be, as Shakespeare says, the mirror of life—and life as we know it never has unity. It's always in conflict—from one moment to another, there's a paradox. Nothing follows in a predictable line—everything is in contradiction. So if the main law of life is contradiction, then I don't think there's anything wrong in trying to mirror that in the theater.

Now, still, in the theater one has to give a structure and a shape to the performance. So unity comes from that, the fact that, still, things have to match—that as contradictory as they are, they have to make sense in their link, in their development.

So the responsibility is that although things seem to go against each other, all in all they should do that for a very clear aim—and the aim is to create in the audience a kind of a fresh impression, a surprising shock as to the experience of that play. If one does *Hamlet*, everybody, when he buys his ticket, also buys the right to be the director of the play. There is an expectation that *Hamlet* should be done according to how "I" see it—every single one of us. Every single one of us has opinions about what *Hamlet* represents, means, and how it should be done. It's very hard to go see *Hamlet* with an innocent eye, to allow yourself to be taken by surprise by what you see, because you know it too well. You know very well that in the play within the play, Claudius has to stay there watching the play with growing impatience, that his eyebrows should be more and more active toward the end, and then he should say "Lights! Lights!" and leave. That's how I made some people very happy and some people very upset—by trying to stage the play within the play so that even the people who knew *Hamlet* well would be surprised by what the hell is going on!

I think that's right! And I don't think that I betrayed Shakespeare by doing that. I just changed the conditions—and by changing the conditions, I obliged the audience to look at that moment in a way that is fresh and unexpected.

So, now, how the unity of it all comes in is that, hopefully, at the very end of the evening, one will have gone through the experience of *Hamlet* in a way that is unexpected, that is new—that makes one hear the words for the first time. And still there is that sense of unity—it aims to do something which is intentional, not just a capricious adding up of things that don't make any sense. Unity means the effort to bring sense to the event.

SC: I'm interested in the way theater like your production of *Hamlet* will reach people who don't go to the theater often. If I've only seen a Neil Simon play, maybe an Ibsen, do I have the wherewithal to appreciate what you're doing in that production?

AS: Well, in rehearsals, we invited a group of children from high school. And when I asked them at the end, "Have you ever seen a Shakespeare play before?" half of them had never seen a Shakespeare play. Some of them have never gone to the theater, and there were many who had never seen or read *Hamlet*. So they were, from that point of view, a totally innocent audience. It could have been the nightmare of a matinee performance, when you have children in the audience who come with this very boisterous energy. We were thinking: "How are we going to keep this wild gathering for a three-and-a-half-hour evening, with extremely complex and subtle metaphysical language that is far beyond their experience? How are we going to keep their attention?" And to our total, delightful surprise, from the moment the play started, until the last image, you could cut the silence with a knife! It was so extraordinary! And then, during the discussion with them afterwards, they said they were completely captivated by everything, and they were totally intrigued and nourished by this.

A play like this—it's a very different kind of nourishment than they get with disco or rock. For me, that was the most valuable response to our work—much more so than an academic audience coming and saying, "Well, you know, that was an interesting evening . . . I liked it . . ." This young audience could really take the play as an experience of now, right there, and in spite of the sophistication, be totally, totally touched. Now, why it is that they were touched is very hard to say—but they were.

SC: These kids grow up watching television and movies. In light of the fact that there are television and film, can theater ever become as important again as it was for Ibsen's audience, for Shaw's audience, Shakespeare's?

AS: Well, it's very difficult to say because it's very hard to predict what will happen in the theater in the twenty-first century. There are voices that wonder if theater will last into the next century or not. When I was younger, before there was so much invasion of other media into the theater, video screens, laser beams, computerized sound and image—there's so much technicality now in the theater! The human element, human exchange between two actors and an audience is interfered with. One wonders what will happen in the theater, because the human factor becomes less and less important.

I don't think that theater can die. It's been there for three thousand years. How can it die in the next hundred years? But I'm not a prophet—I don't know. My responsibility is to just keep working with these very, very old tools. It's like a very old craft. I feel like I'm in the business of repairing roofs in old castles—it's a specialty that is going out of business. Still, there is a need to create in the imagination voyages toward the miraculous, towards the impossible, towards worlds that are invisible and deeply spiritual. Those are the potentials that theater has in its pure form, uncompromised.

So that's how I feel. I'm behind time. I'm not interested in how to use computers. I'm not interested in how to use multimedia. I'm still a believer in the classical form, in the classical tradition. In order to continue it, one has to challenge it, one has to question it—but one should not dismiss it.

At heart I'm very much a classical director. But being a classical director means not respectfully continuing what was done yesterday and doing the same thing, but challenging and questioning in order to keep the tradition fresh.

SC: I was stunned when I saw *Fragments of a Greek Trilogy*.[1] As I understand it, you had a very long rehearsal period, and you no longer do that. Is that right?

AS: It's true that a time limit is a crucial frustration, if one doesn't have two or three years and a group of actors to work together as a team, if they are just in the system of Equity actors, and of the star system. There are some actors who are especially important—you cannot make them improvise endlessly. They get nervous staying in that frame of research, not knowing, not having a solution. The seeking is what makes discovery possible.

Sometimes actors who have an established career look at their watch and say, "This will be faster. I have another appointment." The climate is very hard to find in which all the whole event is the question of "What is theater?" or "What are we trying to explore?" With the Greek plays, we were all younger. Nobody was a star. Everybody was a student, in a way, and had enthusiasm. *Hamlet* was what I could do within the range of a professional situation—[*laughing*] Equity,[2] you know!

SC: I see. So it's a matter of the logistics—it's not a matter of your choice. Did *Fragments of a Greek Trilogy* have the same effect on its audience as the original production did? Do you transmute the play in order to have the same effect on the audience as it did for the ancients?

AS: Well, it's very hard to imagine what it was for the ancients. We don't know because all records are lost. We can reconstruct it in our imagination if we go to Delphi or to any of the Greek ancient theaters. We can imagine this cosmic theater—this theater that really had a multilevel relation that the actor transmitted to the audience at a distance, in open air, without microphones—a message that was received by the stars, by the wind, by the movement of the day, always in connection with the fact that we are not alone. We are part of a cosmos. There are gods up there, and inside the earth there are forces which are mysterious. The energies of the earth and the energies of the above were taken into account. That multilevel aspect of theater as part of something much larger than us is totally lost. We are in a small theater—even a Broadway house is a small place, and it's closed up. Theater can reach a vertical connection, rather than only a horizontal connection—it is something other than just entertainment. We can't connect to that. We have to reinvent it each time in order to make it alive for us today, and to retain some of what it meant two thousand years ago—but that's all we can do.

SC: In *The Magic Behind the Curtain*,[3] Ed Menta quotes you as saying that you don't know the play well before opening night, and that there are levels of meaning that you don't appreciate until you see the play. Can you say more about that?

AS: There are people who think that in every Shakespearean line there are seven levels of meaning. Well, we are lucky sometimes if we even discover one level! So I ask the actors to paraphrase. And than I say, "Okay, if that's what it could mean, what else could it mean?" There is the immediate understanding, and then there is the deeper understanding—the more subtle understanding.

Shakespeare invented new words, in order to catch new meanings to the human aspects of life. Now, in that theater, the people upstairs, the *literati*, could appreciate this new vocabulary. The people downstairs, the rough audience, were totally at a loss with that, because the words are just too hermetic, too elliptic for them. What is so wonderful in Shakespeare is that there are two adjectives, one which is more sophisticated, one which is more simple. The one that's more simple was addressed to the ones downstairs. Just like with the Greeks, you can see different images reaching different levels. The communication was with the people—and with the gods, too. How can a director come to the first rehearsal and say, "I understand it all?"

SC: Yes, yes. Do you adjust the elements of the production according to the audience's reaction?

AS: Very much—that's what the previews are there for. I really change drastically from one preview to another, because I can feel when the audience gets lost. When the audience loses connection with what's going on onstage—that is totally our fault. It's never the audience's fault—it's our fault. Somehow we have not found a way to express a certain aspect of the play.

SC: Ed Menta wrote that you tell your actors exactly what you want them to do. Can you comment on that?

AS: It's not true! I don't tell them exactly what I want them to do because I often don't know myself. The best actors I work with are the ones who completely trust my—my being in a continuous state of doubt. There are actors who would like to be told "Do this—do that." And there are actors who like to discover together with the director what is the best way to approach something. I like those much more. That's why coming opening night, seeing the play for the first time with audience there brings a clarity that I didn't have before. Then I feel: "Oh, my God, if I can just work from beginning again!" Of course—it's too late!

SC: Finally, how do you see that your work has changed, has developed, since, say, the Romanian Theater? How does it look to you?

AS: When I was young, I used to work much more quickly, happy with a certain result or another. I thought that my role in the theater is to create new and beautiful images. The more I work, the more I'm interested in the inner life of the actors, and less in broad strokes of images. So, in a way, the theater I'm doing now seems less spectacular, less exciting than it used to be. I hope that eventually the inner concern of the actor—the person trying to meet a situation through theater—will reach the audience, and that the exchange will be more subtle, less showy—not shocking through images only.

Notes

1. *Fragments of a Greek Trilogy* comprises three plays: *Medea*, *The Trojan Women*, and *Elektra*. It was written and composed by Elizabeth Swados and directed by Mr. Serban. *Medea* was first produced in 1972, by La MaMa E.T.C. I'm speaking of the 1999 La MaMa production, also directed by Mr. Serban.

2. Actors' Equity Association.

3. Ed Menta, *The Magic World Behind the Curtain: Andrei Serban and the American Theatre* (New York: Peter Lang, 1995).

Richard Foreman
New York, March 10, 1999

I'm trying to build myself a little fortification of theory so that I can defend myself to other people who think I'm crazy.

RICHARD FOREMAN FOUNDED the Ontological Hysteric Theater in 1968 and has since then written, directed, and designed fifty highly idiosyncratic productions. He's received several Obie Awards, the Literature Award from the American Academy and Institute of Arts and Letters, a National Endowment for the Arts Award for Lifetime Achievement, and a MacArthur "Genius" Fellowship. Five collections of his plays have been published. He's also directed classical productions internationally.

SC: Let's say that I'm the Lady from Dubuque. I've seen Neil Simon and Ibsen—and I'm expecting Neil Simon and Ibsen when I go to the theater, but I end up at one of your productions at St. Mark's Church. Do I have the wherewithal to appreciate your work? Is it accessible to me?

RF: It's a very difficult question to answer, because . . . would James Joyce be accessible to this lady? I suppose that, the truth be said, it might not be accessible. Now, I think that the reason it might not be accessible is not the fault of the lady. I think it's the fault of the conditioning that the lady has been subjected to through her life, that things that don't make sense in the normal, narrative way that she is expecting the theater to make sense are therefore not understandable.

There probably aren't too many ladies who read Wallace Stevens in Dubuque, but those that did would have no problem with my theater, because there's nothing exceptional about my theater. It simply exploits the strategies of most so-called advanced twentieth-century art, most twentieth-century poetry, and to me that's not experimental or far-out, that's just the normal, logical way to do things in the twentieth century. But people have been scared off, when they were young, to accept that—as Keats said in talking about *negative capability*—one can live amidst doubts and ambiguities, and one must not be too quick to try to resolve all those doubts and ambiguities.

I've often thought, indeed, that's the problem in America. The reason for reactionary forces, non-progressive forces, in America is that people are so afraid of being in a situation where they don't know exactly what's black, what's white—where you go if you take the route that goes to the left as opposed to where you go if you take the route that goes to the right. How interesting it is, when you're on a trip, to sometimes get lost and discover all kinds of fantastic things. Someone who is open to those possibilities and reacts with their gut, rather than with their inherited, disciplined way of understanding things, could have a wonderful time.

SC: I experience your work differently now than I did when I first saw it, in the early '80s. I don't know if I've learned how to appreciate your work, or if it's become more accessible.

RF: I think it's become more accessible in a certain way. Younger people have been trained to perceive tiny little stories in a different way through something like MTV. Now obviously, most of the videos on MTV aren't so great, but nevertheless, it has loosened up their heads so that things can have associative connections, and associative connections can make just as much sense as narrative links can.

SC: I'm very interested in what you've said about moral art and immoral art. You mention immoral art in your Second Manifesto,[1] and in *The Director's Voice*[2] you said to Arthur Bartow: "Stylistic position is a moral position." Can you say more about that? I understand how style reflects levels of consciousness—and even politics—but how can I identify the morality in a style?

RF: Well, it's related to what I just said—that a style such as mine depends upon people having an openness to possibility in the world. Obviously, if you are the kind of person who insists on rigid moral categories, you're going to be insisting on rigid ways to follow a narrative. If you have a style that is a more associative style, that expects the seven types of ambiguity—and the many more types of ambiguity—then the implication is that morality is an open, more fluid kind of thing.

I am not the kind of person who thinks in the ethical and moral sphere *anything goes*. Some people, seeing my work, think: "Oh, wow—he must be some wild character"—and I'm not! I'm a very conventional, bourgeoisie, almost Puritanical character, who realizes in my work that a kind of *therapy* for normal, middle-class people such as myself is required— a therapy that allows one's mind to range freely over all its possibilities. That is a kind of therapeutic exercise. The repressed personality, the person that is not able to entertain all kinds of strange notions, is a more dangerous personality—both to the society, to the people surrounding him, and his family, his loved ones, and to himself, in the end.

SC: So then, while there's nothing overtly political or sociological in your texts, there is a social position, in a way.

RF: Well, I think there is by implication, definitely. My concerns have always been, as I've said before, closet religious concerns—they're a little less these days, in the last couple of years. I don't know why that is, exactly. I used to read very deeply and extensively in all kinds of religious and spiritual literature, and I don't feel that quite speaks to me in the same way anymore—which is a little perplexing to me, a little surprising, but it's a fact.

SC: Has your artistic vision changed much since you wrote the three manifestos?[3]

RF: The general orientation of my character hasn't changed much. I have been circling around slightly different themes and approaches to things in succeeding years, but it's still the same person, and the same basic inclinations.

SC: When you spoke with Mr. Bartow, you also had said that the reason you were producing plays other than your own is to see if your "rhythmic articulation" is applicable to all work.

RF: Yeah. I don't so much do plays other than my own. I don't know if I will in the future. I stopped because my wife was very sick for a while, and I couldn't go to other theaters in Europe and other parts of America where I normally got the opportunity to do those plays. And Joe Papp[4] died in New York—he gave me those opportunities.

But, again—I'm getting older. I don't know how many more years I have left, and I've always felt that my life's task was to do my own plays. The other stuff that I did was to teach me, to stretch me, to force me to touch other worlds, and I don't feel that tremendous need anymore—although if the occasion arises, I probably would do it. But I've never actively sought that other work. It sort of fell into my lap all the time.

SC: You said early on that you were primarily a writer.

RF: Yes. That's still true even though I'm finding it more difficult to write these days. My sensibility—even as a director—is as a writer. I don't really know how to direct plays. What I do know how to do is to keep seeing what's wrong, and just keep changing it and changing it and changing it, until it seems *right*, in my terms. Ernest Hemingway said, in one of the *Paris Review* interviews, that the most important tool for a writer is a built-in shit-detector. Well, I think I have a very good shit-detector.

When I start directing my plays, you would not believe the little resemblance they bear to the play in its finished state. Now, it's interesting: that is not true when I'm directing other people's plays. Perhaps that's because my scripts have a kind of open structure that could go in so many ways. You could pick up on this set of associations and make the scene go this way, or another set of associations and make it go another way. So I sort of flounder around with my own plays until I find what I think is the right central road for me to take with them. But in other plays, I think I'm much more conventional in my approach.

SC: You've also written other scripts . . . librettos. How does your aesthetic position inform that work?

RF: That's very different. I haven't written a libretto in quite a while—and I doubt that I will be writing any more. But for those, I would just think about it—think about it one day, sit down, and then, in two weeks or something, I'd finish. I'd write through from beginning to end. I was thinking *writing to music*, and that enabled me to flow forward in a way that I don't do in my own writing for the theater.

SC: At Brown and Yale, you must have had classical education. How do you unlearn that? How do we unlearn, say, Alexander Dean's *Fundamentals of Play Directing*[5]—or how much of that have you retained and used?

RF: Well, of course, I didn't study directing. I was a literature major, and then I studied playwriting at Yale.

I have two things to say about that. I was a very bright student. I graduated *magna cum laude* and so forth, but I always felt something was wrong—through high school, through college. After I got out of school, I started being introduced, through my association with the downtown underground filmmakers, to contemporary poetry—people like Gertrude

Stein and Charles Olsen. Only at that point did I begin to understand that I felt that every-thing I had been taught was a lie—in the sense that everything I had been taught suppressed a more creative, spiritual tendency that was also present, running through the stream of Western culture—perhaps the underground stream, but the stream that nourished all of the things that are most interesting that have flowered in Western culture. I knew that in-tuitively when I was at Brown, so that, while it was very easy for me, and I was able to snow people with my intelligence and get through things very fast, I was not trapped, I think, by the schooling I was given. I knew something was missing.

I must say, along with that, that since I was a very little boy, I was always interested in the most far-out things I could find in the arts. I remember being in junior high school and drawing a Salvador Dali–type painting. My art teacher—I was a good student, and my art teacher was my friend—sort of mumbled and said, "Well, Richard, you've got to be care-ful, you know. You may be interested in those paintings, but the guys who made those paint-ings were very disturbed people. You don't want to get too deeply into that."

Then, when I went to Yale, I studied playwriting with John Gassner, who had been the literary manager of the Theatre Guild for many years. And John Gassner was amazing. He was very, very rigorous in taking your play apart line by line and analyzing it—and that rigor was a beacon for me. Now, I was interested, generally, in things that were a little fur-ther out than John Gassner, though he was very catholic in his tastes—but still, I think that his example was very important to me, and the understanding that every inch of a work of art had to be mulled over and analyzed.

In the days that I was at Yale, of course, I thought that playwriting was about rewriting and rewriting and rewriting. Then, under the influence of Gertrude Stein and the post–American beat movement—and I certainly was never a beat-type person—I got this idea that what came down on the page was evidence of where you were, where your head was, and it was wrong to lie about that evidence, so you shouldn't rewrite. You should accept what came. I did that for a number of years. These days, I rewrite and rewrite and rewrite. My plays go through many versions, and we change them in rehearsal. But the interesting thing is that, in the end, I think it ends up still being it's own weird, unique, idiosyncratic self.

SC: Right. *Angel Face*[6] is not fundamentally different from *Paradise Hotel*.[7]

RF: Right.

SC: Are your plays directed by other directors often?

RF: Up until a couple of years ago, I had seen five or six productions, all of which I hated—all of which were very embarrassing to me—because they tried to copy me too much. A couple of years ago, this little experimental theater club in New York, Nada, just down here on Ludlow Street, started in the summer doing a Foreman Festival.

So, for two summers now, they've done ten or eleven plays, and there's gonna be another one this year. By the end of this year, they'll have done pretty much all of my plays, in-cluding some I've never done. What I said to them—and what I say in my books—was that directors should take my scripts, they should erase any stage directions, they should erase any indication of who's talking, and they should take them as pure language. Redivide the lines, invent new scenarios. And the people downtown did that. So even though they were a lot of young, inexperienced directors, it was very interesting to me.

Then, last year, in France, for the first time, I saw a major director[8] in France do the play that I was actually doing, *Pearls for Pigs*.[9] About three months after I mounted *Pearls for Pigs*, I went to France and saw the French version, which he directed in a style totally different from the way I direct.[10]

SC: Without the lights, without the thuds . . .

RF: Yes. Very different. Very gentle, very soft, sort of naturalistic relations between the actors. It was very interesting to me—and I think it worked.

SC: Reading about your work—what you've written, what other people have written—has clarified the scripts a lot. But I find less written about the lights and the thuds, the directorial effects. Can you say something about that? Are they for clarification?

RF: You know, I talk a lot, and theorize a lot, and it's always a moot point how much that's just a show with which I'm trying to protect myself. I'm trying to build myself a little fortification of theory so that I can defend myself to other people who think I'm crazy. I had to start doing that many years ago with my parents, who thought: "Well, Richard, we're happy you're getting your picture in the *New York Times*, but why can't you write a play like Neil Simon?" So I would have these internal dialogues with myself, trying to justify what I was doing.

SC: But it's very helpful to us. We need it.

RF: I think that they are things that are framing what's going on in my plays—to provide a certain kind of clarity. I'm starting to work on a play now for next year, and I'm starting to listen to different kinds of music that I might want to use. And when I start the music, and I realize, "Well it just seems funny that the music starts. I need a thud, or a bell, to indicate *Now—music is starting. You're going to be listening a little differently now, because you're going to hear dialogue against music.*" All of those various things are to highlight that the theatrical experience is a collaboration between the object that is passing before you, and the perceptual mechanism you're using to process that object. These various markings are reminders saying, "Wait a minute. Now something's changing," or "Wait a minute. That word that follows that *ping* might be important."

SC: Kate Davy wrote[11] that you believe in *experience*—as opposed to understanding the production. And you yourself talk about the reason for artists to understand.

RF: I live inside the world of my plays, and I've been doing them for thirty years, so I don't think they're hard to understand. I think they're rather simpleminded. I always deal with basic archetypes, basic dramatic situations. To understand the world is to understand that there is a repertoire of types and situations, confrontations that continually recycle, continually interpenetrate themselves in different ways, and life itself juggles with a limited number of basic *givens*. My theater reflects that. Deep understanding is to understand that game—the repetition of these *givens*. They mix together in different ways, so that sometimes it muddies the water. But *accepting* the fact that the water is always muddied is another level of understanding that art should make available and comfortable for us. Because indeed, life never goes as we want it. Life is always surprising us, upsetting our apple cart. We say, "Wait a minute. I want to clear my head. I want things to get clear," but it never does get clear. Progressive, good art helps to acclimate people to such a world, instead of pretending that the world is really understandable—like a post–Paddy Chayefsky TV-movie that says at the end, "Well, you see, if we just get the social worker in, then everything's going to be okay."

SC: It helped me to understand conventional drama, Ibsen and the others, when you criticized them for making too much order, and making the spectator smug.

RF: Yes, I want to make people, myself included, happy and lucid and exhilarated amidst this mess that life always is—and not deny the mess. That's why I say I'm a very middle-class person. I am very ordered. I hate messes. Art is a place to experience what you're scared to experience in life—often for quite reasonable reasons.

SC: Are you still present at all your performances?

RF: I am—only of necessity. For instance, for the play this year, I've been working part of the sound. We have a system where there are sound operators, and all of the music they're turning on comes through my little mixer, and I can make them get louder and softer as I want. I'm the only one that can really do that the way I want to do it. *Pearls for Pigs* toured around the country—I couldn't be with it all the time.

SC: But you no longer think it's vital, a part of the whole process, like you used to.

RF: No. I would always want to be there as much as possible, because performances drift, and I like to keep control of them. Keeping control of my own plays, which is my own blood and guts, is important to me.

SC: Finally, in light of the fact that there are film and television, can theater ever regain the importance that it had for Shaw's audience, and for Ibsen's audience, as a disseminator of ideas?

RF: Probably not. For my whole life, I've never been in that position, to have that kind of influence. I'm always frustrated that I'm not getting a wide enough audience, a big enough audience. We're sold out every night for our runs, but still, there are a lot of my compatriots that I'd like to have a dialogue with on some level. A few come, but a lot don't. So I have had to discipline myself to realize that I am more marginal than I dreamed of being, when I was a young man.

So whether the theater has the kind of influence you're talking about actually doesn't interest me. That would be the kind of influence that, in the glory days, Arthur Miller or Tennessee Williams would dream of having. I will never have that. If the theater closes down, to be a kind of thing that is equivalent to what contemporary poetry is, for instance, that would actually suit my purposes.

Now, I do have to believe that things that really contribute to the society often do it in hidden, tiny, little ways. One little grain of pollen dropping here may have a profound effect. I remember reading, years ago, that Marcel Duchamp went to see, in Paris, some plays of this rather crazy man, Raymond Roussel. He was a very rich man, and he put on his own plays at a very big theater in Paris. Everybody just laughed at them and thought they were crazy, but the surrealists sort of liked them. Duchamp talks about going to see one of Roussel's plays, and how it was about the most important experience in his life and changed his thinking about many things. And then Duchamp, of course, turns out now to be so important, and inspired waves of movement in American art. That gave me courage. I thought: "Well, maybe my little seed will pollinate a few people here, and here, and here . . ."

Notes

1. Richard Foreman, "Ontological-Hysteric Manifesto 1" (1972), in Foreman, *Plays and Manifestos* (New York: New York University Press, 1976).

2. Arthur Bartow, *The Director's Voice: Twenty-one Interviews* (New York: Theatre Communications Group, 1988).

3. Richard Foreman, "Ontological-Hysteric Manifesto 1" (1972), "Ontological-Hysteric Manifesto 2" (1974), and "Ontological-Hysteric Manifesto 3" (1975), in Foreman, *Plays and Manifestos* (New York: New York University Press, 1976).

4. Joseph Papp (1933–1989), founder of the New York Shakespeare Festival and its artistic director from 1954.

5. Alexander Dean, *Fundamentals of Play Directing* (New York: Farrar and Rinehart, 1941).

6. *Angel Face*, by Richard Foreman, was first produced in 1968.

7. *Paradise Hotel*, by Richard Foreman, was first produced in 1998.

8. Bernard Sobel.

9. *Pearls for Pigs*, by Richard Foreman, was first produced in 1997.

10. Mr. Foreman is speaking of the production at the Theatre de Gennvilliers, April 1997.

11. Kate Davy, *Richard Foreman and the Ontological-Hysteric Theatre* (Ann Arbor, Mich.: UMI Research Press, 1981).

Eddie Izzard
April 14, 1998

26

The backup of comedy is to be funny. The bottom line of acting is to be truthful.

EDDIE IZZARD BEGAN his career as a street performer and then became known internationally as a stand-up comedian. He's won two British Comedy Awards for best stand-up, and Emmy Awards as both performer and writer for his comedy *Eddie Izzard: Dress to Kill*. His work as an actor has included playing Lenny Bruce in *Lenny*, directed by Sir Peter Hall, and other West End productions. His solo shows tour extensively.

SC: I saw your act last night!

EI: I hope the audience enjoyed it, 'cause I loved it.

SC: They even understood the French!

EI: Yeah, I know. I just assume everyone speaks French. I quite like assuming vast intelligence from the audience, and playing to the highest common denominator. But also, it's trashy. I'm gonna say "Queen Victoria" and reference *Star Wars*[1] and "Jabba the Hutt."[2] You've got to be watching trash and reading some other stuff—or reading the stuff and knowing a bit about trash. So it's pop culture stand-up.

SC: Has it changed a lot from when you were, say, at the Edinburgh Festival[3]—I think it was '81?

EI: Yeah, I think it has. I've got confidence, I suppose, of being able to link things together in an unusual way. I know roughly where I'm trying to go to.

I'm quite a mainstream head, so I need to drive towards more alternative things. People look at me and think I'm probably very alternative, but in fact, I do watch *Die Hard*[4]—I do go and see big mainstream movies, and I have to push myself to see more subtitled *The Boy with the Fly* type movie. I'm quite intimidated by literature—that's the other thing.

SC: But subject matter aside, the way you jump from one subject to another takes a certain intellectual sharpness from the audience. They really have to be paying attention—they have to be working.

EI: Absolutely. It requires work. Some people buy into it and think: "Hey—oh, I got that one—but I didn't get that one—what was that one?" They either buy into it, or they pull out and say, "No, this is a load of bollocks. What the hell is this guy talking about?"

SC: How do you prepare to get into that very fast, very mentally alert state for two hours?

EI: I do nothing. I really do nothing. I really like being in that state. I've discovered this thing which is sort of linked to newscasters. They could actually say, "The president today set fire to his legs while talking to President Anwar Sadat, who is actually dead, in a small room made out of plywood." There's a certain tonal thing they have in there. If you're not wholly paying attention, you could just think the news is going on. If you just keep going on, people will follow you as long as you've committed to it in this big way, like "My God this is a fascinating story." But you can't do it endlessly; it's got to all sort of flow somewhere—or stop—or jump about.

I'm partially dyslexic. My thinking is very dyslexic. I think a lot of creative people are dyslexic, which gives the sideways thinking—instead of this straight, linear, up-and-down thinking.

That's where the jumping happens. That's where you put Queen Victoria and Jabba the Hutt, and you just say, "Logically, they're very similar, aren't they? They both sat on that big seat . . . walked about a bit." The way I work is very dyslexic. It was a mild dyslexia. Dyslexia can be really hellish for kids—they can be really teased at school, and whatever. But I could do things okay—I was good on numbers.

Literature—it really worked against me. I was looking for an empirical meaning in literature as well, as opposed to personal choice—"What does it mean to you? What do you think of this?" I read very few books. And that's why I don't see many plays.

SC: But you've acted in a number.

EI: Yeah. I prefer acting in them to watching them. Film is this much more open door thing which I link up more with. I'm a film nut. I used to break into film studios. But I like acting in plays.

SC: Isn't it very different from doing stand-up?

EI: I wouldn't say *totally* . . . I've worked three comedy mediums. The first one was sketch comedy—Monte Python[5] influenced. I wanted to go on television and do a sketch show. Live sketch shows are dead in the U.K.—just does not work.

Then I got into street performing and I had to learn that from the ground up.

SC: I'd like to hear about that. Is it really different? Does the venue make a difference? Is the street different from the stage?

EI: So different! Certain things you have to learn which are nothing to do, really, with performing—corralling an audience together. You actually more are linked to the street traders I've read or seen documentaries about on television—the way they talk about *spinning an edge*, and getting a group of people together to watch, and say, "This, now, Madame, this is fantastic! Not six pounds, not five pounds, four pounds, but three pounds!" They work the audience. You have to corral a group of people into a semicircle like this. We learnt over a period of years quite precise details. If you don't actually get a semicircle going of an audience, then your show will never happen. You need to get very close to them and just talk to them—[*softly*] like this. So that other people behind think: "What is going on over there?" It'll encourage them to come over without you shouting, "Come over here! Come over here!" If you tell them to come over, they won't come.

Initially, you have no confidence, and you say, "Can you come and watch my show? I'm gonna do a very funny show." And people listen and they think: "That's not gonna be a funny show. I don't want to watch that." Whereas in the end, after a few years, you go out and say, "I'm gonna do a horrible show. It's a disgusting show. You're gonna hate this. I advise you to leave now." Then people will say, "Well, let's stick around and watch this."

And the character stuff I learned in doing sketches—I took those in and started doing stand-up. And in the end they blended all together to become this energy stand-up which I can pull and twist and take low and high.

SC: I can understand that you've gathered the audience in the street, but to keep them in that sharp mental, intellectual place—to keep them concentrating on you when there's a world around them . . .

EI: Well, it's even worse. You can't actually keep them in an intellectual place. You can't keep them in a thinking place. The attention spans are very low—they're childlike low.

There's sort of three levels of comedy that I notice. One is comedy in the room—which is "Where are you from, Sir? Where did you get that haircut?" . . . talking about stuff in the room. Everyone can see what's going on and they react to it—it's first level.

The second level is observational, which most people get into: "I was in the supermarket the other day," and people know about supermarkets, and they're going, "Yeah, supermarket . . ." ". . . And I was buying this weird stuff they're selling now, these Pop-Tart things . . ." People go, "Yeah, I think I've seen those—I've heard about those things." It's in their realism. They know about it in their world.

And the third level is when you get surreal, when you say, "I was on the moon, and a man came up with a gun, and he was chewing gum and playing piano at the same time." You really have to have them with you and wanting to buy into that world if they're gonna come with it.

I used to do purely surreal stuff, saying I was a waiter in Vietnam and stuff—because I served in Vietnam, so I say I was a waiter there. It was all about foodstuffs in war zones. I was just jumping into this surreal stuff. Sometimes they wouldn't come, and now I do stuff which starts in real and then just flips into surreal when they're not watching.

SC: So there's a structure to the whole act.

EI: The show is structured and the actual technique is structured. The material is like a motorway drive from one city to another, where I can just go off on a side road at any point and start saying, "Oh, I haven't seen that! What's it look like 'round here?" And if I get bogged down, and it gets boring, I just say, "Well, it's back on the motorway!"—and then we start carrying on.

So I know where I'm going. And when I ad-lib, I have the safety net of knowing how to get out of a fuck-up. You know, if it just crashes, I have confidence enough to say, "So, you're not laughing at any of this. You just hate the subject—pig farming? I should never talk about it?" I write on my hand: "Never talk about pig farming again . . ."

Writing on the hand—I use it a lot. You can go, "Oh, God, they hate me now. I am going to die soon." And it gets you out of it, 'cause they laugh out of it, and then you can go on to something else.

So this is a long-winded way of saying—in answer to your original question, about acting—that, having done those three mediums, I realized that you can learn from the ground up if you are willing to let go and say: "Well, I know nothing." I've found I can take anything on board. I can learn, but question everything. So, with acting, the first thing I did was *Cryptogram*,[6] and that was great experience—Gregory Mosher was the director. And I just dumped everything I knew about comedy and just tried to find out what the essence was of acting—what my backup was. The backup of comedy is to be funny. The bottom line of acting is to be truthful.

SC: And so you left your experience behind and started again. That must be really tough.

EI: It is tough, but I've done it three times. When I did street performing, I didn't think I'd have to relearn. I thought: "Street performing—I'll be fine. Two weeks, I'll be on top of this." There was a year of flailing around before I got street performing. Everyone in Britain is very quick to tell me how bad I was when I started doing stand-up. They just say, "Oh, I saw you. You were terrible." It took time learning.

SC: Have you done much stage work? I think you did *Edward II*.[7]

EI: *Edward II*, Elizabethan verse, the area that intimidates the hell out of me—Shakespeare, Marlowe. I like doing things I'm scared of, because you face down your fear.

Coming out as being a transvestite was my big, major, all-consuming fear that I faced down, and feel a lot better for it. And so I'm very into doing things that scare the shit out of me . . . taking risks. I mean, doing photo shoots—when I started I just thought: "God, I'll just do crap in front of those," and then I studied what people do. Now, with photographers, I say, "Okay, I'll trust you. Let's take some risks, see where we go."

SC: You keep discovering new talents in yourself. You've been successful in all of these things, and that's—

EI: Well, the acting has yet to be proved. I've had some good reviews and some bad reviews on the stage thing, and the film stuff hasn't really come out. I want to play psychotic shitheads in films. My agent says, "You want to play *baddies*," and I say, "No, no, it's much more deeper than that." I think there's a link between psychosis and comedy. At the moment, everyone's gonna say, "Hey! We got this transvestite comedy role." I'll say, "I'm not gonna do it. I'm just gonna play straight roles."

SC: You've become internationally famous so quickly, from being famous in the U.K., and that must be a far cry from when you were doing street theater when you were very young. The audience must have a very different set of expectations. Does it make a difference in trying to reach the audience if they paid thirty-five dollars to see somebody that they expect a lot from, rather than somebody that they never heard of, standing on the street corner?

EI: There might be a difference, but I don't assume a difference. David Niven[8] said, "You've got to be a complete egomaniac as a performer, to make it work." So I think the ego probably stays pretty constant. You've got to be about to go onstage and go, "Watch this! See what I'm gonna do?"—as opposed to going, "Hopefully, I'm going to be good today." You can't be apologetic as a performer. You've just got to go on and say, "See where this goes."

So the fact that people paid thirty-five dollars . . . I don't care if they're paying a hundred dollars. It doesn't really matter.

SC: You said that coming out as a transvestite was important to you. Did it make a difference to your audience?

EI: No, No. The bizarre thing is it made zero difference. I don't really have a transvestite audience, because there's not many male TV's who are out. And if there are women TV's who are out, no one knows about it. I don't have a gay audience, really, because there's humor that goes with gay men which is not really my style. My audience is wide open. The fact that I came out . . . I thought there was a chance that my audience would go and just disappear. I thought: "I wanna get this out. I wanna be open. I don't want to end up in a George Michael situation." You know, people say, "We're gonna find secrets." Well, what secrets? I've got no more secrets! It's such a weight off your shoulders!

Notes

1. *Star Wars*, a film directed by George Lucas, 1977.
2. Jabba the Hutt is a character in *Star Wars*.
3. The Edinburgh Fringe Festival.
4. *Die Hard*, a film directed by John McTiernan, 1988.
5. Monty Python, a British comedy troupe.
6. *The Cryptogram*, by David Mamet, opened in the West End in 1994, with Mr. Izzard.
7. *Edward II*, by Christopher Marlowe, was first produced about 1592. I'm speaking of the 1995 production directed by Paul Kerryson at Leicester.
8. David Niven, actor (1909–1983).

Karen Finley
New York State, January 5, 1999

The whole notion of memorization and character is very dated in theater.

KAREN FINLEY HAS PRESENTED performance art, usually monologues, in venues from theaters to nightclubs. Her performances have featured such iconoclastic elements as smearing her body with food. Her work includes *We Keep Our Victims Ready*, *The Return of the Chocolate-Smeared Woman*, and *Shut Up and Love Me*. She won an Obie Award for her stage piece *An American Chestnut*. Her books include *A Different Kind of Intimacy: The Collected Writings of Karen Finley*.

SC: Karen, one writer said that your work can be confused with theater. How about that? Is your work theater?

KF: Yes, it is theater. But I look at myself as being a conceptual artist. I feel more connected with, for example, Marcel Duchamp than with traditional theater artists, because my training is in the visual arts. I'm appropriating different mediums. I've been in the music industry; I've been in the publishing industry. When I do music, it's music. I've done plays, and they are theater. But I'm definitely *playing off of* theater.

Sometimes, for traditional theater critics, there's a naiveté of my work, because I'm breaking tradition. That's my reason I'm interested—I'm *fucking up* expectations—even in myself. I don't like to have the work guaranteed. The beauty of theater is that it can't be guaranteed, because it's live—anything can happen. In theater, now, everyone is struggling to make it guaranteed.

The whole notion of memorization and character is very dated in theater. If you take other art forms, such as just the visual arts, you're gonna show the sketch—in painting, or in drawing. You can see the struggle of the process. I can memorize a piece, but that's boring—this whole idea of suspension of belief, of going into this reality. Many times, I'll just bring the script. If I forget something onstage—that's the human condition. I'm showing that. I'm interested in presenting real time, the struggle, and the time before and after, surrounding the theatrical moment.

SC: The *Village Voice* suggested that your choice to work without artfulness—to call for props when you like, and to start again when you like—was a sort of *trickery*.[1] But it sounds like you're saying that it's much more basic to your work than that.

KF: Well, I think it first came about because I would do a performance the first time and discover the creative element while making it, as opposed to rehearsing a moment until it's perfect. I'm striving to show the magic of a connection happening. That, to me, is much more interesting.

SC: If performance art, or stage work, does progress, can the stage become as important to American culture as it was to, say, the Elizabethans? Or to Ibsen's audience? Or will film and television always get in the way of that?

KF: Well, the reason why I went into theater is that I like the feeling—which I think is an ancient feeling—of everyone coming into the theater and getting dressed. When people go to the movies, they don't get dressed up for the evening in the same way, and go and have the dinner. It isn't as much of an *event*. I enjoy providing an *event* for people—even if they don't like it. I like giving people something to go to, that specialness. I love performing in small places, but I also love performing in big places, just because I love giving people that special feeling.

Now, I'm moving into film. Because of my political problems, I'm moving to Los Angeles next week.

SC: Oh—so we're losing you here in New York!

KF: Yes. My work is over here. My work is finished. Because of my losing the case,[2] I don't have any prospects for new work. I've critically been acclaimed, and I think that if it was a different time, I would have those prospects. I should be having the same access as Robert Wilson—

SC: Right. You should certainly have as much opportunity to work as you would like to—

KF: And I'm not. Every time, it's so much of a struggle.

SC: Was the cancellation at the Whitney Museum[3] the first instance of the reaction to the Supreme Court decision?[4]

KF: Well, many different places just stopped dealing with me.

SC: I'm disappointed to hear that.

KF: Yeah, it is a big disappointment! I think that I do have the critical acclaim. *American Theater* magazine wanted to make me one of the ten most important women in theater. And I told them I didn't want to do it. I had two reasons. One was that I wasn't doing interviews—I just couldn't. It was so difficult to get my mind straight after the NEA decision. It's so emotional. The other was that it meant being marginalized as a woman artist. My work is not just that. I deal with a lot of different situations.

Gay rights are very important to me. I feel it's my responsibility to use my privileges for the pain or the prejudice that occurs to others. These problems I'm having come out of homophobia and sexism, but I get further than many gay and lesbian artists. I'm aware that their suffering is there—and that gives me a great deal of pain. I had to present that emotionality in *The Black Sheep*,[5] and other pieces, because of people that were suffering. Now I feel that's been presented out, and there can be a different level to it. Laughter is also very important. That's what I'm interested in even more—to place those two together.

But I'm gonna move to the West Coast because I think that there'll be support for my work locally. But, you know, I'm still sad that there are certain institutions in New York where I'm not going to be able to perform.

SC: Which institutions are those?

KF: Well, you basically could take every major institution and museum—and I'm not there.

SC: Your work has had a political message. Does art have a political effect?

KF: Yes—obviously, because of what's happened to me politically—going to the Supreme Court, the fact that I have to leave New York because I don't have work. Everything has to be a battle—and I just can't battle anymore for my work. It *is* political. I feel that I'm in a situation similar to the Hollywood Ten[6]—like I'm a red flag. It's all because I've done work that has to deal with sexuality.

SC: When Jesse Helms[7] and the other rightists reacted to your work, did they understand your political points?

KF: No. The only way they could deal with me was through sexual violence. I entered a relationship with Helms which became an abusive relationship. They could only deal with me personally, even though it was public. There was a voyeurism—a *publicness* in the relationship. It was emotionally abusive—really not political. The idea was to create a sense of shame. And I was very young at the time. It took me a long time to realize the abuse that was going on—and my part in the abusive relationship. Then I realized what was happening—how I was victimized, and what I could do to change the relationship. And I have changed.

SC: But you were speaking so much for all of us in your work. Certainly, a lot was accomplished just through the confrontation.

KF: Correct, yes. It's hard for me to leave here. This town has been so good for me. But I don't want to get into a situation like Lenny Bruce. I can't be here at PS 122 again in a year, saying, "Well, these people won't give me this chance . . ." People get tired of it. I do have a lot of different opportunities. If I can turn it around, then I think I can take that energy and I'll have more of a life than other people who have had these problems, like Lenny Bruce or Mae West—even Josephine Baker. Many of these people never recovered— there wasn't a transformation. I'm trying to learn and to see how I can have a laughter and a joy in living. I think there are ways. Some people have been tremendous with it—like John Waters, for example.

SC: Let's say that I'm the Lady from Dubuque, and I haven't been exposed to lower-Manhattan performance art. Can you help me access it? What should I have seen that prepares me for this work?

KF: Setting the table. When the Lady from Dubuque sees my work, she sees, sometimes, the simplicity of the construct. She has these theatrical elements within *her* work—the ceremony, whether it's Sunday dinner and using your best China, or going to the grocery store and saying, "Oh, I'm going to get some holiday paper plates," or just the ritual of making the toast at New Year's eve. Those are special moments which relate to theater. And whether you've got thirty-five cents in your pocket or a million dollars, those rituals are moments which connect all of us together. That genuine impulse, that emotion, is important.

Something that happens many times is that you'll see a piece that's very simple in an alternative space, and then when it gets translated—at BAM,[8] for example—people immediately think they have to have this larger impetus, and that the largeness makes something better. You know, if you're just eating a hot dog, you just want to keep that bun white. You don't want some seven-grain bun hand-made from sprouted wheat—you want to have the bun. And that's important.

Notes

1. Michael Feingold, "Moral Vacuuming," *Village Voice*, September 23, 1997.

2. *National Endowment for the Arts v. Finley et al.*, a 1998 U.S. Supreme Court case in which Ms. Finley and others challenged the cancellation of their funding from the National Endowment for the Arts on the basis of content.

3. In July 1998, the Whitney Museum of American Art, New York, canceled an exhibition in which Ms. Finley would have appeared nude.

4. The decision in *National Endowment for the Arts v. Finley et al.*

5. *The Black Sheep*, by Karen Finley, was first produced 1989 with Ms. Finley.

6. The Hollywood Ten, investigated by the U.S. House Committee on Un-American Activities in 1947, refused to answer questions. They were blacklisted.

7. Jesse Helms: U.S. Senator from North Carolina from 1973 to 2002.

8. The Brooklyn Academy of Music, a performing arts center in New York.

Index

Bold page numbers denote interviews.

About the Author

Steve Capra has worked extensively in the theater as actor, director, and producer. In New York City, he's been involved with La MaMa E.T.C., and with the Theatre for the New City at the New York Shakespeare Festival. In Boston, Massachusetts, he was a founding member of the Playwrights' Platform, a script development company, and later founded his own company, the Artists' Collaborative. On the London fringe, he has directed for the Byt Company. His work in radio is broadcast over the Massachusetts Radio Reading Network.

Capra is on the board of directors of the New England Theatre Conference and chairs its John Gassner Memorial Playwriting Award Committee. His monthly reviews appear in the *New England Entertainment Digest,* and he has also contributed to *Stage Directions* and other theater magazines. His writings for the stage and radio include readings devised from the work of Emily Dickinson and other writers. His play *The Way of a Pilgrim* is based on the Russian inspirational book of that name. He studied acting at HB Studios in New York, and he holds graduate degrees from New York University, Long Island University, and the University of Massachusetts. Capra lives quietly in a Quaker community in New York City.